RATTLER

RATTLER

BARRY ANDREW CHAMBERS

PINNACLE BOOKS
Kensington Publishing Corp.
www.kensingtonbooks.com

PINNACLE BOOKS are published by

Kensington Publishing Corp.
119 West 40th Street
New York, NY 10018

All Kensington titles, imprints, and distributed lines are available at special quantity discounts for bulk purchases for sales promotions, premiums, fund-raising, educational, or institutional use. Special book excerpts or customized printings can also be created to fit specific needs. For details, write or phone the office of the Kensington special sales manager: Kensington Publishing Corp., 119 West 40th Street, New York, NY 10018, attn: Special Sales Department; Phone: 1-800-221-2647.

PINNACLE BOOKS and the P logo are Reg. U.S. Pat. & TM Off.

ISBN-13: 978-0-7860-2207-6
ISBN-10: 0-7860-2207-8

First printing: April 2010

10 9 8 7 6 5 4 3 2 1

Printed in the United States of America

To Bill and Bernice,
who gave me the love of my life.

And to AJ Fenady,
who blazes trails with the likes of
Wister, Grey, and L'Amour.

Prologue

She was shaking so badly she had to hold the cup with both hands as she nervously sipped the hot tea. Wilma Ducette closed her eyes. Soon, very soon, the sheriff would be at her door.

Wilma got up and paced the small parlor, afraid to look out the window. Soon, very soon. She wished the day was over. She wanted to get it over with now. If she looked out the window, she knew she'd see the ghost of her husband. A frightful, unforgiving apparition that would point an accusing finger at her.

"You killed me." His voice would be cold and deep, coming from the other side of life. Stop it, Wilma. Think about what it'll be like an hour from now. It will all be over, with the sheriff's visit. She would play the grieving widow, plan the funeral, and in a week, she'd be on her way to Denver. Back home. Back to the carefree life of a single woman. Back to reliving her days as a social butterfly. Maybe there would be a rich, handsome man available for an attractive young widow.

Wilma glanced up at the clock. It was ten minutes to noon. Ten til noon. Twenty minutes earlier, Charles

Ducette would have met his end at the hands of a highwayman, a vicious killer, whose only aim was to put a bullet in Charles' head and take his money.

The killer, whose unlikely name was Percy Pierpoint, had been hired by Wilma to do the deed. It started two years ago when she came up with the plan. She'd asked her no account cousin who lived in back of a saloon if he knew a man who could do the job. A tough man. A cruel man who killed without mercy. A man like Percy.

Her story had been airtight. "I need a man who can protect Charles when he goes to town."

The cousin, bleary-eyed from a night of drinking and carousing, looked at her dully. "Huh?" was his reply, equally as dull.

Wilma bit her tongue and held in her impatience.

"Charles has a long, daily ride to the bank. People know this. I fear for his safety and I need a man who could shadow him."

"A, uh . . . a body guard?"

She was mildly surprised that her cousin had a coherent thought. "Exactly. I want an outsider . . . someone who doesn't talk to the locals."

With furrowed brow, her cousin rubbed the stubble on his chin. Wilma wasn't sure if he was thinking or about to fall back into a drunken stupor.

"I know someone who knows someone," he said.

The next part of the plan was simple. She presented her gun-shy, derringer-toting husband with a Colt .45.

"For your protection dear. You need it on the long road to town." Charles held the gun away from his body like it was a sleeping skunk.

"This is quite a gift, my love."

"You know I don't like you on that long road, unarmed."

"But dearest, I have my derringer."

"That wouldn't help you against a man with a real gun," she said, patting his cheeks. "I love you. Please carry this gun with you. Do it for me."

He shrugged and gave her a shy smile. "Whatever you say, sweetheart. I'll put it in my briefcase."

Wilma knew two things about her husband. The Colt would stay in the briefcase. And he would never load the gun.

She contacted the man who was recommended by her cousin. He gave her a name and she met the gunslinger in a remote town called Scrubb's Junction. The man called himself Percy, but he looked like the toughest Percy she'd ever seen. A light scar ran from the left corner of his mouth, down his chin. His hair was midnight. His eyes were a deep blue. An alertness in them hid danger. Percy's face was clean shaven, and he wore a scent that was pleasing to her. Pine, she decided. If he'd been in any other line of business, she would have considered him excellent second husband material.

She explained to Percy that she wasn't looking for a bodyguard. She needed a man to kill her husband.

"He beats me!" she cried. "And he consorts with women in town."

Percy showed no emotion. He merely let her speak.

"I have a strange request," she said. "I am going to pay you three hundred dollars as a retainer. In about eighteen months, I will contact you and tell you when I need your services."

Percy Pierpoint's voice was soft and patient. "Believe me, Mrs. Ducette, your request is not so strange. However, my standard retainer fee is five hundred."

"Of course." Without hesitation, she pulled out a handful of bills and counted out five hundred dollars. She had been prepared to pay a thousand. Percy Pierpoint had an impeccable reputation for professionalism and discretion. "I'll be in touch, Mr. Pierpoint."

She shook his black-gloved hand and felt a tingle. His eyes held a gaze with a mixture of killer and sexual allure. He definitely was a dangerous man.

Wilma went back home. She found her cousin at his customary table in the saloon, gulping down cheap whiskey like it was rainwater.

"I talked to the man that your friend recommended."

Her cousin was just starting to drink, so he was as clearheaded as he was going to be for the rest of the day.

"Did he agree to be Charles' bodyguard?"

Wilma shook her head. "He asked for too much money. And he smelled like a polecat." She thought back to the pleasant pine scent of Percy Pierpoint.

Her cousin smirked. "Who cares? You don't have to smell him."

"Yes, but I couldn't pay him the ridiculous price he was asking. You know Charles. He saves pennies like they're gold from El Dorado."

Her cousin took a long swig, then wiped his mouth. He was bored with the conversation.

Wilma continued her tale. "Anyway, I bought Charles a gun. In the long run, it's cheaper and the more I think of it, there hasn't been any crime on that road since the Wells Fargo was robbed three years ago."

Wilma left the bar, satisfied that her cousin would

never connect her talking to Percy Pierpoint with the murder that would happen eighteen months hence.

The day had finally arrived. Wilma knew exactly when Pierpoint would perform the deed and how long it would take. The road was not well traveled, but Charles' corpse would be found by a rancher or farmer who was headed into town. Since the town was closer to the scene of the crime than the house, the excited rancher would go get the sheriff.

Wilma looked up at the clock. 12:07. Seven minutes after noon. The tea in her cup was cold. Her hands still shook. She wasn't nervous about the murder. Her confidence in Percy was solid. It was the waiting. She hated the waiting. She couldn't wait much longer without screaming. Then she heard it.

The clip-clop of hooves was steady, sure. Sheriff Hawkins was approaching the house. He didn't seem to be in a hurry. Of course not. Who was in a hurry to deliver bad news?

She dared not look out the window. Instead, she picked up some sewing and pulled the needle through the cloth. *Look busy. Be calm, then surprised.* Should she cry at the news of her husband's demise? Or should she faint—fall deadweight into the sheriff's arms?

Heavy boots clomped on the wooden porch planks. They stopped. A shadow appeared in the glass. The sharp rap on the door made her jump.

"Yes?" she called out in a strained voice.

"Sheriff Hawkins, Wilma."

She put the sewing down and tried not to hurry to the door. Smile, she thought. Take a breath, she thought. And she did. *Greet him with a pleasant, untroubled smile.*

Wilma opened the door. Sheriff Hawkins stood there with his hat in his hands. He looked like he'd lost his best coon dog.

"Wilma," he said softly.

"Sheriff? What is it?"

She was proud of the alarm she was able to put into her voice. Perhaps she had a flare for the dramatic. She made a mental note to check out some of the fine theatre companies in Denver. They would be looking for a leading lady of beauty and quality.

"I'm afraid I have some bad news, Wilma."

"What? Tell me quickly Sheriff."

"I've come to arrest you, Wilma."

He held up a pair of handcuffs. The shock and disbelief on her face would make any of the finer theatres in Denver proud . . . if she'd been acting. The sheriff stepped into the parlor.

"You are charged with the attempted murder of your husband, Charles."

Without thinking, Wilma dashed to the kitchen to escape through the back door. As she shot out of the house, she was greeted by Percy Pierpoint, who blocked her way.

"Afternoon Mrs. Ducette."

He held up a gold badge. "I'm Randall Foster of The Service, a branch of the U.S. Marshals."

Wilma felt red hot irons puncturing her chest. She put her hand to her throat.

"Wha . . . ? You aren't Percy Pierpoint?"

"No ma'am. Mr. Pierpoint has been rotting in jail for two years. I've been taking his contracts and saving lives . . . such as your husband's."

The sheriff had followed her outside. He caught Wilma in his arms as she fell back in a real faint.

Chapter One

I fell in love with Wilma Ducette the moment I saw her. She was a real firecracker with a wicked glint in her eye to boot. Of course she was now in jail, but my fantasies had been fueled just the same.

My name is Randall "Rattler" Foster. "Randy" to my friends, "Mr. Foster" to anyone under twelve and "Rattler" . . . well, no one knows that name. It's an exclusive code name known to very few people in The Service, which is an offshoot of the U.S. Marshal's Service. My job entails duties such as bringing in escaped prisoners, investigating rustlers and something my boss calls "undercover." I get involved with outlaw gangs as an inside man and send information to my boss.

Harlon Shanks runs the regional office of The Service. It's located in Dodge City, Kansas and our territory goes as far east as St. Louis, as far west as Denver. Wyoming forms the north boundary and New Mexico Territory forms the south.

For a man of fifty-eight years old, Harlon looks a lot younger. His brown hair is grey at the sideburns, and his craggy face could be a lot craggier. At six feet four inches and a lean, muscular, two hundred pounds, Harlon could still hold his own out in the field. The problem is, while he was on a job in the Dakotas, he got shot. In fact, it was the fifteenth time he'd been shot in the line of duty. But the Dakota bullet lodged near his heart. Even though it was small caliber, it couldn't be cut out of him without causing major damage or death.

So Harlon handed in his gun for a desk. To tell you the truth, I think the inactivity and paperwork will do him in sooner.

I came to the attention of The Service when I was just past the age of twenty-one. I lived in Pleasant Valley, Colorado. Both my parents were teachers and like a dutiful son, I trekked to the nearest town that had a school without a teacher and took up the title.

One day in late spring, one of my students, Treva Spurlock, approached me after school.

"Mr. Foster?" she said in a timid voice.

Treva was fifteen, but looked younger. She was a small girl with a big brain. At times, I let her take the younger children out back and teach them their basic *ABC*s.

"What is it Treva?" She walked toward me slowly.

"Mr. Foster, I have a question." For a terrifying moment, I thought she was about to ask me about the birds and the bees.

"Yes, Treva?"

"Well sir, you're really smart. Probably the smartest person in eastern Colorado."

I doubted this, but accepted the compliment with a smile.

"What can I do for you, Treva?"

"My family."

On those two words, I totally understood. The Spurlocks had been in a famous feud with the McMahons for years. No one knew who started the animosity, but these folks just plain didn't like each other.

Bruce McMahon, the grandfather, was said to have stolen a Spurlock pig. David Spurlock, Treva's grandfather, was accused of burning the McMahon's crops in retaliation. Their sons continued the rivalry with petty squabbles to bloody bar fights.

One of the classic bar fights ever, occurred in a skirmish between Spurlocks and McMahons. The Blue Hog was the only bar in Pleasant Valley. Since there were no other watering holes, it was inevitable that a Spurlock and McMahon would meet up and lock horns.

After seeing his place torn up numerous times, the owner of The Blue Hog painted a line right down the middle of his bar. One side was for the McMahons and the other side was for the Spurlocks. For a while, both families respected the boundary.

The trouble started on a lazy Saturday morning in May. Buck Spurlock walked wearily through the swinging doors. He'd been up all night setting fence posts for the northern boundary of the Spurlock property. He sat heavily at the bar and tapped the counter with his dirty fingernails.

"Let's have a whiskey, Sam."

The bartender eyed him in judgment. "A little early, isn't it Buck?"

With bleary eyes, Spurlock slowly held up a silver dollar. "Whiskey," he repeated.

Sam shrugged and poured Buck a shot. He downed the drink and sat at the counter in a stupor. He lowered his head and was soon sound asleep.

What Sam didn't notice and Buck was unaware of, was Buck's elbow had slid over to the McMahon half of the bar. Any neutral stranger who could sit where he wanted, would have gently nudged the elbow away to give himself room. But a neutral person did not show up.

Around noon, Buck was snoring loudly as his body listed to the right, into McMahon territory. Two McMahons, Asa and Creighton, came through the swinging doors. They'd been to town to buy feed. When they saw the slumbering Buck leaning on their side of the bar, their tempers were pricked.

"Lookee here, Creighton. We've got ourselves a trespasser." Sam came in from the back, polishing a glass. His face went white when he took in the situation. He held his hands up at the two McMahons.

"Now wait a minute fellas. I don't want any trouble. Buck here fell asleep. He didn't mean no harm." Sam made a move to pull Buck back over to the Spurlock side of the counter.

"Leave him be," growled Asa. "This piece of Spurlock cow patty needs a lesson in geography." Asa's leg reared back to kick the stool out from under Buck. At that moment, a voice came from the bar's entrance.

"Better not, lessin' you intend to take us all on."

Standing in the doorway were Elmer and Keenan Spurlock and their cousin, Odie. They had come to town to look for Buck since he had not come home the night before. The three men came through the wide swinging doors, shoulder to shoulder.

Asa, who was the biggest man in the room, withdrew his foot and met Elmer halfway.

"Look at him!" shouted Asa. "He's on our side of the bar!"

Creighton joined his brother. "He ain't got no right to be lying on our counter, droolin' all over it."

Sam was in a quandary. He stood there like a statue, trying to figure out what to do. The sheriff was out of town. That meant that Deputy Lawson was in charge. And if things hung true to form, when the sheriff was out of town, Deputy Lawson was most likely up at Beggerman's Creek, fishing. Sam calculated the possible damage and decided on a plan that would save money.

"Drinks are on the house," squeaked Sam, "if you men promise not to squabble." All five men turned their heads to Sam. Buck mumbled something in his peaceful bliss. Creighton licked his lips and rubbed his chin. Free drinks. It was a powerful argument against fighting. Elmer took off his hat and fanned his face. Asa had a tense smile on his face.

"Well . . . maybe we could see our way to let you slide on this one. But you'd better remove that Spurlock from our spot." Odie and Keenan looked at each other and nodded. They warily walked past Asa and Creighton and went over to Buck. Keenan tapped Buck on the shoulder.

"Buck. Time to get up," he said softly.

Buck mumbled again and started to move away from Keenan, which put him farther on the McMahon side. Quickly, Keenan and Odie pulled Buck over to their end of the bar. "Come on Buck, wake up."

Buck opened one eye and spoke in a husky voice, "What are you doing here Keenie?"

With shaking hands, Sam poured whiskey into a glass. The light brown liquid corkscrewed out of the bottle into the tumbler. Keenan took it and held it in front of Buck's opened eye.

"Free whiskey, Buck."

With that, Buck opened his other eye. "Is it Christmas?" he asked.

"No, free whiskey," said Odie.

Buck snatched the glass and took it in one gulp. At that, the Spurlocks and McMahons took their respective sides of the bar as Sam poured glass after glass.

Within half an hour, the piano player showed up and began playing a rousing medley of bawdy songs. The bar was filling up with regular clientele. Katie, the hostess, entered from her upstairs parlor and filtered in and out among the customers. Every Spurlock and McMahon in the place was drunk.

Just as the church bells chimed one o'clock, more Spurlocks and McMahons showed up, looking for their brothers who had not returned from town.

Buddy McMahon, a hot tempered man known for his knee-jerk reactions, was told by a drunk Asa about Buck Spurlock's "crossing the line".

"I'm going to beat Buck to a pulp," threatened Buddy. "We can't let them hornswoggle us."

Asa tried to hold Buddy back. "Wait . . . wait . . . we got free drinks."

Thinking he had diverted disaster, Sam had started charging for drinks after the feuding families had gotten drunk. This made a very sober Buddy McMahon extra angry.

"Free drinks, huh? I'll get my own free drink." Truth be known, Buddy was more upset that his brothers got free drinks than of Buck Spurlock's indiscretion. He brushed off the drunk Asa and walked over into Spurlock Territory. He stopped at a table where Elmer and his brothers were playing poker. Before anyone knew it, Buddy grabbed the whiskey bottle off the table and took two generous gulps.

The piano player took his hands off the keyboard. Katie, the hostess, stopped in mid-giggle at Odie's dirty joke about a nearsighted donkey. The whole place was suddenly a tomb.

Buddy slammed the bottle back down on the table and wiped his mouth with the back of his hand. "Even the liquor tastes rancid on this side of the room," he declared.

Elmer glowered at him. Buck, who was snoozing over in the corner, woke up and looked around. "Wha's matter?" he slurred.

Sam sighed. He pulled out the ledger that was used for recording damages. He licked the lead tip of his pencil and held it poised over the DAMAGE column.

Buddy folded his arms and stood there, challenging everyone at the table. Eight Spurlocks locked eyes on seven McMahons.

Outside The Blue Hog, Minnie Haskell and her twelve-year-old daughter, Nina, were passing by. They heard the explosion of wood on wood. They stopped short of the swinging doors. It probably saved their lives as a forty pound keg of beer flew out, missing them by inches.

"My lands!" shrieked Minnie. Shouts and cursing mixed with banging and crashing assaulted the woman's ears.

"Look, Ma!" cried Nina. Nineteen-year-old Herbie Spurlock crashed through the window and rolled out onto the street. His face, arms and legs were scratched as he lay stunned.

Nina waved. "Hi Herbie!"

"It's those Spurlocks and McMahons," said Minnie. "Let's go dear." She pulled her reluctant daughter away from the roiling Blue Hog.

Katie ran out with her dress torn down the front. "They're killing each other!"

A curious crowd was gathering in front of the noisy bar. Reverend Madison, Bible in hand, started toward the swinging doors. "This is unseemly," he said. "I will play the role of peacemaker."

Katie put both her hands on the Reverend's shoulders. "It's the McMahons and Spurlocks!"

Without hesitating, Reverend Madison turned and headed up the street. "I'll be in my office," he muttered over his shoulder.

A chair with one leg missing was thrown out the door, followed by Buddy, who was pushing Keenan and Buck. They fell into a tangle of arms and legs. In the confusion, Keenan kicked his brother Buck in the face, leaving a dusty print of his boot. Buddy hammered Keenan in his left eye, accompanied by color-ful insults regarding his family.

Trudy 'O Dell held her hands over her ten-year-old son's ears.

A loud clang echoed from inside. Still holding the ledger and pencil Sam the bartender backpedaled out of the swinging doors and hit a support beam. "Oof!" He fell on his butt and groaned. He put his hand to the bump that was swelling on his forehead and scrawled out something with the pencil. "That's one bent spittoon"—he looked down at his torn apron—"and one work vest."

A spine chilling shatter of glass erupted from The Blue Hog. Creighton McMahon staggered out of the bar with shards of glass buried in his bleeding face. "My eye! My eye!" he cried.

Sam wrote furiously into the ledger. "And one very expensive bar mirror."

Ben Carrier, a dry goods clerk, got one good look at Creighton and fainted into the arms of Louise Hampton, the church organist.

Buck lay unconscious in the street. Buddy continued to pound Keenan, who had since rolled himself into a ball. Katie was on Buddy's back, trying to pull him off.

Muted punches of fists on flesh could be heard amidst the crashes and screams. A chair could be heard splintering against the wall. A Spurlock was shouting about "losing his future family", except not in those words. There was a loud *bang* and *whoosh* which brought a gasp from the crowd. A flame flickered inside. "Fire!" yelled a McMahon.

An explosion of flames spit another Spurlock out of the bar. His face was black. Smoke billowed from his hair.

Sam scribbled and mumbled to himself, "One gas heater." He looked up and peered into the bar. Then he went back to his ledger. "One mahogany stairwell."

The piano let out one final wail of protest telling

everyone that a body had been thrown on top of the keys. Then, all went quiet.

Outside, a tired Buddy fell away from the beaten up Keenan. The people stood in the middle of the street, listening for one last punch. A hand appeared on the floor just under the swinging doors. It made a fist and pounded the wooden floor. A soft moan was heard. The fight was over.

Later, Sam the bartender figured damages to be around seven hundred dollars. Two tables were totally destroyed, seven chairs were beyond repair. Numerous glass objects had been broken and the stairwell was suspect because of the fire. The bar itself had deep scratches and several dented places that contained blood and hair.

In the end, the McMahons and Spurlocks grudgingly split the expense. The "fight of the century" became another chapter in the feud. No actual deaths had occurred, but the blood between them remained as bad as a rabid wolf.

The feud had come to a boil again when part of Spurlock's livestock had been rustled. Spurlock sent three of his sons to go shoot up the McMahon's henhouse and burn their stable. If they could recover the stolen cattle, even better.

"Mr. Foster?"

Treva's voice brought me out of my nightmarish thoughts of the Spurlock-McMahon feud. "You want me to help."

The young girl's voice trembled. "We have no sheriff, no law of any kind. I'm afraid my daddy will kill a McMahon, or get himself killed."

I nodded.

She continued, "I thought I could rely on your wisdom to settle this problem."

Yes, I thought. Solomon was my middle name. I had his wisdom. And any man who would get in between the Spurlocks and McMahons was a fool. I knew that much.

"Mr. Foster, could you talk to Daddy? He respects you and so does Mr. McMahon. I know it."

She knew it all right. The fact was, Treva Spurlock was head over heels in love with Danny McMahon. Their generation was longing for peace between the families. This quickened in my mind as I spied a head ducking in the side window. No one could mistake the red hair of a McMahon.

"Danny, come in here," I called out.

Danny McMahon slowly made his way through the front door. At fifteen, he was six feet tall and dwarfed little Treva as he stood by her.

"Hello Mr. Foster."

I looked at both kids with my stern, schoolmaster glare. "What do you propose I do, other than talking to your fathers?"

Danny took Treva's hand in his. His voice was as quiet as hers. "We want you to stop this silly behavior between our families. My brothers did not rustle cattle."

I took my knife out and whittled the wood around the lead point of a pencil. "I understand what you want, but you still haven't told me how."

They looked at each other. Their faces had no answer. Treva spoke. "We thought you might know what to do."

I sharpened the pencil to a fine point and blew the

dust off. For a long moment I was quiet. Both young Spurlock and McMahon stayed as still as stagnant water, watching me with wide eyes. "I'll put a study to your problem. That's all I can promise. If a solution can be found, I'll let you know."

They both gave me sober nods and slowly headed out of the room. Watching them, I was reminded of a Shakespeare play called *Romeo and Juliet*. Centuries after it was written, the play still related to modern times. I also remembered it did not end well.

I rode up to see Jed Spurlock that afternoon. He was not happy that a wet-behind-the-ears teacher was sticking his nose into his ranching business.

"You learned Treva pretty good, Teacher. But you don't know nothing about running cattle."

"Yes sir, but how do you know it was the McMahons who stole your cows?"

Jed gave me a mean smile. "Angus McMahon is crooked as Snake River in winter. I'll bet my granny's glass eye that there are cattle with the Spurlock brand, grazing on the plains of Mexico right now."

Since Mexico was pretty far from Colorado, I was tempted to take that bet and teach Jed a little geography as well. A man never knows when he'll need a glass eye.

"But sir, I—"

Jed held up his hand. "The McMahon's took several prize heifers and sold them. Check around town and see if they haven't been throwing newfound money around."

I could see I was talking to a stone wall. I doffed my hat at Spurlock and thanked him for his time.

"You keep your nose in your books young man,"

said Jed. "If Angus and his thieves come back for more, there will be blood in the streets."

I stopped. "How do you know they'll be back?"

"I'm short hands. Half my men headed for New Mexico territory for that silver strike."

A vein of silver had been discovered near the Gila River down south. Half of Colorado moved in that direction to get rich. Even Mr. Conklin, the staid banker of Pleasant Valley got the fever. He packed up his wife and dogs and put his son-in-law in charge of the Valley Bank.

Spurlock spat into his tin cup. "I'm trying to keep my herds close, but I don't have enough men to keep watch all night."

This gave me an idea. "Excuse me sir, but maybe I could help."

Spurlock looked unconvinced. "How?"

"I'll bet I could round up some extra men to watch over your herd. Let me have a couple nights while your men get their sleep."

Jed Spurlock's face was still as he mentally looked for an argument to this. Apparently, none came to him. "Okay son. My men are tired. But if any cattle are stolen, I'll be after you along with the McMahons."

We shook on it.

The next day, I rode over to see Angus McMahon. Although some of the McMahon clan had gone to seek silver Angus was known for ignoring dreams, schemes and pots of gold. He supposedly kept his money in jars buried on various parts of his land.

I had the feeling of being watched and, as I came to a fork in the road, I heard the click of a trigger. I stopped and held up my hands.

The voice behind me was gruff and hard. "If you take the right fork, you'll find the house of Mc-Mahon. If you take a left, you'll come to the clear pool and lush green pasture . . . also owned by McMahon."

A man, whose voice sounded older than he was, emerged from the bushes. His hair was flaming red, as were his eyes. It was disquieting to have a rifle pointed at me by a man who looked like he hadn't slept for a couple days.

"Either way you go, you're on McMahon property. State your business."

"I came to see Angus McMahon."

"That doesn't tell me your business."

Before I could speak, Danny came riding down the road. "Mr. Foster! Hey, Mr. Foster!"

The man with the rifle gave Danny a scowl. "You know this fella, Danny?"

"He's Mr. Foster, my teacher."

The man lowered his rifle. A look of distant respect crept into his face. "Oh, sorry Teacher. I didn't recognize you without your chalkboard." He guffawed at his own witticism and I smiled, lowering my hands.

Danny gestured to the man. "This is my brother, Alfie. He's watching out for Spurlocks or their agents."

"Glad to know you Alfie."

Danny grabbed the reins of my horse. "Come on Mr. Foster. I'll take you to see Pa."

The McMahon farm was a quarter mile down the road. As we turned a bend, I caught sight of a stable with a charred wall. Four redheaded men were replacing it. All four stopped their hammering and stared at me. When Danny waved them off, they went back to their work.

'Angus McMahon was about as receptive to my invitation to help as was Spurlock. He tapped his corncob pipe impatiently without offering me a seat.

"There's nothing you can do young Foster. This feud has been building for years. It's about time we took those sons of bitches to task!"

To McMahon, they weren't Spurlocks. They were sons of bitches and Jed was the head son of a bitch.

I continued gamely on. "But Mr. McMahon, think of Danny here."

After introducing us, Danny had sat respectfully silent in the corner.

"Wouldn't you like peace with the Spur . . . uh, sons of bitches?"

Angus shook his head.

I pressed on. "Wouldn't it be much better if Danny or Alfie or any of your sons could go to town without worrying about getting into a fight, maybe killed?"

Angus puffed furiously on his pipe, muttering "sons of bitches."

I pled my case. "Mr. McMahon. What would you think if that son of a bitch sent his sons over here to repair your stable and henhouse?"

McMahon froze. Smoke floated over his head. Then, he burst out laughing. "You're plain loco!" He looked over at Danny as he pointed his pipe at me. "He's plain loco!"

"Mr. McMahon, I know you didn't steal any cattle."

He stopped laughing. "How would you know that Teacher?"

"Coming up the trail, I saw no tracks . . . unless your sons herded cows through the woods and mountains.

That's highly unlikely. You have no meat storage. I see no hides being tanned."

Angus McMahon stared holes in me. "Who says we didn't steal 'em, then sell 'em?"

I shrugged. "From what Treva told me, we're talking about a hundred head of cattle. You could have taken them straight to a buyer somewhere, but you're too smart for that."

McMahon sat a little straighter in his chair.

I continued. "You know that someone would have seen you herding them down the road . . . or heard something. Cows moo all the time, and forty or fifty cows can make quite a racket."

He puffed thoughtfully on his pipe. "What do you propose, Teacher?"

A few nights later, I got some volunteers to watch over Spurlock's livestock. It was quiet that evening. It was quiet the next night. On the third night, one of my volunteers saw shadows—about ten of them—on a ridge near the main herd. He alerted me and the other volunteers.

We congregated under some trees and watched the outlaw cowpokes cut about fifty cattle from the herd. These men were good. They were professional rustlers, working quietly and efficiently.

They headed north and we followed, as they took the cattle through the shallow shoals of Chigger Creek. They traveled by water for about a mile, then took their ill-gotten gains up through a mountain pass that lead to Denson County.

"Come on men. We'll take a short cut through

those hills." I pointed. "We'll go past the Denson County line to Briar Forrest and meet them there."

My twenty, well-armed volunteers followed me.

To make a long story short, we caught the rustlers as they came out of the mountains. I let the volunteers beat on them a little and then we got their story. The leader, who received a broken nose and shattered clavicle was eager to tell me what they'd been up to.

"We take a little from each herd," he said, gasping in pain. "We never take any from the same county in the same week. We go where sheriffs are scarce and feuds keep people divided."

The man stopped talking and wiped his bleeding nose.

"We work ten counties. Word was that half the ranchers were shorthanded because of the silver strike. We'd go in, take the cattle, and drive them into Kansas."

"You sell them there?"

He nodded. "We've got a buyer, not partial to the mixed brands. He sends them on to a confederate in Chicago who operates a slaughter house."

As the rooster crowed the next morning, I was at Spurlock's door. He answered, tucking his shirt in. "Did you get 'em? Did you get those dirty McMahons?"

"Good morning Mr. Spurlock. Yes sir, we got 'em. They're out in back of the barn with my volunteers."

Spurlock called back into the house. "Boys? Come on out here!"

Four Spurlocks came down the stairs and one came from the kitchen, wiping egg off his face.

Spurlock smiled. "Looks like we've got some McMahons to deal with. Let's go."

As he headed out, I followed. "Mr. Spurlock, it isn't the McMahons. These rustlers are from Kansas."

Spurlock turned around, stunned.

"Kansas? If they're from Kansas, I'll bet a bee's ransom in honey that Angus McMahon hired 'em."

"I don't think so sir. We questioned them thoroughly."

Spurlock hurried around to the back. There he found the rustlers beaten and tied up. My volunteers sat proudly on their horses, grinning. Spurlock looked up to thank them and was shocked to find that most of the volunteers had red hair. The others were blond as McMahon cousins were prone to be. I walked around the corner of the barn and beamed.

"I asked the McMahons and their cousins from Denson County to help me capture the real rustlers. And they recovered your cattle."

Jed shook his head and slowly smiled. "Well I'll be."

That very day, new lumber arrived at the McMahon farm. Along with it were four Spurlocks to help rebuild. From what I heard, Treva and Danny married two years later. When their baby girl was born, she was celebrated by both the Spurlocks and the McMahons. They named her Foster.

Chapter Two

It was settling the Spurlock-McMahon feud that brought me to the attention of The Service. That summer, I received a letter requesting my presence in St. Louis. The invitation was on government stationary and it said that I was a prime candidate for The Service. Included was a train ticket and twenty-five dollars spending money.

I'd heard of The Service, but was unclear as to the duties involved. At any rate, I looked at it as a free trip to St. Louis.

The city known as the Gateway to the West was a bustling, exciting place. It was huge. Dance halls, saloons, and theatres spread out for blocks. They were lit up so brightly, it was hard to tell whether it was day or night.

When I got off the train, I went to the Hotel D'Arms on Olive Street, as instructed. I was to meet with the director the next morning and had some time to myself.

The innkeeper suggested a restaurant down the

block, noted for it's fried turkey sandwich and cold beer. It was early evening and the eatery was getting busy. I sat at the bar and ordered the fried turkey sandwich and sweet tea.

Munching happily on the sandwich, I did not see the rough-hewn cowboy enter. He walked straight to me and thumped me behind the ear.

"Hey!" I cried as I turned.

"You're in my seat," he said in a gruff voice.

I moved down two stools and gestured toward the stool I'd been sitting on. "Be my guest."

The cowboy took my old seat and ordered a whiskey. Then he looked over at me and growled, "You sure give up your seat easy."

"You said it was your seat." I figured logic would appeal to him. It didn't.

"First come, first served. It's your seat," he said.

I smiled. "I bequeath it to you."

The witticism sailed over his head. The man had no sense of humor. "You give up too easy Tenderfoot. You're a yellow backed coward."

The challenge had been issued. A piece of turkey stuck in my throat. I tried to wash it down with the tea, but all that did was choke me. I started to cough like a madman. The cowboy walked over and shoved me.

"What's the matter . . . coward? 'Fraid?"

I backpedaled into another customer who made no effort to stop my action. Suddenly I was on my back, looking up at a painting on the ceiling. It looked religious in nature with winged devils flying over the flames of Hades.

"Get up boy." The rough cowboy stood over me.

Before I could reply, he pulled me up by my shirt collar and started slapping me.

That was enough. I pushed back, putting the weight on my back foot. The cowboy didn't move. He laughed.

"Are you crazy?" I yelled. "Are you plain loco?"

"Yeah, I'm—"

While he was busy replying, I threw a fist straight at his nose. It caught him by surprise and I was pleased to see blood spurting from his face as he did some backpedaling of his own. The customer who I ran into was still in his place with a Colt revolver sticking out of his belt. I didn't think. I just grabbed the gun.

"Wha . . . ?" the customer protested.

I pointed the Colt at the customer. He didn't say another word. Then I wheeled on the cowboy who was advancing on me.

"Stop right there, mister," I commanded.

He did.

"I've had enough of this and it stops now."

The cowboy smiled and took two steps toward me. "You don't know how to use that."

Actually I'm quite good with firearms. Rifles, pistols, derringers, bow and arrow, you name it. My father was a short, small-boned man who suffered from bullies. To equalize his lifestyle, he learned guns. He became quite the expert sharpshooter.

I'm not a fast draw, but my father taught me well. I could core a silver dollar at twenty-five paces. I aimed the Colt low.

"One more step and I'll blow your knee to pieces."

He hesitated and for the first time, the cowboy looked worried.

I continued, "Do you know what kind of damage a bullet at close range will do to a man's knee? I mean, forget the blind, searing pain. That will be the least of your worries."

The cowboy's eyes turned down, looking at the barrel of the gun.

"The cartilage will just blow through, tearing muscle along with the bullet. A spray of blood—*your* blood—will splash against the wall behind you."

I nodded toward the barkeep. "Yes sir. The gentleman behind the bar will have a real mess to clean up." My eyes shifted to the barkeep. "I hope you've got a lot of clean towels."

The barkeep nodded dumbly.

My eyes shifted back to the cowboy.

"And you . . . you'll spend the rest of your life with a nub. After tonight they will have to amputate, because the bullet will sever tendons, dividing the lower part from the thigh."

Not being a doctor I had no idea of the damage, but having read a McKenzie Medical Digest for a stomach ache, it sounded good.

Although the cowboy grimaced, he kept up a strong bravado. "You're not going to shoot me. You don't have it in you."

I cocked the trigger. "I beg to differ."

His face fell. Then he did an odd thing. He picked up his whiskey glass and downed it in one gulp.

"What are you doing?" I asked.

He didn't reply. He turned the glass in his hand with a simple three quarter turn of his wrist. The whiskey glass caught the light from the overhead chandelier. It wasn't blinding, but it was bright enough to catch my attention. In an instant, the Colt was knocked out of my hand and I saw a fist headed for my face.

I woke up in a bed. My face hurt and my neck hurt. And my back wasn't feeling too good either. My eyes focused on a lamp that hung on the wall. In the room was a chifforobe and a chair. It looked like my hotel room, but mine had a chifforobe on the opposite wall.

Standing over me was an old gentleman holding a glass of something brown.

"Where am I?"

The old man held my face up to the light. "Open your eyes."

"They are open."

"Wider."

I had not realized that my lids were half closed. The room was dim, but the lamp hurt my eyes.

"Open," he said gently.

Against my better judgment, I opened my eyes full wide.

"Look at me," he said.

"Are you a doctor?"

"The best one in St. Louis." He gazed into my eyes. "You'll live. That bump on your head was what worried me."

I reached back and felt the swelling just above my neck. "Ow!"

"Relax."

I leaned back on a soft, eiderdown pillow. It was just like the one in my room. Upon feeling it, I was thinking of taking it home with me. "Where am I?" I asked for a second time.

"Room 34 of the Hotel D' Arms."

That figured. Room 32 was mine.

"Is this your room, doctor?"

"Nope. It belongs to the man who brought you in and called me."

A good Samaritan. "Where is he?"

"He's down the hall taking a bath."

I nodded, but didn't understand. "I have an appointment tomorrow morning."

The doctor shook his head. "You need rest. That bruise isn't going away any too soon." There were no mirrors in the room, but the doctor produced a hand mirror from his bag. "Here you go."

On my forehead was a dark, purple spot. The mark of Cain. I was not going to make a very good impression on my potential employers. The door opened.

"Ah, here's your friend now."

Coming through the door was Harlon Shanks, my future boss and current good Samaritan. He wore a bathrobe and had a wet towel draped across his shoulders. Of course at that moment, I didn't know his name when he walked in the room, but I'd seen him before. He was the cowboy who punched me out.

There are different ways for The Service to approach candidates. If a man showed an extraordinary skill in gunplay or fisticuffs, he would be marked by The Service and contacted. Then he would be tested for how smart he was.

The Service saw that I was smart in handling the

Spurlock-McMahon feud but they needed to test my physical skills, which is what Harlon Shanks proceeded to do in St. Louis. To tell you the truth, I thought I'd failed miserably, but Harlon was impressed.

"I'm not very good with my fists," I told him.

"Nonsense," Harlon said, waving me off. "You pack a mean punch. For a moment there, I thought you'd broken my nose."

I squinted at his nose which now sported a bandage. It was hard to see if I'd actually done any damage.

"You showed other qualities we like Mr. Foster."

"I did? Like what?"

"When I immediately started in on you, you were slow to anger. You held yourself at bay, displaying a cool temper."

I was tempted to tell him that it was because I was scared to death.

"And you showed calm. Here I am, a big bruiser, threatening you. You didn't flinch. In fact, you made a joke."

Again, I was tempted to tell him I didn't flinch, because I was frozen in fear.

"We need men who are slow to anger and can think on their feet. Your little speech about the bullet in the knee"—Harlon shook his head and grinned—"that showed quick thinking and imagination. And I can tell you're very comfortable with a gun, even when it isn't yours."

So I retired as a teacher and went into training as a special agent of The Service. I was taught how to pick a lock, how to read counterfeit money, and how to use my fists. For a while, I thought they were training me to be an outlaw.

"You need to know the world of the criminal," Harlon told me. "You don't have to live the life of one, you just need to understand them."

I qualified on their shooting range with one of The Service's highest scores. I was just glad they didn't test me on my quick draw, which was poorly lacking.

The Service had a course in memorizing. In a month's time, I was able to remember faces, scars, moles, mustaches, plus dates, times, and other numerical exercises. My observation skills were tested. I could remember clothes, horses, all sorts of useful information.

They also had me run, jump, crawl, climb, and swim through a wooded area they called "The Trail", or as we trainees called it, "The Trail of Hell". Some guy from West Point designed it. The first time I tried it, I didn't make it halfway through. The Trail was supposed to train me for survival and to last through a rigorous, physical fight. At the end of six months, not only could I complete The Trail of Hell, I could slice through it like a knife through butter.

My hands grew rough and firm. My muscles hardened. I had more energy than I'd ever had before. As a teacher, my life was sedentary, soft. The Service toughened me up.

I was also trained in the art of pugilism. I learned to throw a whale of a haymaker. I was taught balance and counterbalance so I could throw a man twice my size, by using his momentum.

One day I was called into the director's office. He was a man of white hair and rough skin. His name was Hansel, like the fairy tale, except Hansel was his last name.

"Come in, Mr. Foster."

"Yes sir."

Mr. Hansel sat behind a very large oak desk with a stack of papers scattered across it. His handshake was as firm as the gaze he held on me.

"How is your training going?"

"Very good sir. I have a week left."

He opened a file and jotted a note inside it. When he closed it, I saw my name on it.

"We're assigning you a code name. You will never use it in public. It is a name that only you and certain operators in The Service will know."

I nodded, hoping it would be an easy name to spell.

"You will be known as "Rattler". We logged it into your file."

"Rattler," I repeated. "Yes, Mr. Hansel, thank you sir."

He stood up, signifying it was time I left. He gave me another firm handshake, and I walked to the door. I turned. "Mr. Hansel? Why Rattler?"

He smiled and nodded to himself. "The name "Daisy" was already taken."

I thought Rattler was a much better name.

When I finished my training I was given an agent's license and issued a badge and a six-shooter. The weapon was from a gunsmith in Connecticut. I'd never heard of the brand name, but was assured that it was a quality firearm. I liked its heft. It felt right. It felt like it had been made especially for my hand.

For the next seven years I lived in Dallas, Topeka, Salt Lake City, Denver, New Mexico Territory, and San Francisco. I went wherever I was needed. In

Utah, I was part of a gang that robbed mining payrolls. Somewhere along the line I was found out and almost hung. Instead, the gang's boss decided to stick a Bowie knife in me. I was left for dead, but found by another agent who was playing the outside man on the case. Harlon Shanks. He got me to a doctor who decided the huge knife had missed my vital organs. I was laid up for several weeks after that.

Since joining The Service, my body has been thrown down a mine shaft, shot twice in each shoulder, knifed in the gut, and I broke my leg jumping off a cliff. There's no other job in the world I'd rather have.

Chapter Three

When the Dodge City office opened, I was recovering from my broken leg and doing some filing for The Service. Mr. Hansel retired and was replaced by his nephew, Jacob Specks.

At thirty-three, Jacob was a little green for such a job, but he was a proven field agent and humbled by the appointment. Two days after the cast was removed from my leg, Jacob summoned me to his office.

I found him behind that same oak desk of Hansel's—the one from St. Louis. Jacob was reading a report and didn't look up as he pointed to a chair.

"Take a seat Rattler. I'll be with you in a moment."

I sat quietly as he finished reading the report. He nodded as he read, his lips moving with the words. Then he put the report down and pinched the bridge of his nose.

"I need a drink," he said to no one in particular.

"You're not supposed to drink on duty, sir."

He looked up at the ceiling and smiled ruefully.

"That's exactly right, Rattler." He laughed and kept on laughing.

That's when I realized he'd already had that drink. To remind him that I was still present, I spoke. "Why did you want to see me sir?"

He sobered up immediately.

"I have something for you."

"Yes sir?"

"It's a little dangerous."

So far, this was nothing new. "How can I be of service, Mr. Specks?"

He stood up and looked out the window. What he was looking at, I don't know, but it was something serious. Then he turned. "I was going to assign this job to Gator, but he turned me down."

In The Service, you are not allowed to turn down a job. The fact that Specks allowed it to be turned down was startling enough, but the fact that it was Gator, made it plumb unbelievable. Gator was a legend. His deeds were legend. I'd list his exploits and all of the men he had killed, but you would stop reading and my credibility would be shot.

"Gator turned you down? What do I have to do? Go to the north pole and wrestle a polar bear naked?"

This struck Jacob Specks as terribly funny and he let out a stream of guffaws mixed with profanity. With each guffaw, I smelled scotch.

"No, no, nothing like that," he said, attempting sobriety.

"But you said it was dangerous."

"Hell yes, it's dangerous. Gator just felt that the assignment was beneath him."

"What if I feel it's beneath me?"

"It won't be. You don't have Gator's seniority." He looked down at the report, and then at me. "I want you to go over to Clearview and take my cousin Benita to the opera."

The ex-teacher in me felt a twinge of excitement. I had gone to the opera with my parents in Denver. I didn't understand the language, but the music gloriously washed over me, clinging to the contours of my soul and finding a home in my tongue, which I hummed for years. In The Service I'd had the opportunity to go to the opera houses in St. Louis, Chicago, and Kansas City. I even got Harlon Shanks and his wife to go. Nedda Shanks became a member of The Opera League and was a loyal season subscriber. I do get a little verbose when it comes to expounding on the virtues of Puccini, Mozart, and Handel.

The agent in me was suspicious about this Clearview assignment. Why dangerous? "I don't understand sir. Is Benita a rough girl or something?"

"No Rattler. She's quite nice, but she needs an escort. She told Uncle Hansel that a man has been following her."

"You think the man is a danger to her?"

Specks pushed a file at me. "The man's name is Lewis Featherston. He's head of security at Anglin Cattle Company. Benita works in their office in Clearview."

"Security man, huh? That doesn't sound too bad."

"Open the file."

In the file was a wanted poster of a man named Allan Coletrane, alias Frenchy Duvois, alias Cole Allan.

"Read the file, Rattler." He stood up. "I'll leave

you alone to look it over." With that, he closed the door.

I opened the file. The title read ALLAN COLETRANE-PROFILE. It was broken up in a series of paragraphs with eye witness accounts. The first account was from a Joe Previn. He had been in a bank holdup by Coletrane and his gang. It was written in Joe Previn's hand, in a conversational style. It read as follows:

Date: August 24, 1867
Location: Denton Falls, Kentucky
Subject: Joe Previn

I was in the bank to make a deposit. Dolly Cantwell was there with four other customers. I knew Dolly from her job at the notions shop. I knew the faces of two other customers. One was a man I'd seen at the cattle auctions every month. We had a nodding acquaintance. The other gentleman that I recognized, worked in the courthouse records department. A young couple was also there. Newlyweds I believe. They were there to open a new account.

As I was filling out my payment slip, five masked men entered. The leader was a big man with a red bandana over his face. He had a shotgun. Two had carbines and the others had their pistols. I noticed that one pistol was a .44 revolver. I remember that, because I had one just like it.

Before Monte, the old security guard, could pull his gun, the leader rammed the butt of his weapon into Monte's face. He fell back, hitting his head against the wall. Although he

was unconscious, his breathing was shallow.
He would die an hour later, but at the time I
ad no idea his injury was that serious.

"Everyone empty your hands!" the robber
yelled.

Dolly Cantwell fainted right off. The young
bride squeaked as she dropped her purse.

"Empty your pockets," he commanded.

Wallets hit the floor. I threw my dollar roll
down. Without warning, the one they called
Coletrane shoved the man I knew from the
cattle auction and he fell on his seat.

"Wha . . . ?" Before he could say another
word, Coletrane kicked him in the head. He
was out immediately. Blood spilled from his
nose onto the floor.

"All tellers, out now!" yelled the leader.
The two tellers came out from behind the
counter with their hands up. Two of the
outlaws walked to the money drawers and
started putting money into the carpetbags
they had brought with them. Coletrane
pointed to the two fallen men. "Does anyone
else want this?" We were in shock. No one
made a move. He waved his shotgun at all of
us. "Okay, everyone take off your jewelry and
strip off your clothes—that means you too,
ladies."

The newlyweds held each other. Dolly, who
was coming out of her swoon, looked up from
her position in disbelief. The only reason I
could figure that he wanted us to strip was to

keep us in line. Or maybe he got some sort of pleasure from it. It was hard to tell.

Apparently we didn't react fast enough. Coletrane kicked the nearest teller between the legs. The man crumpled in agony as both of the women screamed. Coletrane pointed to the other teller who was already shucking his coat.

"You. Get undressed and go open the safe." The teller nodded as he unbuttoned his trousers. I was pulling off my tie and tossed my hat over my money roll. One of the bad men kicked my hat.

"Don't get smart," he warned. He picked up my money roll and tossed it to one of the men behind the counter. Coletrane was looking at me with malice. He was about to walk over to me when the man from the cattle auction moaned. It got Coletrane's attention. As he looked back, he spotted the newlyweds. He started to watch the young woman disrobe.

I was down to my underwear. So was the man who worked at the courthouse. Clothes littered the floor. One of the masked men collected the wallets and jewelry that were on the floor. The teller walked to the back where the safe was. A masked man behind the counter followed him.

Dolly was up. She was slowly undressing. I was embarrassed for her. I didn't know if we would survive this ordeal. I did know that we would never be able to look at each other in the same way. I'm a Christian man. I turned as Dolly got down to her bloomers.

The men in the back came out with four

carpetbags loaded with money. Coletrane looked over at his look-out and asked, "How we doing?"

"It's all clear," said the look-out.

Coletrane nodded and leveled his shotgun at the young couple. The husband was skinny with almost hairless legs under his shorts. She wore a corset and bloomers.

"You're coming with us," he told the girl.

"Like hell!" said her husband. He made a move towards Coletrane.

The young girl grabbed him by the shoulder. "Jimmy, please!"

Half of Jimmy's face disappeared with the shotgun blast. For a long, three seconds, he just stood there. Brains and skull dripped to the floor. He let out a groan, then his knees buckled. When both of his kneecaps cracked on the floor, his young wife screamed.

Then, Coletrane laughed. He held his belly and gave a long, lusty laugh. My blood ran cold. I could not understand evil like this.

While Coletrane was laughing, there was another shock. The girl leaped halfway across the lobby. She was on Coletrane like a wildcat. In one move, she scraped her nails across his face and pulled down his bandana. She kicked him in the knee and pulled his hair. Coletrane dropped the shotgun and howled.

"Agguuuh!" She actually had him back-pedaling. I looked out the window and saw people running toward the bank. They had been alerted by the shotgun fire. Leading the pack was Deputy Morris.

"We've got trouble!" yelled the lookout.

Coletrane was getting all the trouble he needed from the girl. Sympathy and admiration coursed through my veins. Then he coldcocked her on the chin. She flew back across the room like a rag doll.

"Take her!" yelled Coletrane. Two of his men grabbed the unconscious girl.

I knew what God wanted of me. I expected a bullet in the gut, but I had to do something. I ran for the nearest masked man. I thought that if I could grab his gun and start firing, it might save some lives. I didn't see the masked fella behind me, but I felt his .44 slap me upside the head. I fell and slid across the floor.

Just as Deputy Morris reached the door, Coletrane blew a hole in him. Seven others in the street reached for their guns to return fire, but Coletrane and his men were throwing a volley of bullets into the crowd.

My eyes were suddenly bleary and my stomach wanted to give back breakfast. Through a haze, I saw the bad men running out of the bank with their carpetbags. One had the young wife slung over his shoulder. They were firing their guns and using her for cover. People were scattering. About that time, I fainted.

Later, the sheriff showed me wanted posters of Allan Coletrane. I recognized him easily and identified him to the law. That day, he killed Deputy Morris, Monte, the young husband, and three others in the street. The young woman they took was found behind a

*dump in the next town. She had been torn up
by Coletrane and his gang. She died a few
weeks later.*

At the bottom of the affidavit was the neat,
thoughtful signature of Joe Previn. I glanced through
similar witness accounts of murder, robbery, and
mayhem. The trail ended in Texas, sixteen years ago
when he killed a Ranger.

I closed the file. Allan Coletrane. Was this also
Lewis Featherston? Was this the man giving his un-
wanted attentions to Benita, Jacob's cousin, niece of
Mr. Hansel, the former Service Director?

The room was still. For the first time, I noticed an
overhead fan clicking in the quiet. I pushed the file
away from me. I felt slimy reading those accounts . . .
getting inside Coletrane's world. After a few moments,
Jacob Specks entered the office. I slapped my hand on
the top of the file.

"Lewis Featherson?" I asked.

"We think so." This man had a long list of crimes
from armed robbery to murder, to rape.

"He's vermin . . . pure vermin," I said.

"We have another file on him."

"There's another file?"

He nodded. "We started a new one when our man
in Clearview spotted him."

The Service had agents working in mining camps,
banks, cattle companies, all sorts of places where
crime could happen.

Specks continued, "He's not sure if Featherston is
Alan Coletrane. You have to add about twenty years

to that picture and a little more weight in the face. Shave off the mustache in your mind."

I did all of that as I looked at the picture.

"As luck would have it, Featherston spotted Benita in the office. He asked her to go to some dance with him, but she didn't like him. He's sent her flowers and goes by the office frequently, but she keeps rejecting his advances."

I nodded, working out a scenario in my head. It was the logical choice. "So I put up a front. I'm Benita's out of town boyfriend. He'll either leave her alone, or if he really is Coletrane, he might come after me."

"Something like that. When our man spotted Featherston about two months ago, we put in a second agent. Then, Featherston turned his attentions on Benita."

"Who are your agents?"

"Bear and Arrow."

I didn't recognize the two names.

"Bear will contact you when you get to Clearview."

I nodded.

"What's my cover?"

Specks laughed. "You're going to be a school teacher."

Chapter Four

Taking a woman to the opera didn't sound too dangerous, but not finding the right horse can be. I suppose I'd better explain.

As a school teacher, I owned a nag named Shelley. When I went to work for The Service, I gave Shelley to Spider Lee Templeton, a fourteen-year-old who won our annual spelling bee. Spider looked at the old girl with the battered saddle and asked me if she was the prize for winning the spelling bee. I said yes. His eyes glistened.

"I've always wanted a horse like her," said Spider. "Maybe arithmetic should be my next subject to conquer." I was perplexed by his statement. He saw that I was confused and added, "I expect to get a rickety, old wagon to go with Shelley when I win the arithmetic contest."

In The Service, I rode buckboards, stage coaches, trains, and boats. I even rented a horse now and then. On the job where I jumped off the cliff and broke my leg, I decided I needed a horse of my own.

A week before leaving for Clearview, I stopped off at the Dodge City Livery. I was already in my character as a school teacher. Mr. Cavez, who ran the stable, showed me some handsome mounts.

"I don't have a lot to spend, being a teacher and all." This was true. I played my role to the hilt.

Mr. Cavez scratched his chin. "I believe I have what you're looking for young fella. Follow me."

He took me in back where there was a horse tethered to a hitching post. It was not a large horse . . . sort of overweight. Short and stumpy. She was red with a black mane and black tail.

"There she is. Her name is Pandora."

"Pandora," I muttered.

The horse looked up as if she'd heard me. Then, the strangest thing happened. She grinned at me. At least it looked like she grinned.

"She was with the circus," said Cavez. "Trick horse or something."

"Why is she here?"

"The circus gave her to me when they came through town."

"Gave her to you? What's wrong with her?"

"They told me she wouldn't jump off a diving board into a tank of water."

Smart horse, I thought.

Mr. Cavez unhitched her as he spoke. "They gave another horse the job—told me Pandora was worthless when it came to diving off high places. I tried her as a plow horse, but that didn't work. She wouldn't pull a plow or haul rocks."

He gave me a sly look as he patted her flank.

"She's a gentle ride though. You can have her for twenty dollars."

The deal was too good. "Why should I pay you twenty dollars if you got her for free?"

"The saddle that comes with her is worth twenty dollars."

Pandora spied a carton of empty milk bottles. She put her mouth on one and pulled it out of the box. Then she tossed her head back, sending the milk bottle flying through the air. It shattered on a discarded anvil about twenty feet away. There were more broken bottles lying at the base of the anvil, previous victims of Pandora. She sure had good aim.

"Is that one of her tricks?" I asked.

"No," Cavez said darkly. "I'll let you have her for ten dollars."

Pandora looked back over her shoulder at me and gave that smile. Cavez was sweating. "Okay, I'll let her go for five dollars. Five dollars! You can't turn that down."

I could turn it down, but something told me that Pandora was the horse for me. Besides, five dollars for a twenty dollar saddle wasn't something to sniff at. I stuck my hand out. "Deal."

Cavez pumped my hand enthusiastically. I think I saw a tear of gratitude form at the corner of his right eye. "Gracias. Mucho gracias sir."

I took Pandora out for our first ride. There was a grassy area outside of Dodge City that was relatively flat. I gave her a light slap on the rump and she cantered along a wooden fence that outlined the meadow.

"Okay Pandora, let's go."

At my command, I was genuinely surprised when she went into a gentle, steady lope. We passed the fence and were in the open field. I reached back and popped her on the rump once more. "Come on girl, show me your stuff!"

She stayed at the gentle lope.

I slapped her rump harder. "Let's go Pandora!"

The gentle lope turned into a faster lope.

This was it? I hit her as hard as I could. "Come on Pandora! Pour it on! Yeeha!"

She looked back at me with annoyance, but attempted to pick up her speed. Her pace quickened, her head bobbed and I noticed she had churned up pieces of turf in her wake.

As I told you, I wasn't a quick draw, but I could pull a gun a lot faster than this horse could run. I began to think she was doing it on purpose.

"Okay, whoa, whoa girl." Since she wasn't going that fast, she went from clippity-clop to clip-clop in two strides.

I turned her around and we went back to town. I bought my first pair of spurs. This horse thing was becoming expensive, but I was determined.

We headed back to the meadow area. Pandora was prancing in a small circle like she was in the center ring. I leaned over and whispered in her ear, "Okay Pandora. Show me what you've got."

I whipped those spurs into her with a brisk kick. At once, we were at that familiar, easy gallop. That wouldn't do. With all of my leg strength, I dug those spurs in hard. "Go! Go! Go!"

She sped up a little, then abruptly stopped. I went flying, head over heels and landed on my back.

"Oof!" I lay there, stunned. Then, I felt a wet, slippery tongue in my ear. "Hey!" I rolled away from Pandora, feeling a soreness in my ribs.

She followed, and gently nudged me on the back of the neck.

"Okay, okay, I'm all right." I got up. Pandora put her nose lightly on my chest.

"I guess you're not a speed demon."

She shook her head.

"I guess you didn't like the spurs."

She shook her head once more. "I guess you have other talents."

Pandora whinnied softly and used her head to push me to her side. I took off the spurs and tossed them on the ground. I mounted Pandora and stroked her mane. "Let's go home, girl."

During that week, I got to know Pandora and she got to know me. We had an uneasy relationship, but I liked her and she liked me. I hoped.

I stopped in Andre's Hats For Men to accumulate my "teacher disguise".

"I should get a straw hat," I told Pandora as I looped her reins around a hitching post. "What do you think about a straw hat?"

She looked at me with no emotion. I shrugged. "I'll get a real dandy with a red band."

In the hat shop, there was a large assortment of western wear. As a school teacher, I'd worn black pants with a white or grey shirt. Most of the time I wore a bow tie with a black coat. Margie Furman, who was a whiz at geography and science, had told me that I looked like a funeral director.

For my undercover look, I wanted to appear light, non-threatening. That meant light grey or tan pants, a pale pink or blue pastel shirt, and a bleached white straw hat. A red stringed bolero tie would complete the outfit.

I plucked a little number with a red band off the straw hat rack. I put it on my head at a cocky angle and checked it in the mirror. I looked like a carnival barker or worse, a dealer in a casino.

"Hey! Get out of here you!"

I turned and saw the shopkeeper. He was a bald, slightly built man with a sunken-in chest. His voice squeaked when he yelled. "That's right, I mean you!"

Then I saw who he was yelling at. Pandora's head was sticking inside the doorway. The clerk took a brown Stetson off the hat tree and waved it at her. "Shoo! Shoo!"

I ran over and grabbed the reins. "I'm sorry sir, she's . . . she's uh . . ." I looked into Pandora's eyes. They were sparkling. "She likes hats." I led her out and lashed her back to the hitching post. "How did you get loose?" I looked down the street to see if any truant schoolboys were lurking behind a rain barrel trying to hold in their mirth. It was obviously some schoolboy trick.

After returning to the shop and purchasing my outfit, I rode over to the house where I rented a room. I put on the teacher clothes and looked in the mirror. "Now that's what a real school teacher looks like," I told my reflection. I tilted the straw hat to the side. Yep, that was the look I was going for.

Not far from the center of town was a German beer garden. Mr. Stienhaus from Chicago ran a successful establishment. He'd started others in Indiana and southern Illinois, but this was the first one in Kansas. People liked to sit outside at long tables and feast on thick bratwurst sandwiches and cold beer.

I wound Pandora's rein an extra time around the hitching post and walked into the front of the beer garden to place my order. After a few minutes, I took my food on a tray to the back where a man pumped a hand organ to entertain the open air-diners. Near the hedge was a long table where two cowboys and a banker sat, exchanging dirty stories. I took the end spot and tried to look like a school teacher. It never occurred to me to just be myself. After all, I had actually been a teacher. I took out a copy of *Les Miserables* and read as I ate.

As I took a big bite of bratwurst, my straw hat blew off—but the air was as still as pond water. The cowboys and banker laughed. A little girl eating with her parents laughed and pointed at me.

I turned and saw Pandora on the other side of the hedge. She had my straw hat in her mouth and backed away.

"Hey! Come back! How did you get loose?!"

She started to canter off. There was an opening in the hedge and I shot through it. I caught the slow loping Pandora by the reins. "Give me that hat!"

She nickered and turned away.

I grabbed the brim, but she held it tight in her teeth. "Let go! Give it to me Pandora!" I pulled. The straw stretched and the hat went from round to oblong. I let go and it sprang back into shape. "Okay! Fine! Keep it!" I yelled.

I started to walk away. As I did so, a shadow

followed. I felt the hat drop onto my head. "Well that's more like it."

Rather than return to the beer garden, I decided to go to a saloon. I lashed Pandora to the hitching post and went inside. I ordered a beer, sat at a table, and watched her. For a full two minutes, she didn't move. Then she drew her face close to the reins around the post. Her head bobbed. She moved away from the post with the leather in her mouth. She flipped the reins in a reverse order from how they were wound.

"Impossible," I whispered.

She moved back to the post, ducking under it and catching the reins with her teeth. It looked like she was blowing with her mouth as the reins flipped back up over the post, toward her. After repeating these actions three more times, she was loose.

"Impossible," I said once more. Then, I laughed. I laughed so hard, people began staring at me. "Impossible!" I yelled, laughing and slapping the table.

After that, I was asked to leave.

I took a circuitous route to Clearview. My plan was to approach the area as if I were coming from Colorado. It would be on the edge of Comanche territory, but I wanted no witness seeing me approach the town from the east. My story was that I was from Tenbone, Colorado and it had to look true.

About thirty miles out, I camped in a clearing amid gently rolling hills. I shared some beef jerky with Pandora who proved to have a taste that ranged from old leather to sweet potato pie. She was acting a little edgy that night as I lay by the fire. She neighed quietly.

"What?"

She neighed and nodded.

"No. I don't feel like singing. I sang for you last night."

Pandora turned her head to the right. I followed her gaze to a thick, dark, pine tree.

"What is it you want?"

She pranced over to the tree and gave a hop. Both her front hooves landed on the trunk. She was standing on her hind legs. It was such a strange sight, I almost rolled into the fire, laughing. Then she took one hind leg and shook it. She put it down and shook the other hind leg.

"What in blazes are you doing?"

She pushed away from the tree and landed on all fours, then reared up on her hind legs. That smile was on her face again. So I clapped for her.

"Good girl! Good trick, Pandora." On the word "trick", she stood still, looking at me soberly. Then she keeled over.

"Pandora!" I crept up to her and patted her shoulder. "Pandora? Are you okay?"

She jumped up and pranced around the campfire, neighing. No, not neighing. She was laughing.

I clapped some more.

Before I knew it, she trotted over to my stuff, grabbed the saddle by the horn and flipped it over her head. It landed square on her back.

I stood there in the glow of the fire, my mouth agape. "You want to go for a ride?"

She nodded.

I secured the saddle and mounted her. "Let's go girl."

She pranced around the fire at a leisurely pace. Then, with one front leg forward and the other bending, she bowed to some unseen monarch.

"Good girl." I dismounted and stood there looking at her with awe. Just how many tricks did she have? "Can you count?" I asked. "How many is four?"

I was really expecting her to toe the ground and give it four strokes. Instead, she just stared at me.

"Four. How many is four, Pandora?"

She shook her head.

"What, you don't know how to add?"

She pranced back over to the pine tree with a jaunty gait. She picked up a pine cone with her teeth and faced me. Then she jutted her head up, letting go of the pine cone. It flew right at me. I lost it in the dark and the pine cone struck me in the chest. She nodded, smiling.

"You want me to throw it back?"

She whinnied. I lobbed the pine cone under-handed. It flew to her right. She stepped into the throw and caught the pine cone in her mouth.

"Incredible," I whispered.

We played catch for a few moments, then she lowered her head.

"Are you tired girl?"

She slowly waddled over to the fire and peered into the flames.

For some crazy reason, I thought that maybe she had psychic powers. Maybe staring into the fire, she could tell the future. She stood there for a long time.

"What is it girl? Do you see the future? Do you see happy days and fields of grass?" I was babbling, but at least I was babbling out in the middle of nowhere with just a horse as a witness. "Do you see the future girl?"

She turned her head, looking at me. Did I see wet in her eyes? Do horses have tear ducts? Then she did a strange thing. That is, if you could say the other things she had done were normal. She walked over to me and put her head next to mine. And she stood there, touching me. And for a brief moment, I felt touched.

The next day, Pandora, the wonder horse, and I broke camp and headed toward Clearview. With luck, we'd be there in the early morning hours of the next day. I was singing a bawdy sailor's song to entertain Pandora when I caught a glimpse of white on a hill top. The lyrics, "She sailed the ocean blue with sailors two by two" stuck in my throat when I recognized the white as war feathers of the Comanche.

There were seven of them. All braves. Without making a big move, I bucked my legs, spurring Pandora into a solemn canter. The Comanche's were to my left, about a quarter mile away, and moving toward me. A flat prairie lay ahead, dotted with sagebrush.

"Come on girl. You're going to have to run like you never ran before! Eeyaa!"

I kicked her and Pandora went into that slow, familiar gallop.

"Come on! Come on girl! Go!"

I kicked her again. She didn't speed up. I looked back and saw The Comanche's headed my way.

"Pandora! Eeyaa!"

With mounting hope, the wind picked up. She was running a tad bit faster. The Comanche's were whooping. It was a chilling sound, mixed with anger, triumph, and blood lust.

"Pandora! Please!"

She looked back. Her eyes were wide with fear. Good! Maybe she would speed up.

"Yow! Yow! Yow!" came the cries behind me.

Pandora did not speed up. I think she was running as fast as her fat little legs would carry her. I didn't look back. I kept looking at the wide, endless expanse in front of me. No cover. I was a dead man.

"Yow! Yow! Yow!"

They were probably fifty feet behind me. I tensed, waiting for the deadly arrow or spear to pierce my back. Pandora whinnied in panic. Without my command, she started to zigzag in a defensive strategy.

Out of the corner of my eye, I caught sight of a Comanche brave. The whooping sounded horrendous as they pulled up beside me. There were two on each side of me. Gathering my courage, I looked into the face of a young brave.

Then the whooping turned to laughter. They were laughing! They were laughing at Pandora, slowest horse in the west.

One of the braves beside me pointed and continued laughing. He shouted something in Comanche to the others and another laughed so hard, he fell off his horse. I glanced back and saw him rolling in the dust, still laughing.

After about half a mile, the Comanches broke off and let me gallop slowly away from them. Pandora, not realizing they had stopped their pursuit, was still zigzagging through the sage. I looked back and saw all of them sitting on their horses, coughing and laughing uncontrollably.

"Okay Pandora, it's okay. It's okay girl."

I stroked her mane and she stopped her zigzagging. After two more miles, I checked to see if the Comanche's had followed us. I saw no telltale dust. We were apparently out of danger.

Chapter Five

Clearview, Kansas was about forty-five miles southwest of Dodge City. Eventually it would join many others on a list of ghost towns, but that spring, it was the fourth largest city in the state with a population of twelve thousand.

There were three main streets and six side streets filled with stores, shops, and saloons. Pandora and I came riding in around six a.m. There was actually a café open on the empty Main Street, so I decided to get some breakfast. I walked into the unoccupied dining room and sat at a table. A girl behind the counter gave me a wave.

"Be with you in a minute mister."

My plan for later was to stand outside the Anglin Cattle Company and get a good look at Benita before she got to work. The picture that Jacob Specks gave me showed an out of focus girl with long, curly hair and two very dark eyes. That's about all one could tell. I wanted to see Benita Brooks in the flesh.

Benita knew I was coming. She did not know I was

with The Service. From her point of view, I was the man that Cousin Jacob sent to protect her from Featherston. She knew my cover story was that of an itinerate school teacher who was coming to Clearview to offer private tutoring. She also knew that I was an actual school teacher with bodyguard experience.

Jacob had gotten me a room at The Berkshire, a three story, twenty room, grand hotel. It was all set. Benita was to meet me at the train station at noon.

Earlier, I mentioned my attraction to the would-be husband killer, Wilma Ducette. That needs clarification. I have one problem with women. God gave me handsome features. He also gave me the shyness of a naked possum in the midst of jackals. I'm not afraid of women, mind you, I just have a tendency to fall in love with any female whose feet reach the ground. Then I get tongue-tied. I sweat a little. Even a dowdy matron with two grown sons can give me a coquettish smile and I'm thrown into romantic turmoil.

I hoped Benita would be different. She was a job. And Specks said he'd make sure I'd never have children if I tried something funny with his cousin.

The waitress came up to me with a pad. Her name was sewn into the pocket of her blouse. It read CALLIE. She was young and pretty. Her hair was honey-colored and tied in a severe bun, but her features were fragile.

"May I take your order sir?"

"Let me have toast, scrambled eggs, and coffee."

She gave me a friendly smile as she poured water from a tin pitcher into the empty glass in front of me. "I'll be right back."

A few moments later, as I ate my scrambled eggs,

a familiar face showed up. He was a hefty, mustached man with a gun on each hip and a gold badge on a green shirt. It was Lewis Featherston in the flesh.

He gave me a curious look, then took a seat in the corner. He plopped two heavy boots on the table and leaned back in his chair.

"One steak and eggs, Callie!" he yelled. "And burn 'em."

His voice was like sandpaper and he had wide nostrils that flared out when he talked. That was all well and good, but I didn't like the way he seemed to take over the place.

"Coffee Callie!" He was bossy.

Callie came from the back with a steaming pot. "I've got it Lewis."

He turned his cup over and let her pour. His eyes made a waterfall motion down her body. "You have a nice looking form under that dress, Callie."

I admired the fact that she didn't seem flustered by his leer and comment.

"It's one of the few I can afford."

Was she talking about her body or her dress? He made a move to caress her hip, but she was already headed back to the kitchen. She didn't seem to notice his lecherous attention.

Featherston let out a rough laugh and gave me a wink. I went back to my own coffee, watching the man out of the corner of my eye. A shadow fell over me.

"More coffee sir?" Callie stood next to me with the pot of coffee.

"Yes, please." I held up the cup and she poured.

"You're new," she said straight out.

"Yes ma'am. I'm a school teacher."

Callie nodded, then shot a look over at Featherston. "Some people around here could use some schooling."

Featherston was eyeing us both with a hard stare. "How's my steak coming, Callie? I've got to go to work."

"Keep your powder dry Lewis. We're killing that cow out back right now."

Featherston let out a bone shattering cry of laughter. Brown spittle flecked the white tablecloth in front of him. A tobacco man. Alan Coletrane was said to have had the chaw habit.

"Get in there girl and tell that no-good cook to hurry up."

Callie hid a smirk that she gave only to me. Okay. I was officially in love. I watched her head back to the kitchen.

"Hey you!" It was Featherston.

I decided to ignore him, waiting for the inevitable, "I'm talking to you!"

"I'm talking to you, mister!"

Mister. I hadn't counted on the mister part. I slowly turned. "Yes sir?" I tried to play it bold, but guarded. I was a teacher, new in town, not ready for any confrontation.

Featherston was giving me the meanest look he could come up with. He'd probably practiced it in the mirror when he woke up that morning. I had to admit, it was a pretty mean look.

"You're new in town," he said. It was a statement, not a question.

"Yes sir. I'm a teacher."

"Teacher," he said under his breath. He might as well have said, "Polecat."

"What do you teach?"

"Geography, history, arithmetic, spelling, grammar. Just about everything there is to teach." I pulled a McGuffey's Reader from my pack and held it up. "I also teach reading. Do you know how to read?"

It might have been my imagination, but I think I heard Callie give a muted shriek of amusement from the back.

Featherston's face went from insulted to outrage. "I can read better than anybody!" He stood up.

I felt for my gun, but realized I was now a teacher, not an officer of the law. There was no holstered gun at my side.

"You give me something to read. I'll show ya."

Apparently I'd hit a sore spot with Featherston. "I assumed you could sir. I was only inquiring, because I thought you might have children who don't."

He sat back down. "Don't have kids," he said with a nasty grin, "at least, none that I know of." He slapped his knee, letting out another shattering stream of laughter and tobacco. He called back to the kitchen, "You hear that Callie?! None that I know of!?"

Callie came out and wiped down the counter.

His humor turned off like tap water and he scowled. "More coffee Callie."

She took the pot and walked back to his table. His eyes followed her every move. "You sure are a good looking woman."

Between Callie and Benita, I wagered that Featherston was using up his best lines. Callie poured the coffee and quick as a bullet, she was over at my table.

"More coffee sir?"

I waved her off. "No thank you ma'am. I'm pretty well set."

At that moment, a little man not quite five feet tall and almost a hundred pounds if he had a bag of dimes in his pocket, came rushing in. He had the posture of a bent oak tree and a totally bald head. It was hard to determine his age. He was either an old looking fifty or a young looking eighty. His gait was between a hobble and a shuffle as he hurried over to Featherston.

"What is it Pee Wee?"

The man stood there, gulping in air. Featherston tapped a fork impatiently on the table.

Between breaths, Pee Wee spoke. "Mr. Anglin says some contracts are coming in on the noon train."

Featherston looked over at Callie. "Hey Callie, when my food gets done, throw it in one of those paper bags. Then give it to Pee Wee here." He slapped some money on the table and hurried out.

Why the hurry? He had over five hours before the noon train. What was so important about cattle contracts?

I was tempted to follow the man, but it was unseemly for a new school teacher in town to skulk around in the shadows. It was better to let my food digest. Then I would head over to The Berkshire Hotel and check my room out.

With much effort, Pee Wee climbed on a high stool at the counter. "What's good today Callie?"

Without a word, she sliced a piece of apple pie and set it in front of him. "Coffee?" she asked.

"Yes ma'am. Thank you ma'am."

I finished my breakfast and wondered about Pee Wee, contracts on a train, and Featherston. I'd been in town for twenty minutes and already my mind was intrigued.

I headed over to The Berkshire Hotel. Pandora clopped along slowly, letting me know she had not gotten her beauty sleep. I stopped in front of the hotel and looked up at the three story structure. "We're here." I climbed off Pandora and lashed her to the hitching post. Then I went inside.

The Berkshire wasn't as elaborate as my hotel in St. Louis, but it had fur rugs in the lobby. A silver-haired woman of about fifty and of large proportions greeted me with a smile. "Good morning."

I doffed my hat. "Good morning. My name is Randy Foster. I believe you have a room for me."

"Yes Mr. Foster. We've been expecting you." She thumbed through a box of cards. "You're a school teacher I hear."

How she found out so quick, I didn't know. Maybe it was on the reservation card. Specks would have given that out.

"Yes ma'am. I am."

"I have a nephew who could use some private tutoring."

"When I'm settled, I'd be happy to meet him."

She pulled out a card. "Ah, here we are. You are in Room 101."

The first floor. I was hoping for a room on the third floor that had a balcony overlooking Main Street. Of course, The Service was frugal when it came to hotels. I was pretty confident that my room would be a glorified broom closet.

"Will you need a livery service for your horse?"

I thought of Pandora and envisioned her tossing

milk bottles. "No ma'am. I'll just keep her tethered to the hitching post out front."

The woman looked past me, toward the front door of the hotel. "I'm sure she would be more comfortable in a stable," she said.

I turned. Pandora was standing halfway in the lobby.

"I'm sorry ma'am. I'll secure her out front." I had forgotten that the only way to keep her secured was to actually tie a knot in the reins to the post. I left the hotel desk and walked over to Pandora. "Behave!" I violently whispered to her. I took her outside and came up with the best threat that came to mind. "You get loose again, and I'm taking you over to the livery."

She nodded her head and allowed me to tie her to the post.

My room was small and narrow with a bed, lamp, table, and chair. It was truly the size of a large closet. The bed, which was only a single, took up most of the floor space. There was a window that looked on to Main Street. The room inspired me to go out and scout the town. I left the hotel and to Pandora's chagrin, I traveled on foot.

Clearview was waking up. Farmers brought in wagons of produce toward the market down by the railroad depot. Shopkeepers were unlocking their doors and pulling down their awnings. The newspaper, the *Journal*, was already running its presses. A newsboy came out on the street with the morning edition. I bought a paper and continued my walk around town.

I found out that on the corner of Second Street and Mesa, there was a row of restaurants and shops known as The Spanish Quarter. Lively Mexican music was playing in one of the cantinas. Who in their right mind was dancing to lively music at this time of the morning? Anglin Cattle Company was on Third Street. It was a long, red brick building with glass windows. It was two stories tall. In front of it was a shoe shine stand. Across the street was a confection/tobacco shop. I went inside and bought some chewing gum. I hoped that chewing the gum would make people think I was working on a large piece of tobacco. Of course, I wouldn't be doing much spitting. I decided the newspaper was a good cover. I could pretend to read, while getting a good view of Anglin Cattle.

Around nine o'clock, people began milling about. Pee Wee showed up and unlocked the shoe shine box. He instantly had two black booted customers. I saw a man who was tall and broad. He had a salt and pepper beard and looked to be in his thirties. He lurched down the boardwalk, weaving to the right. People side-stepped him with utter distaste. He had all the markings of the town drunk. His shirt was dirty and his trousers had mud on them. After a block, he disappeared into an alley. More and more people entered the Anglin office.

It didn't take long for Benita Brooks to show up. Thanks to the out of focus pictures, I recognized her in focus immediately. She wore a simple, pale green skirt with a white blouse. A bonnet covered her long, brown hair. Her eyes were not dark like in the picture. They were bright, brown buttons that had a smile to them. She was just over five feet tall and carried her small frame erect and proud. Her cheeks had a natural glow on tanned skin. My bet was, she had Comanche blood. Her nose had a hook to it like her cousin Jacob. No, not that hooked. You are picturing too much of a hook.

It was a cute, downward turn. She was definitely cute. Even pretty. Yep, I was in love.

I had time to kill before I met Benita at the depot. That was where all strangers meet whether they came in on the train or not. I moseyed over to the Prairie Saloon on Second Street to have a beer.

The saloon also served food, so the place was busy with late breakfast and early lunch. I found a table in the corner and took out the *Journal*. I actually read it this time. There was a story of a bank robbery in Midvale, a town not too far from Clearview.

A group of seven men robbed a Wells Fargo coach up near the Nebraska border. The driver was beaten along with the two male passengers. Two females were also robbed and according to this report, violated. I shook my head.

"We are in the End Times," I declared quietly.

And this, I was sure of. The world had grown crazy. As the west got civilized, men became more uncivilized. As if to support my point, I heard a shotgun blast from outside. There were some screams and the sound of a galloping horse. Everyone jumped up and ran to the window. A woman continued screaming. I got up with the others to see what happened.

Lying facedown in front of the saloon was a man with a big, red, gurgling hole in his back. His head lay to the side. Blood trickled from one corner of his mouth and his eyes had the glaze of death. He wore the clothes of a cowpuncher. One spur was still on a boot, the other was eight feet away. The impact of the blast sent the man sprawling several feet forward. I looked up Second Street and saw a cloud of dust in the distance.

One of the bystanders cried out, pointing to the dead figure. "It's Tom Addington!"

A woman screamed and fainted. I'm not sure if she was screaming at the name of the dead man or the sight of Tom Addington lying in the street.

"Someone get the sheriff!"

Two more people stood over the dead man. "That's Tom, all right."

"We need to send word to Hogan."

I surmised that Hogan was the man's boss.

A man in a straw hat, white shirt, and blue vest, ran up to the crowd. "What happened here?" he asked. He pulled out a pencil and notepad. A reporter.

But he was no reporter. I'd seen his face before. But where? He was about my age, had curly blond hair under the straw hat, and a small, white scar through his left eyebrow.

"Tom Addington was shot," said an on-looker.

The woman who had swooned was being led to the steps in front of the saloon. Several people were giving their stories to the *Journal* reporter. Others were coming out of the stores and peering down the street at the still, bleeding body in the dust. It was pure chaos.

The reporter held up his hands. "All right, all right, one at a time, people. Don't everybody speak at once." He scribbled furiously as an eye witness gave his account.

"I was leaving the feed store and saw Tom Addington headed to the saloon. One of his spurs was loose and I was about to call out to him."

I admired the eyewitness's observation skills.

"Then, before I could say anything, this man came

galloping by. He wore a long coat, and had a bandana over his face. He had a shotgun. Without slowing down, he popped Tom in the back and flew down the street." The eyewitness pointed where the cloud of dust had cleared.

The reporter continued to write as he spoke. "What color was his horse?"

The eyewitness started to speak, then looked blank.

The reporter tried to prompt him. "Was it a paint? All black? Black with white spots?"

The eyewitness shook his head in confusion.

The reporter scribbled some more then continued. "You said he wore a mask. Did you see his eyes? Hair color?"

"I couldn't see his face too good with that bandana."

"Was he a big man? Average?"

The witness shook his head once more. "What color was his long coat?" asked the reporter.

The man's eyes lit up. He smiled. "Black! A long, black coat. And he wore round toed boots. Black boots. And his hat was black. A broad-brimmed black hat."

"Did it have a hat-band?"

The witness scrunched his eyes in concentration. "I don't remember."

"Other than the shotgun, did he have any other weapons visible under the long, black coat?" asked the reporter.

I realized that the reporter was questioning the witness, not as a newsman, but as a lawman. He was definitely with The Service. Was he called Bear or Arrow? Those were my two contacts. Would they know me? They had to.

Suddenly, an old man wandered through the crowd.

His hair was white, as was his mustache. He must have been well past seventy as he slowly lowered himself over the dead man. He wore a sheriff's badge. "Who is it?" he asked.

"Tom Addington, Sheriff."

The old sheriff took out some bifocals. He eyed the wound and gently felt for a pulse. He put the back of his hand to the man's brow like he was taking Tom Addington's temperature.

"I'm here, Sheriff Daily!"

The sheriff looked up, confusion filling his face. Featherston broke through the crowd with two of his own men. They too, wore badges and green shirts.

"That you Lewis?" asked the sheriff.

Featherston put a hand on Daily's shoulder. "I'm here. You don't have to worry your old head about this." Featherston nodded to his two men. "Take Sheriff Daily back to his office and get him out of the sun."

Sheriff Daily looked befuddled, but went willingly with the two Anglin security officers.

Featherston waved everybody off. "Clear out, I'm in charge here!" He pointed to Pee Wee who was at the edge of the group. "Pee Wee, go get Doc Fenton."

The crowd began to disperse.

Featherston took hold of the reporter's arm. "Wha'cha got Farly?"

Farly slowly took his arm from Featherston's grasp. He pointed his pencil down at the dead man. "This is Tom Addington—one of Hogan's hands."

"No, I mean the man who shot him."

Farly shrugged. "He wore a long, black coat, used a shot gun, and had his face covered." Farly pointed the pencil at several people, naming them off. "Trey,

Mr. Kennedy, Carl—you might ask them what they saw." He slapped the notebook on his thigh. "I've got enough for my story."

So this was how it worked. Featherston was the real law in Clearview. Sheriff Daily was a figurehead. I followed Farly as he headed back to the newspaper office.

"Hi," I said. "I guess a killing in Clearview is big news."

Farly stopped. He looked at me and frowned. "It's the fifth killing this year. The third one with a shotgun. You must be new in town."

"Fresh off the trail." I offered my hand. "Randy Foster. I'm a teacher."

A smile instantly appeared on his face. Then it instantly disappeared. He shook my hand. "Well sir, the *Journal* could use your services."

"How so?"

"The old sot of an editor and myself are responsible for the paper's grammar and we are lacking in that skill. Perhaps you could look over our work and make corrections before we put it in print."

I nodded. "That would be good. Why don't I buy you a beer?"

"No thanks. I've got to get this story to press." Farly walked briskly up on the boardwalk.

I followed.

"Then I'll look over your story when you're finished."

"Excellent," he said. As an afterthought, he added, "I'm Farly Wilson."

He took my arm as we entered the office of the *Journal*. The place smelled of ink and paper. The press was right up in the show window. Two cluttered desks took up half the space of the small room. Farly gestured to a desk that had the editor's nameplate on it. "He's over at the saloon soaking his liver."

Farly went over to a door and checked inside a smaller room. It was more like a large closet with files and a cot. "Wanted to make sure he wasn't sleeping off a drunk," Farly said. Then he walked back over to me and shook my hand. "Welcome to Clearview, Rattler."

Chapter Six

After shaking Farly Wilson's hand, I had to ask, "Are you Arrow or Bear?"

"Arrow. Bear will contact us for a meeting. Right now you need to get your feet wet and get acquainted with the landscape."

"Yep. Been doing that. What about the other shotgun killings?"

"First of all, I think Lewis Featherston is our man, but I have no proof. Even if he isn't, he's up to no-good."

"I see how he took over that killing. The sheriff must be a puppet."

"The man has "old folks disease", but he keeps getting elected. I'm sure Featherston is behind that. He doesn't want a strong-minded lawman around."

"But how does Featherston get away with doing the sheriff's job?"

"He is an official deputy. So are all of his men."

I pondered this. "So Featherston investigated the other killings."

"Right. I don't see a relationship. One was a bank teller. He lived just outside of town. The milkman found him."

"Clearview has a milk delivery service?"

"As good as St. Louis. You would not believe what this town has. Trev Olfman came down from Wisconsin and started his own dairy. He's got several ice-houses and a pasteurizing system."

Fresh, cold milk was a treat I experienced in Denver and St. Louis. I looked forward to having a glass.

Arrow continued, "Anyway, the bank teller had been shot in his sleep. I took some pictures."

"Not for the newspaper."

"Oh no. I sent the pictures back to The Service."

"How long ago was that?"

"Eight months."

"You've been here for eight months?"

It wasn't a record. Gator was undercover with a gambling syndicate on the Barbary Coast for sixteen months. It was an essential part of The Service that an agent became part of the community. It gained trust.

Arrow shrugged. "I was in Mexico for three months. It felt like three years."

I rewarded him with a short laugh. "What about the other killing?"

"The last killing before today was a man who worked in the Anglin cattle office. He was an accountant."

"Any witnesses?"

"Nope. He was working late one night. Someone came in and took off the back of his head. Terry Hill was his name."

"There was evidence of a break in?"

"No. Terry must have left the door unlocked when he went in to work."

"What was the bank teller's name?"

"Mike Reese."

"Hmm. A bank teller, an accountant and a cowpoke." I failed to see the connection. Arrow peered out the window. A short, fat man, red as a rose, was staggering toward the newspaper office.

"That's Teddy Bartly, editor in chief."

I headed for the door. "Guess I'd better go."

"Hey Rattler, come back tomorrow and I'll have you edit some of our copy."

I nodded.

The editor stumbled through the door and looked at me with bleary eyes. "Want to buy some advertising son?"

Before I could answer, Arrow took the man by the arm. "Sit Teddy. This is Randy Foster, a new teacher in town."

Teddy looked up at me. He widened his eyes, trying to see past the alcoholic haze. "You don't say."

"Yes sir. And Randy's going to help us with our grammar."

Teddy pointed at me. "A dollar and fifty cents a day. It's all I can afford."

"That will be sufficient sir." I half bowed to the old sot.

Teddy leaned back in his chair and rubbed his neck. There was a creak. I didn't know whether it was the chair or his neck. He looked up at the ceiling.

"Of course if we're too grammatical, the citizenry won't be able to understand it."

Before Arrow could speak, I held up my hand in a

pledge position. "I believe in writing the way people talk. But I will make sure that every word is spelled correctly and no participle will dangle."

Before I finished that speech, Teddy Bartly was limp and snoring loudly.

At the depot, I sat on the bench with my trusty newspaper. The street was bustling with activity. A yellow milk wagon turned the corner and stopped in front of the Mercantile. It had red lettering on it that read BUTTERMILK DIARY—TREV OLFMAN, PROPRIETOR. Ladies in their "city finery" entered several shops. They all left with bags, hatboxes, or new clothes on hangers. Near noon, more people appeared on the boardwalk, heading into various saloons and restaurants. The post office across the street closed down for the lunch hour. Some town boys in their early to late teens met in an alley next to the post office and proceeded to shoot craps. There were cries of triumph and groans of defeat, sprinkled with cursing and laughter. I could not tell if they were truants or rabble-rousers. Since they were acting loud and obnoxious, I ruled out the possibility of truancy. Clearview was not going to make one forget Denver or St. Louis, but for a small town, it had its share of movement and commerce.

Before the train arrived, Featherston rode up and stationed himself next to the telegraph office. He looked over my way curiously, but ignored me. At seven minutes before noon, he walked over to me.

"Leaving so soon, teacher?"

"Oh, I'm not leaving. I'm meeting someone."

Before he could ask who it was, I asked him a question. "How is your murder case going?"

A deep scowl played across his face. "What murder?"

"The man who was killed this morning." It was as if I'd reminded him to pull his boots on before going outside.

"Oh yeah. I didn't really think of it as some unsolved murder case."

"It's not?"

His sly smile told me the answer before he could tell it himself. "We know who did it," he said.

I put on my best "teacher who is not used to violent crime" look of surprise. "Do tell. Who was it?"

"A varmint we have on a wanted poster. Nick Starrett."

Upon passing the post office and the sheriff's office on my early morning walk, I had not seen any wanted poster with a man named Nick Starrett.

Featherston toed the dirt with his boot as he spoke. "Yeah, he's wanted in three states for bank robbery and murder."

I clucked my tongue like an old biddy who was a veteran gossip. "My, my. Is he in jail now?"

Featherston toed the ground harder, not looking at me. "No. Me and the boys had him cornered in a barn just outside of Midvale. We had a shoot-out and that egg sucker is now dead."

As I put up a face of frightened disbelief, I smiled to myself. Featherston was not real good at thinking on his feet.

"That's big news. Maybe you ought to tell that reporter over at the *Journal*."

Beads of sweat were forming under the brim of his hat. "Yeah, maybe I—" He stopped.

We heard a train whistle off in the distance. We both looked down the tracks and saw smoke over the tree line.

Also in our sights was Benita Brooks who stood on the platform. She too, was looking down the tracks at the approaching train.

Featherston waved both his arms wildly. "Hey, Benita!"

She turned slowly like she was about to see a slaughtered bull. Then she smiled thinly. "Hello Lewis."

"What are you doing here?" he asked.

I stood up. "She's here to meet me."

At my words, Benita's face froze. This was not good. She was supposed to know me. Of course, we weren't planning on Featherston being at our first meeting.

I held out my arms and smiled broadly. "I fooled you. Instead of taking the train, I rode in early."

Benita recovered quickly and went into a very convincing act of true love. "Randy! Oh Randy!"

She ran past Featherston and flew into my arms.

"Why didn't you tell me you were coming in early?"

"I didn't take the time to send a wire. I couldn't wait to see you."

Lewis Featherston's mouth was agape. He was totally speechless.

We continued our charade. "Did you find a room in town, darling?"

"I did. I freshened up so we could have a fast lunch before you have to get back to work."

She took my hand. "I know the perfect place. It's on Second Street."

Before we headed off, Featherston found his voice. "Who is this man Benita?"

"Oh, Randy Foster, this is Lewis Featherston."

"Yes, we've already met," I said.

Benita's eyes were bright and happy. I was beginning to think that she was really glad to see me.

"Randy and I are old friends, Lewis. He's going to be teaching here in Clearview." Then she turned to me. "Lewis is head of security at the cattle company."

"You seem to be very capable," I offered.

Featherston's face was a frozen portrait of restrained fury. The train slowly pulled into the depot and his attention turned toward it. "Well, I've got to pick up some mail for Anglin." He looked at me none-to-friendly, nodded curtly, and said, "Guess I'll see you around."

I gave him a prissy salute, then offered my arm to Benita. "Most definitely. Come my dear."

We headed toward Second Street. As we walked, Benita's hand tightened on mine, but her voice was cooler. "Thanks for the warning Mr. Foster. I hope I didn't overact."

I ignored the sudden frost she was throwing on me. "You were perfect. But I was hoping to meet you without the man who's been bothering you."

She looked back toward the station. "That was him all right. He gives me candy and flowers, but it's always with a leer. He makes me very nervous."

"Well now that he's had a look at your beau, maybe he'll leave you alone."

"That's what I was hoping." A brief fear passed through her eyes. "I think he watches me at night."

"You think, or you know?"

Her face fell. "I'd had the feeling that I was being

watched. It's hard to describe, but I knew it. I have to go outside to pump water for my bath. It usually takes about four trips with the water bucket."

I could feel the blood rushing to my face at the image of Benita taking a bath. "Go on," I said.

"On my third trip to the pump I saw a face in the bushes. It was Lewis. I pretended I didn't see him and went back in. I didn't make a fourth trip to the pump." Her hand gripped mine tighter as we headed down the boardwalk of Second Street. "I keep my curtains drawn, but sometimes I peek through them with my lamp off. I've seen him out there."

"Your bedroom curtains?"

She nodded and blushed. Before entering The Blue Bird Café, Benita stopped at the door. "Randy, I asked my cousin to help. He sent you. I'm not expecting trouble. I just hope Lewis will see that I'm spoken for and leave me alone."

Before I could reply, she led me into the café. We had lunch and got to know each other. At least she got to know me as a teacher, not as an undercover member of The Service.

I didn't need to know a lot about Benita. I already knew her brown eyes were liquid and I was drowning in them. I wanted to brush a stray strand of luscious brown hair that draped across her cheek. She had a freckle at the top left corner of her lips. I wanted to kiss it.

The good news was, she was a client. A job. I was playing a part, so my shyness wasn't a factor. Nothing was on the line. My only regret was, I would never be able to tell her the truth about me. If I did, I'd turn into a blathering idiot.

"Mr. Anglin is such a nice man," she was saying. "He lost his wife and son in that horrible flood up in West Virginia ten years ago. He moved to Kansas and started his business."

"Anglin Cattle has turned into a pretty big business," I said.

"That's why I'm here," she replied. "I hope to have my own business."

This was news. Whoever heard of a woman having her own business? Except of course, a madam. "You want to be in the cattle business?"

She reached across the table and flicked me on the shoulder. "Of course not, silly."

I hoped to say something else silly so she would flick me on the shoulder again.

"I want to have my own dress shop. That's why I got the job at Anglin. I want to know all there is to financing, payroll, and filing. I started as a file clerk, but got promoted to the accounting division."

My thoughts went to Terry Hill, whose head was blown off by a shotgun in the accounting department.

Benita continued, "Mr. Anglin is a dear. Once I proved my mettle, he wanted to stake me for the dress shop, but I couldn't do it. I want to make it on my own."

It was unseeming for a young woman to want these things. I thought all women wanted a house, children, and a husband who had a good job. Benita Brooks seemed soft and vulnerable on the outside, but on the inside, she had ambition of stone.

"Did you ever see a cattle contract?" I asked. I thought maybe I'd learn why Featherston was so interested in the contracts he picked up.

"No, but that's my next step. I hope to be working

with Mr. Leslie by the end of the year. Mr. Leslie is the cattle company's legal counsel. I know they'd never let a woman in that position, but Mr. Anglin has confidence in me."

"So Mr. Leslie is the one who looks over the contracts."

She nodded as she sipped her tea. "He's the vice president. Mr. Leslie has his own law office on Main Street."

I wanted to ask her more questions, but Benita changed the subject on me. "So Mr. Randy Foster, how do you like opera?"

"Very much. I usually don't understand the words, but the music tells me all I need to know."

She let out a deep, throaty laugh. Very deep and throaty for such a small woman. I found it enchanting.

She nodded. "Then I'll pick you up at your hotel at seven. I have a buckboard I bought for cheap."

"Oh no, Miss Brooks. I am to escort you. I'll ride over to your house and we'll take the buckboard to the theatre."

Benita smiled softly.

I was doing all I could to keep from jumping across the table and kissing her. Instead, I buttered a roll.

"Why Mr. Foster, I think I'm going to like you a lot."

I buttered a second roll. Apparently, while I had become charmed by Benita Brooks, she too, had fallen for my handsome face. No brag, just fact.

"I, uh . . . I think I like you too," I said. It was me talking, not the character I was playing. I started to stutter. "I-I-" I picked up another roll and buttered it.

She nodded to the roll, lathered in yellow. "You've already buttered two of those."

Before I could panic, and jam the three rolls into my mouth all at once, a man in a blue suit approached the table. He held a cane in one hand and a derby in the other. He was a handsome man in his late sixties. His hair was steel gray, as were his eyes. They were kind eyes and he smiled down at us from his six-foot-three frame.

"Miss Brooks. Who is your friend?"

I rose from my chair as did Benita. "Mr. Anglin, this is Randy Foster from Tenbone, Colorado. We're old friends."

His handshake was warm. His hands were as soft as cotton. "How are you young man? I'm Warren Anglin."

"A pleasure sir."

Anglin put an arm around Benita. "Why didn't you tell me you had a young gentleman under your affections?"

"You know me sir. I'm all business and I keep my private life, private."

Anglin nodded, chuckling quietly. He put a fatherly hand on my shoulder. "Benita is my best worker. And she's like a daughter to me. So welcome Mr. Foster of Colorado. If she's always this happy around you, then you're a keeper."

"Thank you sir."

Mr. Anglin put on his derby and held up his cane. "I will leave you two to your lunch. Mr. Foster, if you need anything, let me know."

"Again, I thank you sir. It was a pleasure meeting you."

Benita and I sat back down. I watched the tall man in the blue suit walk out the door. I liked Warren Anglin.

"He must really like you," said Benita.

"Why is that?"

"Mr. Anglin doesn't eat here. Apparently he was passing by and saw us in the window. The fact that he made a special effort to come in and introduce himself speaks volumes."

Speaks volumes. I'd never heard that expression. "Speaks volumes of what?"

Benita held her arms out. "Volumes of whatever you can think of. The important thing is, he likes you. Warren Anglin is a straight shooter. He means a lot to this town, and he can do a lot of good things for you."

"I like him too."

"So. Let's talk opera. The one tonight is called *La Bohème*."

"I've never seen that one, but I'm looking forward to it." I stood up and held out my hand. "But we need to get you back to work. We can't have Mr. Anglin catching you coming in late. He might stop liking me."

Chapter Seven

I couldn't just walk around town all day to learn any more than I had. Like Arrow, I had to insert myself into the community. My first stop was at the Clearview Bank and Trust.

It was a new building made of brown brick. A big glass window revealed three teller windows and a customer at one of them. As I walked closer, I could see a green shirted deputy sitting in a chair near the door. Even in daylight, it was easy to see inside. This bank was built to discourage any lowlife who might consider robbing it.

I walked inside. A bell over the door rang out, announcing my arrival. The customer, a middle aged woman, left the teller window. I tipped my hat to her and she returned a smile. Friendly people. I stepped back and held the door for her.

"Thank you, kind sir," she said.

The bell rang as the door closed. The deputy/guard held a shotgun across his lap. He gave me a good once over and scowled. His face said, "Tip your hat at me and I'll blow it off your head." Yep. Real friendly.

The interior of the bank was painted a pale green. A fan whistled overhead, creating a pleasant breeze. The place had the feel of a library, very calm, very serene. Although there were three windows, only one teller was on duty. The skin wrinkled down his face like a fleshy waterfall. He had two dark circles under his eyes. He looked like a hound dog in an undertaker's suit. His smile lifted the wrinkles and brightened his entire countenance.

"Yes sir, may I help you?"

I walked over to the counter and put both hands on the counter. "Hello. My name is Randy Foster."

The man slipped a wrinkled hand through the bars and shook my right hand in greeting. "Great to know you Randy. I'm Clarence Biggs." With the hint of a ceremony, he pulled a card from his pocket and slipped it to me. "My card, sir." It was a fancy business card. It was grey with glossy green printing and dollar signs on all four corners. The name, Clarence Adams Biggs was embossed along with the title, HEAD TELLER.

I tapped the card on the counter. "It's nice to meet you, Mr. Biggs."

"How can I be of service, Mr. Foster?"

"Well, I'm new here in Clearview. I hope to start teaching in the fall."

"That's good to hear. Our school marm is getting on in years. Miss Parker is a good teacher, but she couldn't hear the wail of a banshee." Mr. Biggs clucked sympathetically. "Can't see too good either. Last week she was talking to the barber pole, telling "Nate Hensley" how much she liked his red and blue striped tie."

A laugh erupted from the sour-faced deputy. Biggs smirked. "I'm only kidding son. It's nice to find out we're getting a teacher that can see and hear at the same time."

"I'm not sure I'll be pushing Miss Parker out of her position. I'm a private tutor."

A quick frown crossed his face, then he brightened. "Oh, well. Even better. My daughter has a ten-year-old who needs special attention." He leaned into the bars and whispered. "She's slow."

I nodded.

"So how can I be of service, Mr. Foster? Are you here to open an account?"

"Yes sir. I am gainfully employed at the *Journal* as a proofreader."

"Ah, Bartly's a good man. Even when he's drunk, he can write a news story that will put ice cubes down your shirt. He's got an account with us. So does that young reporter, Farly."

"Then it looks like I'm in the right place, but tell me . . . how safe is my money?"

Mr. Biggs looked insulted. "Why Mr. Foster, this is the best place in Kansas to lay down your green and coinage. Let me give you a tour to assuage your fears." He walked around to the door that led to the area behind the windows. "Come right in, Mr. Foster."

He led me down a corridor. As we passed an office, he threw a thumb in its direction.

"That's the office of Mr. Spiels, the bank president." We passed a larger room with a table. It looked sort of like a jury room. "Board room," he explained. "Did you see Anglin Cattle Company when you came into town?"

"Yes sir."

"Mr. Anglin is the head of our board of directors. The design of this bank was his idea."

With this information, I had even more respect for Mr. Anglin.

"He said he wanted a bank that was more . . . what was the word?" Biggs scratched his head in thought. "Ah! Unrobbable. Now isn't that a word? Unrobbable." We stopped in the middle of the corridor. He pointed down toward the end of it. "Private wash room for Mr. Spiels. Brass fittings, ceramic basin." He tapped an iron door in the middle of the hall. "The bank safe is in here. The walls of this building are a foot thick," he said as he took out a ring full of keys. "Enough dynamite would blow a hole in the walls, but they'd still have to get to the safe."

He unlocked the door. I peered into total darkness. Mr. Biggs stepped in and took out a lamp. He lit it and nodded into the dark. "This is where we keep our depositor's money."

I followed him down a stairwell. It was narrow with walls on each side. He rapped his wrinkled knuckles against them, causing a dull thump. "Stone," he said solemnly.

We walked down ten more feet and came to a huge steel door. "I hear they put gold in Ft. Knox," he said. "They really should put it in here." He unlocked the door and motioned for me to follow. As the light filled the room, he waved his arm around it proudly. "It's a natural cave." The ceiling and sides were all rock. There were rows of shelves with metal boxes lined up for about a hundred feet. "We do not leave cash exposed." He pulled out a box and opened it with a smaller key. Inside were stacks of bills. "I won't tell you how much you are looking at. But even if a hoodlum were to get this far, to make it worth his while, he would have to haul out a number of these boxes. They each weigh ten pounds."

I gave a low, impressed whistle. I didn't have the heart to tell him that a real robber would have a potato sack to put the bills in. He would not deal with carrying heavy boxes. Of course that person would have a lot of trouble trying to get the boxes open.

"You've sold me, Mr. Biggs."

As we tramped back up the stairs, Mr. Biggs turned and spoke, "The old bank has been robbed twice since I've been here. Jesse James and his boys did it once. The other time it was a group of banditos from New Mexico Territory."

When we entered the corridor, I said to Mr. Biggs, "One thing sir. When I got into town, a man was murdered."

Biggs gave the sign of the cross. "Yes, Mr. Addington. His boss, Mr. Hogan has a very large account here. I wasn't there, but customers who saw it told me that it was a horrible sight."

"And I also heard that before, a bank teller had been killed."

A look of sadness crossed Biggs' face. "Mike Reese. He was one of ours." He shook his head. "Poor boy. Poor, poor, boy. He was a loyal worker. Very fastidious. Very good with numbers." He shook his head once more, then looked up. "But he wasn't killed here at the bank if that's your worry."

I nodded sheepishly.

"You have my assurance, your money is safe here."

"I'm sure it is, Mr. Biggs. I just thought that maybe his murder had something to do with the bank." I was fishing, but all I was netting were minnows so far.

Biggs shook his head once more. "I don't think so. Tom Addington didn't have an account here."

I had nothing to say to that, so I babbled, "I like you sir. I just want you and the other people who work here to be safe."

He patted his jacket. "I keep a gun on me at all times"—we walked to the end of the corridor and he turned once more—"and I'm a very good shot. I killed a turkey once."

I wanted to ask him if the turkey had a gun and tried to shoot back.

We were behind the teller cages and he ushered me through the door that led to the lobby. The guard watched me with grave suspicion as I walked around to the window and plunked down fifty dollars.

"There it is, Mr. Biggs. It's all I have, save the five dollars in my wallet."

"Very good sir," he said crisply. With expert deftness he counted out the bills and tapped them on the counter into a neat, orderly rectangle of paper. "I just need you to fill out a simple application and this deposit slip."

The bell over the door rang and a farmer entered. Biggs face lit up. "Good afternoon Mr. Watson."

The farmer dipped his head in greeting and took off his battered straw hat. Biggs sidled over to the next window so I could fill out the forms. Watson, the farmer, had a ruddy face with watery blue eyes. His hands were gnarled and rough as he clumsily laid two dollars and some coins in front of Mr. Biggs.

"Where's them other boys today?" asked Watson.

"Taylor is home sick, and Gil took a late lunch. Mr. Spiels is having steaks with the businessmen over at The Sagebrush." He gave Mr. Watson a deposit slip and walked back over to me. "Are you ready, Mr. Foster?"

I handed him the application. It was a simple form asking for my name, address and occupation. Although I had references, there was not a space for that. Biggs took out a pen and dipped it in the ink well. With meticulous penmanship, he entered a number on his ledger. Then he wrote the number on my application. After that, he wrote the number on a second business card and handed it to me. "This is your account number. Let me get you a receipt."

The bank looked like a dead end. Apparently Clarence Biggs had no clue as to who killed Mike Reese or why. I thanked him and headed out. Farmer Watson looked up and gave me a glance before he went back to laboriously filling out his deposit slip. The green shirted bank guard watched my every move as I exited through the door.

Out on the street, I felt the guard's eyes on me. I needed a place to find out information and figured a good source was the barbershop. I rubbed my hand on my face, feeling the emerging bristles. Yep, a good shave was what I needed.

Clarence Biggs was right. There was a blue and red striped pole out front. I chuckled at the thought of an old school teacher talking to the pole like it was a person. The sign painted on the window read CLEMENT AND SON—TONSORIAL PROFESSIONALS. A smaller placard read HAIRCUTS-THIRTY-FIVE CENTS. A second placard read SHAVE-FIFTEEN CENTS. A third

placard read SHAVE AND A HAIRCUT JUST FIFTY CENTS.
My quick mind did the arithmetic. Whether you got
the hair cut and shave separately or together, it would
still cost fifty cents. I went inside.

There were two, high, barber chairs with customers
in both of them. The first barber was a tall, skinny
man in his forties with a thick mustache and thin hair
laid across a balding pate. I figured he was Clement,
and the second was his son. The ten-year-old boy
stood on an apple crate as he carefully shaved the
sideburns of the customer. Clement Jr. had a full head
of curly red hair, reminding me of Danny McMahon.
The boy wore a white apron as did his father. His
hands were as skilled and adept as his old man's. Like
father, like son. Except the father had black hair, so
maybe the son looked more like his redheaded
mother. Who knew? Maybe she was a McMahon.

There was one more customer before me, a broad
shouldered man with long, black, greasy hair. It was
speckled with grey cinders. Perhaps they were the
cinders from the fires he'd forged, because his strong,
tanned arms told me that he was a blacksmith. His
crude, jagged nails were grimy from hard labor. His
face was round, with kind, brown eyes. Thick tufts of
hair rose from his chest and over his shirt collar. A
fourth man sat near a spittoon, reading a newspaper.
He was bald and beardless, so I figured he was just
there for the gossip.

All five men and the boy looked at me as I came in.
Whatever talk had been going on fell silent. A stranger
was in their midst. A newcomer. Clement offered
a smile.

"Come on in, stranger. Have a seat. It won't be long."

I sat two chairs down from the blacksmith. He looked over at me and offered a large, dirty paw. "The name's Nelson."

I didn't ignore his friendly gesture. As I shook his hand, it felt rough, but the grip was soft, like he was afraid he would hurt me if he squeezed too hard. "Randy Foster," I said.

He tossed his head at the bald man who nodded back to me. "That's Hank. He's with me."

Clement waved a pair of scissors at me. "I'm Marcel Clement. This is my son, A.J."

A.J. gave me a quick nod and with steady concentration, finished the customer's sideburns. His customer was also reading a newspaper. He spoke to me. "You new in town?"

"Yes. I'm a tutor."

A.J. looked up for just an instant, before putting his attention back to his task. Here was a boy who obviously wasn't in school. Perhaps he was hoping for a little schooling.

"I'm a private tutor," I clarified. "I teach history, English, arithmetic, whatever needs teaching to whomever needs it." I wished I had a fancy business card to hand out like Clarence Biggs. Instead, I'd have to rely on my fancy words. If I had any. "Presently I'm employed by the *Journal*."

"You a reporter?" asked Clement's customer.

"No sir. I'm an editor. Proofreader really. I make sure the spelling is correct and all new paragraphs are indented."

Hank tapped the paper that he was reading. "You're going to have a lot of spelling and indenting tomorrow."

"That's right," said Nelson. "After that killing this morning, there will be plenty to read in the newspaper tomorrow."

Since the two customers having their hair cut had not introduced themselves, I thought of Clement's man as Customer One and A.J.'s as Customer Two.

Customer One spoke, "This place is turning into one of those wild west towns you read about."

"I thought this *was* a wild west town," said Clement. I hid a smile.

"Yeah, but it used to be, you could walk across the street without having half your head blown off," said Customer One.

"Tom Addington was shot in the back," said Nelson.

Customer One waved him off. "Yeah, yeah, and he's just as dead."

This was the opening I was looking for to get some information. "Does anyone here know the fella who was shot?"

"He was a cowpuncher for Hogan out at his ranch," said Customer One.

I was getting tired of hearing this part of Addington's biography. Was that all anyone knew about the man? "Who would want to kill him?" I ventured.

"Tom was not a real friendly fella. Kept mostly to himself," said Hank.

"Every time I cut his hair, he tipped me a nickel," said A.J. "I find no fault with him."

"He was a surly son of a bitch," said Nelson. "I shoed his horse once and he complained about my price."

"That's because he gave all his money in tips to A.J.," laughed Clement.

No one found this to be particularly funny, so Clement went back to cutting hair.

I tried a new approach. "The reporter at the *Journal*—Farly—told me a bank teller and another man were killed. They too, had been murdered with a shotgun to the back. Maybe the killings are related."

Customer Two lowered his paper and looked at me. The room grew quiet as everyone pondered this.

"Yeah, there was that bank teller," said Hank. "Killed in his sleep, I believe it was."

"And the other man worked over at the Anglin Cattle Company," said Clement.

"That's right," said Nelson. "He worked up there in the office one night and someone plugged him in the back too."

Again, the room fell silent, the men thinking about the Anglin accountant. The only sound was the metal clicking of the scissors. A.J. took a soft brush and lightly powdered Customer Two's neck.

"All done Mr. Fryer."

Fryer. Customer Two was Fryer.

With a well practiced move, A.J. whipped the sheet off Fryer. Brown hair scattered on the floor. That's when I saw what Fryer was wearing. A green shirt and a badge. He gave me a curious look as he reached into his pocket. A.J. jumped off his box.

"There you are A.J.," Fryer said as he dropped thirty-five cents into the boy's palm.

No tip, I noticed. He put on his hat. A white hat, I might add. He gave me one last curious glance and left. Great. I'm in town for one day and he reports to

Featherston that I'm asking about the shotgun killings. Of course, being the mild mannered, very curious school teacher that I am, it would only be natural to be intrigued by killings in a wild west town.

Since the damage was done, I mused aloud, "What would a bank teller, a cowpoke and an accountant have in common?"

A.J. swept up the floor and mounted his apple crate. "Ready for you, Mr. Nelson."

The big blacksmith got up and filled the large barber chair. For a moment, I thought A.J. would need another crate to reach him. Nelson adjusted and settled into the chair. With his foot, A.J. hit a lever on the chair and it lowered a few inches. Perfect.

"I didn't know the accountant," said Clement with a hint of distaste. "He grew his hair long and he had a full beard."

"Pa offered to knock off ten cents for a shave and a haircut, but that man wouldn't go for it," said A.J.

Forty cents for a shave and a haircut. Now that was a deal. "What about the teller?" I asked.

"Mike Reese. Nice fella," said Customer One. "He was always friendly. Every time you entered the bank, he would greet you with a smile." Clement was powdering Customer One's neck. He'd plastered down the man's hair with a pleasant smelling cream.

"You're done, Bill." As Clement whipped the sheet off, I expected to see another green shirt. Bill, who was Customer One, wore a white shirt with a wide, red tie. Clement gave me a conspiratorial wink. "Bill here likes to see friendly service. He runs the Kithen Oven."

Kithen Oven. Did he mean "kitchen" oven? Did Clement have a speech impediment?

Now that he was out of the chair, Customer One offered his hand. "Bill Kithen. We not only bake bread, we bake cakes, pies, donuts, you name it. And we offer great, friendly service to our customers."

"Greet 'em with a smile, huh?" I grinned as I shook his hand.

"You betcha." Bill gave Clement a fifty cent piece. While waiting for his change, Bill took his coat off the rack and put it on. "Come see me when you get a sweet tooth."

"I will, Mr. Kithen."

Kithen collected his change and left. Clement shook the sheet free of hair and patted the back of the seat.

"Ready for you, teacher."

"Just a shave today, Clement."

"You've got it, pardner."

Nelson was mumbling under his breath.

"What's that, Nelson?" asked Clement.

A.J. was using a pair of sharp, heavy shears to cut through Nelson's thick hair. They looked like the kind used on sheep.

"I was just thinking was all," said Nelson. "I don't see any connection to those three men."

"They might have been killed by the same person," said Hank.

"Yes," said Clement. "You're right. The men were unrelated. One was killed in his sleep—one was shot at his office—and the third was killed in broad daylight, on a busy street." Clement was cranking the chair back so that he could shave me.

I had to admit, I couldn't argue with his logic.

"I reckon all three of them could have enemies," said A.J. "None of us really knew them."

I had come in here for answers and the only answers I got were that the murders were all unrelated. Nothing new there.

With my head all the way back, I could see the ceiling of the barbershop. I had not noticed before, but plastered up there were pictures of half dressed women. They were mostly newspaper ads for various burlesque shows. Some were underwear ads out of a mail order catalogue.

"Do you like our ladies?" A.J. asked innocently.

"Guess it gives you something to look at."

Clement was patting a cold tonic on my face. It stung like mint, but instantly began to soothe as it seeped into my pores. I couldn't see anyone except for Clement as he stood over me. I could hear Hank snoring and Nelson talking.

"I saw one of them burlesque shows up Kansas City way. There was some pretty wild stuff in 'em—not for your eyes A.J."

"Ah, those women don't scare me none," was the boy's reply.

Clement dipped a brush into the mug and applied lather over my gristled cheeks and chin. I could hear the steady slap of the razor as he sharpened it.

"Come on in and have a seat. It won't be long," Clement told a customer who had just entered.

"Hey there," I heard Nelson say to the newcomer.

Clement took the razor and gently shaved the short, stiff hairs under my lip. I did not speak for fear of getting nicked.

"Mike Reese rented a buggy from me last year," said Nelson. "I remember now."

I felt the blade stop just under my lower lip.

"Oh yeah, that's right," said Clement. "He was seeing that young lady . . ." The blade stopped once more as Clement tried to remember the name. "She goes to our church."

Now A.J. spoke, "He came in here to get all gussied up for the big hoedown they have at the city park."

"I never go to those things," said Nelson. "I can't square dance—tried it once and nearly crippled ten people."

Clement was making a nice, smooth stroke down my chin. I could feel and hear the hairs protesting as they were cleared away by the blade.

"Brooks!" Clement said with returning memory. "Benita Brooks, that girl who works for Anglin. That's who Mike was seeing."

When Clement said "Brooks", his hand was steady. Despite my shock at hearing her name, I impressed myself by reacting calmly.

Clement looked down at me with a worried expression. "You're bleeding." I don't remember jerking my head but I felt a trickle run down my collar.

"Let me get a towel." He dabbed the blood off my neck with the towel and pressed it over the cut. "Don't worry, I have a salve for this." He took the towel away and peered at the wound. "It's not bad. Just a nick." He dried off my left cheek and rubbed some ointment on it. Then he stuck a small patch of cotton over it. "There. No harm done. You can take the patch off in a few minutes. I'll finish you up."

"I don't remember the girl," said Nelson. "But he rented that fancy white carriage I reserve for weddings."

"I don't think they were getting married," said Clement.

"He didn't mention marriage," said Nelson, "but he was willing to pay the extra charge for that carriage."

I couldn't breathe. Of course Benita was apt to have beaus before me. But of all people, Mike Reese? Did she tell Jacob Specks about this? I would think a murder would be worth mentioning.

"There, my friend. All done," said Clement. He pumped the lever under the seat and in one, smooth move, I was upright again. The sudden shift in position made me woozy. My eyes were unfocused for a brief moment. When they cleared, I was looking at my own clean, shaven face with a white cotton patch on my left cheek. Clement was holding a hand mirror in front of my face.

"Good, huh?"

"Good," I told Clement. He took the mirror away and I was staring at the customer who had come in. It was Lewis Featherston. There was a catch in my throat. I couldn't speak. Fryer had told him I was here. Yet, he could use a shave, a haircut, and a bath. A long bath. He was grinning.

"Yes sir," said Lewis Featherston. "That girl of yours gets around." Then the grin faded. "To bad her boyfriend got murdered."

Chapter Eight

At fifteen minutes to seven, that night, I left The Berkshire and mounted Pandora. Benita had given me directions to her house and I was ready to venture into the Clearview neighborhood.

It did not escape my attention that a man sat on a cracker barrel outside the hotel, reading a newspaper. I recognized him as one of Featherston's men, but he wasn't wearing a badge or green shirt. Neither his eyes nor lips were moving. He was staring at the top of the page, which meant he was staring at me. I pretended to be ignorant of his spying, but Pandora didn't. As we pulled away from the hitching post, she stopped right in front of the man. She wanted to make sure he knew that she knew. For an undercover horse, Pandora was more than lacking.

"Come on Pandora," I whispered, "let's go."

She didn't budge.

"Come on girl."

The man lowered his paper. The short, plump, red

horse stood like a statue in the middle of the street, challenging the man to a staring contest.

I gave him an embarrassed smile. "She's got a lot of mule blood in her." I leaned down and whispered harshly in her ear, "You keep this up and I'm sending you back to the circus. Remember that high dive you're so scared of?"

Satisfied she'd made her point, Pandora walked on.

Two blocks from town, four roads led out in a westerly direction. Each road was about a quarter mile long with rows of houses. Past those houses were farms and ranches.

Benita's house was on Cedar Dust. Pandora plodded slowly along, seemingly in her own little world. The road was narrow and dusty. While Kansas City and Topeka had electric street lights, Clearview still had gas street lamps. Every fifty feet, a flare kept the ride from being too dark.

I pondered how I was going to approach Benita about Mike Reese. It was delicate. Should I even mention it yet? Was it too soon? I decided to see how the evening played out. If I saw an opening, I'd take it.

I found the small house with a tiny front yard and a picket fence. This was really a cottage. It could only have two rooms, three at the most. An outhouse was on the side next to the water pump. The buckboard was parked near the front porch.

Before dismounting Pandora, I saw a shadow disappear around the corner of the house next door. The person was shorter than the man sitting on the cracker barrel. Another man from Featherston?

I lashed Pandora to a tree branch and walked onto the porch. Before I could knock, Benita opened the door.

"Randy, come on in."

She was dressed in an outfit with lots of ruffles and printed flowers. She smelled good. I had worn a brown suit with my black dress boots. I regretted not putting on more tonsorial water. The house smelled vaguely of baked cinnamon rolls.

"I'm ready," she said. "Do you want to put your horse out back? I've got some feed in a trough."

"Sounds good. Pandora eats anything put in front of her."

"Then after you feed her, let's go." She smiled.

I took Pandora around to the trough. Next to it was an iron post. I knotted the reins twice. "Stay here. Eat. I'll see you later." I patted Pandora on the head. She ignored me as she chowed down on the oats.

As we headed into town on the buckboard, I kept an eye out for shadows following us. It was what was ahead that got my attention. A fellow stood under a street lamp smoking a cigar. He took out a pocket watch and looked at it as we passed. I did not recognize the man, but I did recognize the tail. He wasn't waiting for anyone. He was watching us. Taking out the watch was a signal to someone else. I turned the buckboard down an alley between houses.

"Why did you do that?" Benita asked.

"I've already seen Cedar Dust. I thought I'd check out the next street."

She laughed. "You are an odd man."

"I like to know all about the places I visit."

She laughed again. I loved that laugh. Low and throaty always got to me.

It was obvious that Featherston was having me watched. He probably wanted to see what I was going to do with "his girl." We got to the theatre called The Grand where Benita had box seats for all the shows. In the lobby, we grabbed a program and Benita led me over to a booth.

"Oh Randy, can we rent opera glasses?" They looked like binoculars, but each double glass had a stick attached to it as a handle. We rented a pair and an usher took us upstairs where the box seats were. Our box overlooked the large auditorium. Benita gripped my hand.

"This is so exciting. See? See the orchestra down in the pit?"

I could hear a horn giving out some short bursts. Every second or so, a violin would play for a few notes.

"I'm very excited, Benita. There are so many people here. It's like an election or something."

In addition to the operas, I'd been to a circus and a bullfight. Each event seemed important—like a battle of sorts. I could feel the tension in the air.

Benita looked through her glasses. "There's Mr. Anglin. He's in his box across the way." On the other side of the auditorium, Mr. Anglin sat in a box with Sheriff Daily and a redheaded woman in her late forties.

"Who is the woman with him?" I asked.

"That's Bessie Corbin. She's the cream of Wichita society. She and Mr. Anglin are "special friends", but I don't think it's serious. She always comes down for the opera and other major events."

I scanned the large room as it filled with opera

goers. The waitress, Callie, entered wearing a simple white dress. Her escort was a cavalry lieutenant in his dress blue uniform.

"Who is that soldier?"

Benita peered down at the couple. "That's Lt. Martin from Fort Carmel. For the last few months, he's been seeing Callie, the lady who is with him."

"Yes, I met Callie when I first got in."

Benita frowned as she watched the couple. "Callie is very pretty," she said.

That was why she was frowning. I knew the look on her face. I'd seen it at times when I was in the vicinity of two women.

Benita looked up at me. "And you are very handsome."

My handsome face turned red. "Thanks . . . thanks Benita."

"Do you think she's pretty?"

"I . . . who?"

"Callie."

"Who? Callie?" I attempted to laugh and shrug it off, but Benita's eyes were serious. "Benita, are you jealous?"

She turned away in a pout. "Sorry Randy. It's a fault I need to work on."

I leaned into her.

"Benita," I whispered. "Do you already like me enough to be jealous?"

She bit her lip and nodded briskly.

For some reason, I didn't feel nervous any longer. I took her hand. "Hey. I like you too. You better not make eyes at that handsome soldier with Callie."

She looked up at me and smiled. "Really?"

"Really."

She kissed me on the cheek. "You are a sweet man."

I was still blushing, but I was grinning like Pandora when she snatched the hat off my head.

The lights went down. Benita applauded along with the audience. I reached over for the opera glasses. "Can I see your binoculars?"

"Of course," she said with a laugh.

The auditorium was illuminated by the footlights. I scanned the crowd in the darkness. In the back corner, standing near the exit door was the man who had stood under the street lamp, checking his watch. He too, had opera glasses. And he was looking in our direction.

La Bohème was exhilarating. Letting the music wash over me, I took Benita's hand in the second act. She gave it an answering squeeze. I was definitely falling down the endless well of love.

When the opera ended we rode back to Benita's at a slow pace. She spoke excitedly about the opera and hummed some of the music from it. I kept my eyes open for Featherston's men. When we pulled up to the house, Benita put her head on my shoulder. "Would you like to sit out on my porch?"

"I've been known to sit on a porch or two." Love makes you babble. I took a seat in the swing on the edge of the porch and Benita went inside to make us some lemonade.

As I sat there, keeping my eyes and ears open, I could feel the presence of Featherston's men. They were out there in the dark. I could hear Benita stirring in the kitchen. An insect of unknown origin, chirped from the trees. I heard a slight rustle from the bushes across the street, but the soft touch of air on my face told me it was only a breeze.

After some time, the breeze stopped and the chirping from the tree fell silent. It was a peaceful silence. Peaceful. It was a *deadly* silence. I knew at that very moment, there was a gun pointed at me from out there in the dark. I used the moon's glow and peered at the bushes across the street. Was that the black gleam from a Henry rifle? Or merely leaves, yielding to the stillness of the night? I knew Featherston's deputies were out there. Of course an agent's best weapon is paranoia.

"Here we are!" Benita said brightly. I almost jumped when she appeared in the doorway with the dainty cups of lemonade. "You don't have to stand, Randy. My goodness, you are a gentleman to a fault. You looked like you were shot out of a cannon."

"I guess I was thirstier than I thought."

The cup of lemonade was tangy and sweet. I would have preferred scotch, but it was inappropriate for the occasion.

"What do you teach back in Tenbone?"

"Almost everything. I like history and arithmetic. Science can be very exciting, but the field is developing so fast, it's hard to keep up."

Benita nodded as she sipped her drink. My cup was already empty after two healthy gulps. It was time to get down to business.

"Benita, tell me all you know about Lewis Featherston."

"Must we talk of him and spoil our evening?"

"That's why your cousin sent me here."

She sighed. "I know. Tonight made me forget why you're here. The music, the performance, the applause . . ." She sighed again. Then she gave me a nudge and a wink. "And you, looking handsome in that brown suit."

The old shyness was creeping back in. I awkwardly set the cup to the side and looked at the suit like it suddenly appeared on me. "What, this suit? I bought it at a general merchandise in Covington."

"Well I like it."

I had to take control before the stammering started. "So what about Featherston?"

A sour look crossed her face. I don't think it was the lemonade.

"He's a brute. His manners are coarse, and his breath smells like food gone bad."

"How long has he worked for Anglin?"

"He was there before I was. I wouldn't know when he was hired. He was just there. He leers at me all the time. At first, I tried to be nice. I should never have accepted those early gifts." She held up a finger to me. "Of course I protested him giving me the flowers and candy. And I never promised him anything." She chewed on her lip in deep thought. "Whenever he asked me out, I refused. The man can't take no for an answer."

"Did you complain to Mr. Anglin?"

"Oh no, I couldn't. It's hard enough being a female in that office. Mr. Anglin needs a self-sufficient person, not a whiner."

"I admire that."

She seemed genuinely surprised at my comment.

"You do? A lot of men don't like women who exhibit a little vinegar."

I was terrified of women with a little vinegar, but I smiled anyway. "No, I like strength and confidence in a woman. I knew a woman like that back home. She chewed tobacco, told dirty jokes, and could shoot better than any man." I was babbling and Benita was frowning at me. I babbled on. "Not that I would think you should chew tobacco or something."

Her face softened. "Oh no, of course not. I'm not good at telling jokes and I'm really afraid of guns."

Now this was my kind of woman.

"Which leads me into telling you something about Lewis," she added.

"Tell me."

"I think he's a vicious, dangerous man. Be very careful of him."

"Why do you say that? He's a law officer." Law officer my crooked hind foot. I was glad Benita could see through him.

"He uses that badge of his to scare people. He swings his weight around the office all the time."

"He's a bully?"

"Worse. Once, Mr. Anglin fired a man for stealing money. The man protested. I really thought he was innocent. He was pleading his case to Mr. Anglin and Lewis walked in. He collared him and led him out into the hallway. There, he kicked the man down the stairs into our office."

I gave a sympathetic grimace.

"He took the stunned man by the lapels of his shirt and started to curse him. Next . . ."

Benita started to shake. I put my arm around her.

Instead of comforting her with words like, "Say no more", I said, "Go on."

"Oh Randy, it was awful. Lewis pistol-whipped him. You could hear the bones cracking in his face. I screamed for Lewis to stop, but his eyes were crazy. Two clerks tried to pull him off." She stopped and took a sip of lemonade. Her hand was shaking. "The man's jaw went slack to the side like it was broken. Blood was pouring out of his mouth, his nose, even his forehead. The skin was broken." Benita shook her head slowly as she spoke. "It was horrible. Lewis finally stopped. He dropped the man to the floor and kicked him. The clerks tried to restrain him and Lewis shrugged them off like rag dolls. Three of his deputies watched the whole thing. They just stood around, enjoying the show. He told them to drag the man out to the street and leave him there."

"Horrible," I replied, "simply horrible."

Benita had stopped shaking. She was so lost in the story, re-living the memory. "As his men took that poor soul, Lewis walked over to my desk and smiled as if nothing had happened. He wanted to know if I would have lunch with him." She looked up at me. "Lunch? He wanted me to eat lunch with him?" Benita shook her head in disbelief. "I told him I was going home for lunch. He insisted. He kept insisting. I kept shaking my head. I could tell he was about to lose his temper again and almost said yes."

I shifted uncomfortably, trying to imagine Benita in the clutches of this animal.

"Before I could say yes, one of his men returned and said that Doc Fenton had been summoned. Lewis waved him off and gave me a look. He had a funny

glint in his eye. He said, 'I'll see you later.' I wanted
to scream." She took another sip of lemonade, then a
long swallow, draining her cup. "He left the office. I
sat down at my desk. I had been going over some figures. There was blood drying on the ledger. It had
flown across the office from that man's face to my
desk." She looked like she was about to cry.

I hugged her, patting her on the shoulder. "There
now, don't fret." I smiled down at her. "I'm here now.
Lewis Featherston won't bother you anymore."

She looked at me with a soft, sad smile. She
reached over and touched the pale scar that ran from
the left corner of my mouth to my chin. "How did you
get that?"

There were a million stories I could tell her. A
childhood accident with a fish hook. Catching the end
of an errant pitchfork while baling hay. Getting stuck
while traversing under a barbed wire fence. Running
into a wagon with iron spikes during the summer
while working for the railroad. Cutting myself shav-
ing. The truth almost stumbled out of my mouth like
a drunk through a swinging door. I was feeling comfortable enough to tell her the truth about my scar,
but now was not the time.

The scar. It happened in Dothan, Colorado about
ten miles east of Boulder. I was on my second undercover job.

When an agent is undercover, the rules are a bit
different. Sometimes he is put in a position where
he might have to kill innocent people. The code was
DO NOT HARM A SOUL UNLESS ABSOLUTELY NECESSARY.

It was drummed into our brains during training. It was not, however, a rule wrapped up in pretty pink ribbon. I prayed I would never be put into such a position.

The Bester Gang had been robbing mining payrolls. Cheek Bester and his brother Thumb—no, I'm not making up those names—had a lot of success in New Mexico and Arizona and had moved to Colorado, along with four others. All had criminal records. With the help of an ex-con, I was able to get in good with Thumb. He said he would try me out in Dothan. So far, my false credentials had held up.

The assignment was simple. We—me, along with the Bester gang—would wait for the mining payroll to be shipped to Denver. We would ambush the four guards and blow up the armored wagon to get to the money. I would have time to alert "Tiger", the agent who was the outside man. His job was to contact the Denver office. Before the wagon got to the designated spot, agents would swarm the gang. We would all be arrested and I would eventually "escape" from jail. It was always good to keep the criminal persona alive for future jobs.

Cheek had other plans. On the morning we were to take our positions at Cross Roads Station, he got us all in a circle. "Here's what we're going to do," he said. "I decided we'll catch 'em better at Bumper's Pass."

That was two miles before Cross Roads Station. Cheek was smart. The last minute change kept people like me from being effective. Maybe he suspected me. At that moment, I couldn't protest his decision. In fact, I smiled and nodded at the others.

"I like it. We'll have that wagon down in the Pass. It will be like shooting fish in a barrel."

Thumb laughed and slapped me on the shoulder. "I told you, Cheek, this guy knows a good plan when he hears it."

Cheek gave me a short nod. His eyes were full of distrust.

The original reason for ambushing the wagon at Cross Roads Station was because Bumper's Pass was the obvious choice. Cheek had good instincts. He must have felt that Cross Roads Station had been compromised. And he had a new member he didn't entirely trust.

Here's where it got complicated. He pointed at his brother. "Thumb, take Sewell, Smith, and Johnson to the north ridge. Me, Jones, and Brown will set up on the south." Smith, Jones, Johnson, and Brown. Every gang had them. They were popular alias names. My alias, Sewell, stood out like a wolf at a sheep's square dance. Next time I was going to be John White.

About thirty minutes before the wagon was to hit the pass we took our positions on the lower ridge so we could get clear shots at the wagon. Unbeknownst to us the Dothan Mining Company had sent ten security men to protect Bumper's Pass. They were hidden on the higher ridge so they could rain hell down on any potential trouble makers.

The air was damp as I took my place behind a rock. The sounds of nature provided a mixture of grackles and larks screeching and calling a discordant symphony. The Bumper's Pass Concerto.

I was in a panic. My thoughts were on The Service posse that was forming up at Cross Roads Station. My only hope was, when they saw that we weren't there, they would go to the next obvious spot, Bumper's Pass. Even then, it would be too late.

For a crazy moment, I thought I could take the Bester's on my own. Thumb was behind a tree. I could see the crown of his grey hat. It would be a head shot. I could do it. Smith was over to my right, up on a rock. I couldn't get a good shot at him. Johnson was in some bushes behind me. I would be exposed. But if I could kill two of them when the wagon arrived, it would alert the wagon guards. Of course they would focus on the north ridge where the shots were heard. It was an impossible plan. In the end, I decided to shoot above the guards' heads and hoped our people would arrive in time. I would abide by the rule.

I checked my watch. The armored wagon would be rolling through the pass at any moment. Thumb's grey hat moved behind another tree. I could hear Johnson behind me. He was pissing in the bushes. Not a bad idea. I suddenly felt bladder pressure myself. At that moment, I had no idea that Dothan security men had their rifles pointed at every Bester gang member, including me.

Then, we could hear it. The slow, steady creak of a wagon wheel. It was echoing in the pass. I moved an inch to my left to peek out from the rock I was hiding behind. Squeak . . . squeak . . . squeak. It seemed like that wagon wheel was the only sound in the world. Even the grackles and swallows had fallen silent. My shirt was heavy and wet in the morning air. Sweat trickled down my neck. The armored wagon was just around the bend. In the quiet, I heard Thumb cock his pistol. Smith and Johnson followed suit.

The sun was a hazy light, throwing a weak brightness against the canyon wall. Squeak . . . squeak . . . squeak. It wasn't quite a shadow, but the wagon threw a dark spot on the rocks as it made the turn. I cocked my gun. I moved farther to my left to get a good look. That saved my life, as the bullet shattered the rock next to my face. To the sound of gun blasts, I hit the dirt and cursed. Thoughts ran through my mind . . . Johnson was shooting at me. He knew I wasn't one of them. But no. Johnson's body was tumbling down the crevice. I could see every detail as his limp body rolled and bounced like a rag doll. A gunshot wound in his back was marked by an angry red hole. The bones of his leg snapped as he hit a ledge. A bone popped out of his thigh in a burst of blood and his teeth cracked on a blunt stone. Johnson was beyond caring.

Across the pass, I could see the smoke from several guns. Cheek had his own battle with men on the higher ridge. At that time, I thought it was The Service. But a bullet zinged over my head. They were shooting at me. It hit me that it was Dothan men and maybe even the sheriff and his crew. They were shooting to kill.

"They're killing us!" came Thumb's panicked scream.

Fish in a barrel. Bullets were hitting rock and dirt all around me, missing by inches.

"Aim for the flashes!" Thumb yelled.

Even though the Dothan men were shooting at me, I couldn't shoot back and kill "the good guys." Smith had been shot in the shoulder. He was dodging bullets, running between the trees. He saw me frozen on the ground. "Shoot, you coward!"

I nodded. I drew a bead on the Dothan man who had

been unloading his rifle on me. It was an easy shot. I pulled the trigger and the man yelped as he dropped the rifle. He ducked under a thick bush. I spotted another man firing from behind a pine tree. I shot the bark where his face was hidden. My plan was to pin him down until Thumb and Smith were killed. Then, maybe I could surrender and explain who I was. That plan was shattered when a bullet caught me in my hand. I turned. Not only was hell raining *down* on me, the wagon guards were shooting *up* at us. I rolled under some bushes for better cover. They were thorn bushes. Their stickers took my mind off the graze on my hand.

Through the thick bushes, I could see the opposite wall of the pass. Cheek had been hit. His chin was red. Blood was cascading out of his mouth. He was walking in short, jerky steps. His shooting arm hung limp. With his other hand, he was scatter shooting with his sawed off shotgun. Then, it clicked impotently when it was empty. Cheek kept walking and pulling the useless trigger. A bullet hit him in the head. A piece of his scalp flew off and he collapsed.

"Aagguuh!" Smith screamed. He fell back, clutching his chest.

"Die!" commanded Thumb, who laid a barrage of fire at the Dothan men. His body flew into the tree. One of the guards had gotten him from behind.

Then, it was quiet. I played possum.

Someone was shouting, "Let's go check the damage boys!"

I could hear them making their way down the rocks. "Careful"—the voice continued—"keep your eyes open, make sure they're dead."

A boot nudged me. I moved and very slowly rolled over. I didn't want to make any fast moves.

"Hey! I've got one!"

I looked up. It was the man whose rifle I'd shot out of his hands. Blood dripped down his wrist.

"I-I'm Randy Foster. I'm with The Service. You can—" Before I could finish saying "You can contact Dodge City. There's a group of agents on their way right now", the man kicked me in the face.

I woke up, flat on my back on a wooden table. I was in the mining office. Toby, the outside man on the job was standing over me. He held up a bottle. "Whiskey?" he offered.

My face felt numb. "What happened?"

"You got kicked in the face. The man was wearing spurs." I felt the bandage on my chin. A scar was born.

Suddenly, I realized that Benita was staring at my scar. "How did you get that?" she repeated.

"I was kicked by a horse."

"Oh dear!" she gasped, her face full of horror.

"I got it while I was guarding the Mayor of Abilene and tutoring his young son, Ben."

She put a hand on my wrist. "You don't have to tell me this Randy."

I shook my head. "It really wasn't that dramatic. The Mayor had gone to town to look for a bonnet for his wife. He took Ben along with him. Of course I had to go, too. As the Mayor was in the hat shop, Ben wanted to run across the street to a toy store. Without asking for permission, he dashed out of the hat shop. As he ran into the street, a stage coach was bearing down on him.

I sped out of there as fast as my boots would carry me. I dove for Ben and pulled him out of the path of the stage coach, but got kicked in the mouth by a hoof."

"How terrible."

"It was the first time I'd ever visited a dentist."

Benita rubbed her hand across my wrist in a soothing manner.

I had never known the Mayor of Abilene. I doubt whether he actually had a son named Ben. And the trip to the dentist was a hundred percent imagination on my part, but I'd learned that details gave a story the ring of truth.

"I'm really sorry, Randy," she said as she rubbed my wrist sympathetically.

I gave a dismissive wave in the air with the wrist she was not rubbing. "Doesn't bother me. Someone told me that a scar gives a face character." I touched the scar. "Does it repel you?"

"Oh no! Not at all!" she protested. Then she lightly drew her finger over it, tracing it's path gently. "To tell you the truth, it looks a little . . . well, it looks attractive." She blushed. "And it makes your face more interesting."

Her eyes lingered on my lips. I'd seen that look in other women and rarely followed through. This time I was going to do it. I closed my eyes. She closed hers. I moved in and felt . . . hair? How did I miss her face? A shock ran through me. It was a beard! All of this happened in an instant as Benita screamed. Pandora had stuck her head between us!

"Pandora!" I screamed.

Benita was spitting and feeling her lips for hair. "I kissed your horse!"

"So did I!"

"How did she get loose?"

"She's good at undoing her tether. I've tried all sorts of knots, but she finds a way." I tried to push Pandora's head away, but she just dug in harder. "Pandora, stop it!"

Then Benita laughed. "I think Pandora is like me. She's a jealous girl." She stroked Pandora's neck. For a moment, I was afraid Pandora would bite Benita, but Pandora liked it. She nodded at Benita for more stroking.

I was not happy. "I guess we need to call it a night, Benita."

She too, had lost the mood. "I really had a good time, Randy."

"Other than kissing my horse, I had a pretty good time too."

Chapter Nine

The next couple days were uneventful. I met with Farly "Arrow" Wilson at the *Journal* and he put me on the payroll, editing news copy and selling advertising. He told me that he was in touch with Bear and the three of us would meet soon.

I got into the habit of eating at the café where Callie worked. Occasionally, I saw the army lieutenant, Martin, at the café. Callie would sit at his usual table and they would talk softly. It looked like true love.

Speaking of love, I was constantly thinking of Benita. She'd had me over for dinner and I was feeling a deep attachment toward her, but I had just met her. It bothered me. An agent was not supposed to be emotionally involved. Although I was sent to protect her, I was also lying to her. Benita thought I was a school teacher/bodyguard. Because I was with The Service, I knew I would be moving on when the job in Clearview was done.

Arrow didn't talk a lot about Lewis Featherston, simply because he didn't know any more than I did.

He kept up the role as ace reporter, while I played the role of school teacher turned editor/ad man. The editor in chief, Teddy Bartly, spent most of his time in the saloon. His sober moments were late in the afternoon when he'd come in and spit out a scathing editorial against the migration of easterners invading the west. Bartly was from Newark, New Jersey.

I asked Arrow about Bear. He assured me that Bear would contact us when the time was right.

I was reading through some old editorials that Teddy Bartly had written, trying to catch his style. One was a real barn burner about water rights and why Clearview should dam up the Little Cimarron River. It actually made a lot of sense, considering he wrote most of his stuff under the influence of the brothers Scotch, Hard Rye, and O'Sullivans Cream Liquor.

A shadow crossed the *Journal*'s door and I looked up. He was close to six feet tall, thin as a sapling with shoulders beginning to broaden out. He had coal black skin, and short, curly hair. His voice was soft, almost a whisper.

"S'cuse me suh." The young man wore patched pants that he had clearly outgrown. His faded blue shirt had all of its buttons, but there were brown stains on the collar, lapels, and right sleeve. Maybe it was blood . . . could have been tobacco. He held a worn, brown felt hat that was torn at the brim.

"What can I do for you son?"

His head was bowed in humility, a familiar pose for people of dark skin. He looked up for a moment and revealed startling grey eyes. They looked into my blue eyes and it was hard to ignore their dark, determination. Despite his air of supplication, I felt there was a moral strength inside his skin.

"I hear you teach folks readin' and writin'."

"I do. Come in."

He shook his head. "No suh. I'm not allowed in."

"But I'm inviting you."

He leaned back and looked up and down the street. "No suh. People might not like it."

I stood up and gestured to a chair. "Those people don't count. Come. Have a seat."

He took one last look at the street and walked in. Then, he hurried over to the chair and sat.

"So you want to learn to read?"

He nodded. "Yes. I can write my name. I know some letters, but I need to know it all."

I pushed a sheet of paper at him and handed him a pencil. "Write your name."

He looked at me with a mixture of hurt and anger. "I can write my own name," he said defiantly. He proceeded to slowly print out his name in large letters.

I looked at it. "Noah Smith."

"Yes suh. I don't have any way to pay you exceptin' for some beans and tomatoes." He was expecting rejection.

I pondered what sort of courage it took him to make this move.

"I could also stake you to some corn and potatoes. I could cook you meals. I'm a good cook."

"That would be a good deal, Noah. I haven't had much time for home cooking."

A broad grin spread across his face. "Thank you. Thank you suh."

I held out my hand. "Deal?"

He looked at my lily-white hand as if it had appeared out of thin air. Then, hesitantly he took it and shook. The beaming smile returned. "Yes suh! Thank you, suh!"

"How old are you Noah?"

"I don't rightly know. I remember hearing about General Custer when I was small. I figure I'm at least fifteen." He was maybe closer to eighteen. It was hard to tell.

"Well Noah, you're almost a man. You call me Randy."

Noah nodded, the grin melting from happiness to sobriety. "Yes suh. I mean, yes Mr. Randy."

I did not expect him to call me "mister", but Noah had good manners. I wasn't going to correct him.

We set a time and place for his lessons. The time would be around three o'clock. The place would be the *Journal*. I didn't know how people would take my educating Noah, but it helped emphasize my cover as a teacher.

Later, I checked with Arrow to make sure having Noah over was not a problem. He had no objection. I knew that my assignment in Clearview would not last long enough to complete Noah's lessons. I would inquire around after the Featherston case was done and get Noah a real teacher.

The next day, Noah appeared at the *Journal* right as the church bells rang three peals. He wore the same blue shirt, but now had a pair of black, baggy pants that were rolled up around his ankles. He saw that I'd noticed his attire. He tightened his rope belt on the generous waistband.

"My brother Saul left these pants when he went out west to work on the railroad."

"Your brother must be a pretty big man."

"Yes su—I mean, yes Mr. Randy. If he were here, he'd be the biggest man in town." Noah hefted a potato sack onto my desk.

"What is this?" I asked.

"My first payment," he replied. He took a battered canteen out of the sack and held it up. "Sweet tea." He set it down and pulled out a tobacco tin.

"Tobacco?" I guessed.

He shook his head and opened it. "Beans baked on my stove." Next he produced an ice cream carton.

"Ice cream?"

He shook his head once more. "Mashed potatoes." Then he laid four huge biscuits on the table. "I don't have any oleo for the biscuits, but I did bring dessert." He reached into the potato sack and pulled out two large peaches. "I swept out the Mercantile and cleaned their outhouse for these." He held up his hands. "Don't put your head to worry. I wash my hands when I cook and I washed them before I came."

I smiled and pulled a chair out from the desk. "Sit down. We'll eat before we learn."

The food was delicious. Noah had a talent for seasoning the potatoes to perfection.

"You could get a job as a trail cook, Noah."

"I reckon. I know what to do with a barbeque spit."

"Maybe I could get you on with the Anglin Cattle Company. They know all of the big trail bosses."

His dark face hid a deeper darkness. "No thank you. I go my own way." He dunked his biscuit in a tin of gravy. "Don't take to being insulted Mr. Randy. I had a run in with some of those men who work for Mr. Anglin. They aren't right."

I cocked my head. "What do you mean?"

"Said too much," he mumbled.

"What's that Noah?"

He looked at me with displeasure and merely shook his head. "I shouldn't talk about that."

My curiosity was piqued. "Shouldn't talk about what? What do you mean they're not right?"

He put down his biscuit and licked his fingers. "My grandma had second sight. She could see how people were before they got a stone's throw from her. I don't have that . . . but I get tinglings."

"Tinglings?"

He nodded and chewed slowly on the biscuit. I was quiet, giving him time to finish.

He continued, "I feel it go up my spine to my neck. It's cold, dark." He took a breath, like the room was suddenly sucked dry of air. "That's what I felt when I crossed the path of that big deputy."

Featherston. "What about people who are . . . right."

He smiled. "I feel a warm spot. Right here." He patted his chest.

I wasn't sure if I believed him. "What did you feel when you met me, Noah?"

"Nothing Mr. Randy. Nothing at all."

I wasn't sure if I felt insulted or relieved. Maybe I did believe him a little bit.

Noah leaned forward. "Mr. Randy . . . I don't feel it on everybody. Not like my grandma. But I know you're a good man."

I felt better. A little. "Let's finish this delicious meal so we can work on your lessons."

* * *

He was a quick learner. Noah understood certain letter arrangements that formed words. Within the hour he could recite half of the alphabet. We went through all twenty-six letters and I taught him how the letters sounded.

"*Tuh . . . tuh . . .*" Noah formed the letter sounds with his lips. "*Tu . . . T.*"

"Very good. Now *C* is tricky. Remember *S*? *Sssss*? Well *C* can be a lot like that." I pursed my lips. "*Cee. Cee.* But it also can sound like a *K. Cuh. Cuh.*"

With repetition, I was sure Noah would catch on. We were finishing up when Editor in Chief Teddy Bartly, staggered in from the bar. He looked at Noah in startled silence.

"My word. I have drunk myself to the Ivory Coast." He fixed his expression on Noah, squinting his eyes. "Are you a tribal prince?"

Noah looked at me for help. I shrugged.

Bartly stumbled across the room and poked a finger into Noah's shoulder. "Hard muscle. He's real. I can feel him." The dawn of realization hit his face. "You're the young fellow who sweeps out the Mercantile."

"Yes suh."

Bartly gave a sharp clap of his hands. "Ah! Thought so!" He looked over at me. "Is he sweeping up here?"

I shook my head.

Bartly walked over to his desk and sat down hard. "You don't look natural sitting there. Never saw any of your kind in this office."

I was about to speak, but Noah quickly patted his chest. He smiled.

Bartly found some whiskey in a drawer and un-corked it. He took a swig and pointed the bottle at us.

"What's he doing here Randall?"

"I'm teaching him his letters."

The editor wiped his mouth and leaned back in his chair. "That's okay, I guess." He finished off the bottle in one, long swallow as Noah gathered his tins and canteen.

"Maybe you could come out to my place tomorrow," said Noah. "I could make you a hot meal."

I mentally ran through my schedule. Nothing seemed pressing. "Okay. Where do you live?"

"I live down by Easy Springs, just past Shanty Town. My grandpa got the land after the war. Three acres owned by Smith," he said with pride. "When you get to Shanty Town, ask for "Old Hermps Place". They'll tell you."

That night I asked the hotel clerk about Shanty Town.

"Don't go down there without a gun," he warned. "That place is full of cutthroats and card sharks. Why would you want to go down there anyway?"

"I have a student."

The clerk looked at me like he swallowed a rotten egg. "Don't take any money with you, Mr. Foster. And you might leave a note here with the name of your next of kin."

I gave him a hard grimace and headed back to my room.

The next day, I packed up my books and two new pencils. Then I took Pandora down Shed Road. Soon she was clopping down the dirt road that led northwest out of town. It narrowed down to a footpath two miles out. Meeting another horse would be a burden. One rider would have to pull into thick, thorn bushes to give way.

I felt that the clerk exaggerated the danger, but only a fool would not heed his warning. I wore my gun with belt and holster. I wanted it to be visible to all.

About a half mile farther, Pandora lifted her head. "What is it, girl?"

She was sniffing the air. I took a whiff, but came away with nothing. "What do you smell? Skunk? Do you smell a skunk, girl?"

Without my urging, Pandora picked up her pace and headed down the trail. She wasn't exactly at a full gallop, but with Pandora it was hard to tell. I was glad that the narrow trail bore straight through the trees and I ducked to avoid the occasional low hanging limb.

"What's the hurry girl?" I shouted. Then I smelled it. It was a pleasant odor of meat smoking over wood. Noah was cooking. Smoke rose over the tree line.

A quarter mile later, the trail opened into a clearing. There were about fifteen shacks made of cardboard and old tents. Two children as black as Noah played chase with canes. They ran in between the narrow paths of the abodes, swiping at each other's head. A bent old man stirred a galvanized tub of brown soup with black chunks.

Just past the old man, a wild boar was roasting over a pit. These people had nothing, but they ate well. Pandora eyed the cooking pig. She was nickering, hopping from one front hoof to the other.

I stroked her mane. "Not yours. Behave."

There were three men and a woman tending to the boar. The woman basted the carcass with a gooey black substance on a wooden spoon. The children stopped their game and looked up at me. The grownups looked at me suspiciously. No one spoke.

I doffed my hat. "Excuse me. I'm looking for Old Hermps Place."

This was met with silence. One of the men wiped a dirty rag across his face.

"Hermps is dead. Died last winter of the consumption. What's your business, mister?"

Hermps must have been Noah's grandfather.

One of the other men spat into the fire. He was one of the few white men there.

He pointed at me and said, "You the school teacher?"

"Yes sir."

He pointed to the woods to the right. "You go right through those woods. Easy Springs, they call it. Hermp's place is to the left of the water."

I doffed my hat once more as thanks and pulled on the reins. "Let's go girl."

Pandora gave a last wistful glance at the boar and trodded into the thick forest.

Through an overgrown path, I could hear the gurgling of a brook. Up on a pine tree was a homemade sign reading EASY SPRINGS. Just up a short hill, I saw a rusty, tin roof. The cabin was one room with an outhouse to the side. Noah was at the door, hailing me.

"Welcome Mr. Randy! Welcome!"

"Hello Noah." I dismounted Pandora.

Noah had an apple in his hand. "Your horse looks hungry."

Pandora's eyes were big, the apple in her sites. Noah went straight to her and held the apple to her mouth. "It's okay Pandora," he said. "It's yours."

She gave that broad horse grin and took the apple in her mouth.

"Let's go Randy. You don't have to tie her up. She'll stay."

As we headed for the cabin, it struck me. How did he know Pandora's name?

Noah worked the farm. He lived off the land. He grew tomatoes, beans, corn, and potatoes. He trapped rabbit, squirrels, even wild boars. It was he, who supplied Shanty Town with the wild boar.

Upon entering the cabin, I felt like I'd grown into a giant, the place was so small. It had a stove, a table, a chair that was falling apart, and a feather bed. Something sweet was baking in the oven. Noah went over to it.

"I need to chop some more wood. This old stove eats it real good." He motioned toward the table. "Have a seat over there. I've got a rabbit, refried beans, and corn." He rattled a pan on the stove. Apple and cinnamon wafted through the small cabin. "I've made us an apple pie."

"You must have done a lot of sweeping at the Mercantile."

"These are the green apples I get off my tree." He pointed to a cupboard of salt, flour, and sugar. "I got me a job of building coffins down at the funeral parlor. Mr.

Stands, the undertaker, pays me five cents a coffin. Then I do my tradin' at the Mercantile before they close." A sad look crossed his face. "The only way they let me inside during the day is to let me sweep. Then I gets to trade with 'em when they close up."

I wondered how such a young man had gotten along by himself.

As if reading my mind, Noah spoke. "My folks worked at a plantation down south. Actually, they were owned. I got sold to a family in Tennessee. Grandpa was a key maker up north. After the war, he looked me and my brother up. Saul and I had not been separated. He tried to find my parents, but they were long gone. That plantation had been burned to the ground."

"So your grandfather brought you and Saul up?"

He nodded. "And my grandma. We moved here when she died and Saul left to work on the railroad. Grandpa taught me how to use my hands and how to farm." He held up his hands. "I am clumsy, but I work extra hard to get stuff right." He went to the bed and pulled something out from under it. "This was his." It was a musket . . . very old, but in good condition.

"Well I'll be. Let me see that."

He handed the ancient weapon to me and said, "I make my own iron balls. I don't get enough powder, but it's accurate."

"Did you kill the boar with this?"

"Yes. I had to get close . . . or I guess I had to let him get close. When he charged me, I aimed for the snout. It wouldn't kill him, but it would stop him. Then I sliced his neck while he was down." As he spoke, Noah never took his eyes off my holstered gun.

I touched the handle. "Ever fire a pistol Noah?"

He shook his head, almost in a trance. My gun held his entire attention.

"You're pretty good with a musket. Would you like to try mine?"

He suddenly looked up at me, his eyes hopeful, yet disbelieving. "You-you mean it?"

I flipped my gun out and grabbed it by the barrel, offering the grip to him. "Let's go outside."

"Yes sir, Mr. Randy. Let's."

When we came out of the cabin, Pandora nodded and smiled at Noah. I think she was in love.

"I've got me tobacco tins." Noah handed the gun back to me and collected four tins. He walked toward a tree.

I noticed an empty, brown bottle lying under some chopped wood. "Here's a bottle to aim at."

Noah placed the four tins at the base of a tree, all in a row. "Let me go get some twine," he said and hurried into the cabin.

I heard a board being lifted by the protests of screeching nails. Apparently Noah had a cubbyhole of hidden treasure in his floor. He returned with a two foot length of twine.

"Let me see that bottle, Mr. Randy." He made a tiny noose in the twine and looped it over the neck of the bottle. "That's good. Real good," he said quietly. Then he went over to the tree and tied the twine to a limb. He held the hanging bottle at an angle, then let go. The bottle swung back and forth. Noah hurried back to me and took my gun. I watched the bottle as its arch shortened and it slowed. It was still a difficult target.

"You know, shooting a pistol is a lot different than using a long barrel."

Noah ignored my remark. He watched the bottle. Then he stood up straight. "Mr. Randy, could I borrow your belt?"

"Of course." I unbuckled my belt and handed it to him. He fastened it around his waist and awkwardly put the gun in the holster. He eyed the bottle as it swung slowly, back and forth. I watched it too. The slow movement was hypnotic.

"Real good," Noah said once more.

The brown bottle glinted in the sun like a glass pendulum. I saw movement out of the corner of my eye as the bottle shattered with the explosion.

"Wha . . . ?" My head swiveled, looking into the woods. "Who?"

Noah stood there, the gun in its holster.

"Where did that shot come from?"

"It was me, Mr. Randy."

I looked down at my holster. Smoke was whiffing from the barrel. I shook my head in disbelief. "I never saw you draw it."

"I shot it."

The four tins under the tree jumped as each bullet hit center. Before the last two hit the ground, Noah had the gun back in its holster. His arm had been a blur. I saw it briefly, defined in sure stillness as he pulled the trigger four times. No one was that fast. Pandora was up on her hind legs neighing in tribute. This was one horse who appreciated real speed.

"It's the first time I did it with a holster," he said.

My brain was empty. I had no words to describe what I'd just witnessed. I know there are fish stories out there. You know the kind. The four-foot catfish that got away. This was not a fish story. If I hadn't seen Noah's fast draw, I wouldn't be telling it. Noah unbuckled the belt and handed it back to me.

"Thank you, Mr. Randy." He headed over to a warped table on the side of the cabin. He picked up an object and headed back my way. What was in his hand?

"This is what I practice with." He held up a crude, wooden pistol. He stuck it through the rope around his waist. "Your holster made it a lot easier, Mr. Randy."

I finally found my voice. "You never shot a gun before?"

"Just that old musket." He held up the wooden toy. "My grandpa made this for me. I've played with it ever since I was little."

"What I just saw was impossible."

Noah toed the ground. He looked . . . awkward?

"I can cook, Mr. Randy. I can grow things. I can scale fish and skin hogs." He kept his head down as he held the wooden gun. "I tried my hand at carvin' and almost cut off my fingers." He looked up at me. "Like I said, I'm clumsy. I drop pots and pans. I drop the hoe when I'm weeding. I can't draw no pictures. But God gave my hands quickness, and a quick eye. And a quick mind."

"That's a good thing Noah." I said quietly. I saw water forming in his odd, grey eyes.

"Don't like my life much here. That's why I want to learn to read."

I looked over at the remains of the brown bottle, hanging in the noose . . . it's jagged shards shining in the sun.

Chapter Ten

There was another element of Clearview that affected my life—the men who were following me. I labeled them Cracker Barrel, Shadow, and Lamppost. That's how I'd first seen them. Cracker Barrel was usually outside the hotel sitting on a cracker barrel. I also saw him having lunch with Featherston at Callie's café, so I knew he definitely worked on Featherston's security team. Shadow came out of the shadows and did a bad job of trailing me all day on Saturday. He was short, with prematurely graying hair, but his face was unlined. Lamppost was usually stationed on Cedar Dust. He was a large man, prone to blowing his nose. His eyes were always red and swollen and he was constantly checking his pocket watch.

Starting into my second week, it all came to a head. I left the hotel and saw Cracker Barrel in his usual spot. I headed over to the café. Shadow was a block away, trying to look like he was on a stroll. Lamppost wasn't anywhere in sight.

I entered the café, and took a seat where I could look out to the street. Callie approached my table as I sat.

"Morning Randy. The usual?"

"You know it, Callie."

She poured me coffee and called back to the cook, "Three scrambled eggs, four bacon, one biscuit and grits!" She looked at me, cocking her head. "How do you like working at the *Journal*?"

"It's a job. I plan on applying at one of the local schools before autumn." Of course, by autumn, I'd probably be on another assignment.

"Clearview could use a good teacher. There are some unruly boys that come in on Saturday nights, smoking and cursing. They need a teacher who will give them lots of homework to keep them occupied."

I laughed. "How do you know I would assign a lot of homework?"

She laughed back. "Because you eat slow. School teachers who eat slow are calculating, reflective. From that comes a lot of thinking, which results in a lot of work for the students."

I blinked at her. "That's a real mouthful, Callie. You sound a tad educated yourself."

"My father taught school." As she walked back to the counter, she spoke over her shoulder. "He was a fast eater."

Through the window, I saw Shadow across the street. He was showing an unusual amount of interest in a shovel that was in the hardware store window. There was still no sign of Lamppost.

Lt. Martin came in as I was finishing my grits. Our eyes met and we each gave friendly nods. He walked over to the counter. "Hey! Where's my girl?!"

Callie came out from the back. "Hi darling. Take a seat. I'll bring you breakfast."

The lieutenant moved with a slow, quiet confidence. He eased to a seat at his usual table and set his Cavalry-issued hat on his knee.

"How are you Lieutenant?"

"I'm working hard this morning. How about you teacher?"

"I'm about to start working hard."

He gave me an easy smile and casual salute. "Don't work too hard."

I nodded as Callie brought me my breakfast.

"Here's your eggs," she said. "We browned them just the way you like them."

"Thanks Callie."

I ate slowly while Callie sat for a few moments with Lt. Martin. Their voices were soft and intimate. I felt like I was intruding so I gobbled up the eggs like a teacher who doesn't give out much homework. Slamming down the breakfast, I stood up. I left a half dollar on the table which took care of the meal and a generous tip for Callie.

When I turned up the street, Shadow started to follow. Good. Up ahead, Cracker Barrel was not sitting on his cracker barrel. He was walking toward me with his hands on his holster. I didn't like the determined look on his face.

Sensing trouble in the air, I decided to turn down a side street. Sure enough, Cracker Barrel followed me and he didn't care if I knew it or not. I picked up my pace and was chagrined to see Cracker Barrel do the same.

At the end of the street I saw another figure approaching me. It was Shadow. Between a warehouse and The Happy Gables Hotel was a narrow alley. I made a sudden turn down that passageway and immediately regretted my decision. Lamppost was standing there, straight and tall. He wasn't looking at his watch, but he did have a Louisville Slugger in his hands. I wasn't partial to the bat as a weapon. Of course the baseball team in Dodge City didn't have very good hitters. I turned to go back, but Shadow and Cracker Barrel had me blocked off.

"You got any money, mister?" Cracker Barrel asked.

So that was their scenario. No mention of Featherston. No mention that they were there to warn me off Benita. Just three thugs intent on robbery and grievous, personal assault.

"I just spent my last thirty-five cents on breakfast." No reason to think I was rich. I held out my arms. "No more money until pay day."

All three men moved in on me. Lamppost tapped the bat against the brick wall of The Happy Gables. Cracker Barrel remained the spokesman of the group.

"Your boots must be worth something."

"What, these? I found them at an old Civil War surplus store in St. Louis." Shadow pulled out a knife. Cracker Barrel kept looking at my boots.

"Yep, those are some fine looking boots." I saw Lamppost's shadow on the wall of the warehouse. He was behind me and he was lifting the bat over his head.

"You like my boots? You can have them." I kicked my right boot into Cracker Barrel's groin. In the shadow, the bat was coming down toward my head. I ducked and rolled. Lamppost missed by an inch, coming away with nothing but air.

"Get him!" Cracker Barrel yelled through gritted

teeth. He lay on his side, holding his groin. I found some purchase with the ground and jumped up, throwing dirt in Lamppost's face as he wheeled around with the bat. Shadow charged me with the knife.

"I'll kill you!" he screamed. In one move, I side-stepped Shadow, grabbed his wrist and twisted the knife out of his hand.

"My wrist! You broke my wrist!" he howled. While he was worrying about his wrist, I rammed his head into the brick side of the hotel. He fell like a sack of potatoes.

The move on Shadow was effective, but it took time. Lamppost was swinging the bat at my ribs. I jumped back but the bat caught me in the chest with a glancing blow. I fell on my back. Lamppost had a murderous look in his eyes as he pounded the bat at me. I kept rolling and he kept hitting dirt. The man was in a very unhealthy rage. Did he hate me this much, or was he just a dedicated stooge for Feather-ston? His emotions were working in my favor, because he was swinging blindly. I had time to grab the knife as I jumped to my feet.

"Get back!" I yelled, wielding the knife. He swung for my head. I ducked and thrust the knife forward. It caught him in the stomach, but it was a shallow slice. He yelped in pain.

As I prepared a deeper thrust, Lamppost gave the bat a backswing. It was so sudden and surprising, the ash popped me in the shoulder, hard.

"Oof!" The air went out of me as pain rampaged down my shoulder and into my arm. I dropped the knife and he kicked at it. The backswing and the kick put Lamppost off balance. Ignoring my screaming shoulder, I kicked the big man backwards. He fell, hitting his head on the hardwood of the warehouse. He was dazed, but not out. I grabbed the bat and using the end of it, I gave him a sharp poke in his Adam's Apple.

"Auugghh!" He grabbed his throat and gasped for breath. The blow was not lethal, but it kept the subject's mind off me and on the subject of breathing normally. I threw the bat down at the three groaning men and walked out of the alley.

Arrow saw me approaching the *Journal* office and immediately knew something was wrong. Maybe it was me clutching my shoulder or the tears running down my cheek. Either way, he pulled the shades down as soon as I entered the office. He eyed my torn shirt and the blood soaking through.

"What happened?"

"Three of Featherston's henchmen attacked me."

"Where are they?"

"Lying in the alley by The Happy Gables Hotel."

"Did you kill any of them?"

"Nah. I just roughed 'em up a little. Where's Bartly?"

"He's sleeping off a drunk in back of Hazel's Bar. Let's look at your shoulder."

I unbuttoned my shirt and he gently pulled it off. A deep, purple bruise covered the top part of my shoulder. It was topped off by a bulbous, white knot.

"It doesn't look too bad," said Arrow. "Sit down and let me pour you a whiskey."

I sat down hard, feeling the shoulder yell back in protest.

"Can you move your arm?" he asked.

Painfully, slowly, I rotated my arm. It hurt like hell. I spoke through gritted teeth, "Guess it's not broken."

Arrow brought me the drink and I gulped it down. The liquor stung its way down my throat and settled nicely. I held up the glass with my good arm. "Two more of these and I won't feel a thing."

Arrow shook his head. "Go see Doc Fenton. He'll probably send you over to the icehouse. Then, go back to your room and await my message. Bear's called a meeting for tonight."

"Where?"

"In a room over the café. We'll wait for Callie to close up. She usually locks up around eight o'clock. Then you, me, and Bear will have a talk."

Doc Fenton worked out of an office on the second floor of the Prairie Saloon. This was a saloon like those in St. Louis. It was lit up and loud whether it was day or night. Gunplay and fistfights were not tolerated, but enough happened to give Doc enough business to pay his rent. Like many of the businesses, The Prairie Saloon had a back stairwell. This led to Doc Fenton's office. As I climbed the fourteen steps, I was glad I didn't have gout of the foot or a broken leg.

Doc gingerly examined my injured shoulder. "How did it happen?" he asked.

"I was carrying a box of books down some stairs and fell. I guess my shoulder took all of the punishment." There was a red bump where the bat had brushed me in the chest. The Doc was eyeing that.

I touched the bump. "Yeah, *Crisswell's History of America* did that one. The book flew out of the box and I landed on it."

Doc Fenton slowly nodded. "Well son, you're lucky it's not broken."

He walked over to the wall and pulled down a chart. It was a color diagram of how the insides of a human body looked. I could see the heart, the intestines, and all sorts of parts of the male anatomy I wasn't too interested in.

"This is the human body."

I felt that Doc Fenton was leading up to a lecture that he'd given many times. I waved my good arm at him. "Get on with it, Doc."

He sighed and pulled down another chart. It showed muscles and the bones of a man. Doc pointed to a brown colored muscle between the upper arm and shoulder. "Your muscle here, is severely swollen, but nothing is broken. The bone is still intact." He walked over to an icebox. "I'm going to give you an ice pack for the swelling and an ointment to help with the healing." As he got the materials, he continued to speak. "Good thing you aren't a rancher or farmer. You'd be laid up for a few days. I suppose sitting at a desk up there at the *Journal* won't kill you." He placed a cloth bag of ice on my shoulder and gently bandaged it so it wouldn't slip off. "The swelling will go down, then carefully, and I mean carefully, rub the ointment in." He held up a black tube. "Petroleum jelly." Then he held up a bottle. "This is aspirin for the pain. Tomorrow you'll really be feeling it, but you might be able to sleep. You won't be sleeping tonight."

Doc Fenton's bedside manner had little to be desired.

"Thanks Doc. If I'm not better quickly, you have my permission to shoot me."

Doc let out a laugh and clapped me on my good

shoulder. My bad shoulder felt the vibration and for a brief moment, I went blind with pain.

Walking back to the hotel, I thought about the training that The Service gave me in St. Louis. I had questioned the hours of exercise I did, developing quickness and balance. I'd questioned the fencing class they gave us. Looking back, it was all of that training that saved my life in the alley.

I entered my room cautiously. One of Featherston's men could be waiting for me. A bottle of whiskey was on the little end table with a note attached. It read: *Take one glass for the pain, but remember our editorial meeting later*. It was signed Farly Wilson. Arrow was a good man. I hoped Bear was a good man, too. Today, my job had become dangerous.

Chapter Eleven

By late afternoon, the swelling in my shoulder had gone down a little. The pain level had gone up a lot. I resisted whiskey. I wanted to have a clear head for my meeting with Arrow and Bear. I chewed several aspirin tablets and washed them down with water.

The hotel clerk knocked on my door at five minutes to eight. "It's time sir," came the muffled voice on the other side of the door.

Since I didn't have a watch, I'd tipped the clerk to alert me. I put my gun in a holster under my coat. If a fast draw was necessary, I'd be dead.

Arrow was sitting on the steps of the hardware store across from the café. Callie was inside, sweeping up. The street was dark. An occasional buggy passed by. I joined Arrow on the steps.

He nodded to a window above the café. "We'll meet Bear in that room up there. I've got a key to get us in." In the distance, the sound of music and laughter echoed from the bars and saloons on Second Street. "How's the shoulder?"

"It's throbbing. I need more ice." I popped an aspirin in my mouth and chewed on it.

"I've had some pretty painful injuries," said Arrow. For the next few minutes, Arrow and I traded injury stories. We both tried not to exaggerate as each wound we revealed raised the ante. Arrow was threatening to show me a scar on his buttocks when Callie started turning out the gas lamps in the café.

"Let's give it about two more minutes, then go up," Arrow said softly.

At that moment, a man staggered down the street. It was that town drunk I'd seen on my first day in Clearview. He stopped in front of the dark café and took out a bottle. He looked both ways, then took a long swallow. Then he burped and tripped down the alley. Bear. Of course. What better way to find out information than to hang around the bar with that glazed look. No one would pay any attention to you.

I looked at Arrow and smiled. "Brilliant."

He gave me a quizzical look and shrugged. Then he slapped me on the knee. "Let's go," he said.

Arrow led me to a side door in the alley. We went up a very narrow staircase which led to a very narrow hallway. I held my hand in front of my face, but couldn't see it. I did see a thin slit of light on the floor. It was coming from a closed door. Arrow gave two, quick, soft raps on the door. Then he opened it.

The room was dim. I had to adjust my eyes for the dark.

"Rattler, meet Bear."

Sitting in a chair in the corner was a woman. "Hello, Rattler." It was Callie.

* * *

The Service had an undercover program that was designed for finding out information before a crime was committed. In most cases, an agent was put in place. The underground agent was called a "mole". The mole would become part of the community and look for nefarious activities. Arrow was the mole in Clearview. When the mole detected something untoward, such as a possible wanted fugitive like Lewis Featherston, he would contact Dodge City. A second mole, such as Bear, was sent in to collaborate and build evidence.

Callie was in a position like Arrow. The café was perfect when it came to gossip. And sometimes, gossip, idle chatter, and overheard conversations produced results. The three of us sat at a small table, while Bear/Callie and Arrow brought me up to date.

Bear started off. "When Arrow found Lewis Featherston, I came in and got the job at the café. I found out some good information."

As I watched her speak, I thought of Benita. Callie was a high ranking officer in The Service. Benita wanted to own a business. What was with women these days?

"Anglin Cattle has clients all over the west," Bear said. "Their biggest client is the U.S. government. They supply cattle and beef to Fort Carmel. Fort Carmel is the distribution outlet to every military post west of the Mississippi."

"And that's why you're seeing Lt. Martin."

She nodded. "He is chief supply officer. There is a lot of money going into the Anglin tills."

"What about Anglin himself?" I asked.

"He's clean as far as we know," said Arrow. "I did

some research on him. Benita probably told you about his losing his family in the flood."

"He seems like a nice man," I said. "Obviously he doesn't know of Featherston's background."

Arrow shook his head. "He hired Featherston about four years ago to head up security. We believe Lewis gave him a fake story about working as a sheriff in Illinois."

Bear continued, "As a security man, Featherston has a good record. Anglin had a lot of cattle rustling problems and Lewis put a stop to that. His violent methods get results."

"Benita told me about a man that he beat up in the office."

Bear looked over at Arrow. He spoke, "That guy was a local. He'd been hired to help with the payroll. After two trips to Wichita, Featherston noticed that the ledger had been changed. It was actually good law enforcement on Featherston's part."

"He didn't have to pistolwhip that man," said Bear. "He should have turned him over to Sheriff Daily, who in turn, would have released him to the U. S. Marshals."

"So what do you think Featherston's doing? It sounds like he's doing an effective job."

"Jerry . . . I mean, Lt. Martin, has been keeping records of the monies that the fort pays Anglin. We think Featherston might be cooking the books."

I saw the light. "That's why he beat up the guy. Featherston was afraid this crook was going to find out about his own crookedness."

"Exactly," said Bear.

A look passed between the two.

"What is it?" I asked.

Bear cleared her throat before she spoke. "To make the case, we need to see the ledger on the Anglin side."

"I tried breaking into their office several times," said Arrow.

Bear smiled. "Arrow can get into any lock in the country."

"That's it!" I shouted.

They both shushed me.

I pointed at Arrow. "Five years ago, you taught safe cracking in St. Louis."

He shrugged modestly.

"But you had a mustache then. And your hair was a different color."

Arrow laughed. "I'd been on a job and they dyed my hair black."

"And it was straight," I said.

He twirled his curly blond locks. "The natural curl is hard to iron down."

Bear looked irritated. "Can we continue please?"

"Sorry."

"I tried to break in," said Arrow. "Featherston has his green shirts all over the place, twenty-four hours a day. I timed out their rounds and figured I had four minutes and thirty-seven seconds to break in and find the ledger. Unfortunately, while I could get into the office in seconds, the ledger is locked in a file cabinet and the cabinet is locked in a bank vault. I can break into a vault, but it takes a while."

"So where does that leave us?" I asked. Then I remembered the look they'd given each other. "You want me to break into the vault?"

"No," said Bear. "But during business hours, Benita could."

Before I could say anything, Arrow spoke, "It was fortunate for us that Featherston started throwing his attention to Benita. That brought you into the picture and—"

Bear finished his sentence for him, "she is in love with you."

There it was, all on the table.

"So I'm supposed to use her love for me to convince her to break into the safe."

"That's what we're paid for," said Arrow.

"Besides, she has keys to the vault. She won't have to break in."

Everything they said was true. My job depended on deceit. The problem was, I realized I loved Benita, too. I could never marry her. Few agents married, and the few who did, never had a happy marriage. It was just that type of job.

"I don't know. How much does Benita have to know? I'll have to tell her who I am."

"You can't Rattler," said Bear. "You have to convince her to get that ledger without revealing your true purpose."

I pondered early retirement. "What have you got on the people who were shotgunned? I asked.

Bear folded her hands on the table. "When Featherston was known as Coletrane, his method was to ambush people from behind. He would ride by on a horse and shoot the victim in the back."

"Who were Coletrane's victims?"

"They were prominent people. Bankers, businessmen, politicians. There are people who paid Featherston to get rid of them."

"He was a hit man?"

"Yes," said Bear. "He worked with a group in Chicago—a group known as The Black Hand. Very deadly, very organized."

I was thinking hard. "Obviously it wasn't Featherston who shot the man the other day. Are you saying he knows the killer? Probably taught him how to do it?"

"It connects," said Arrow.

I absentmindedly tapped on the table with my knuckle. It sent a shock up my arm to my sore shoulder. I switched the tapping to the left hand. "We have three people who were killed by a shotgun in the past eighteen months." I looked over at Arrow. "What were the names of the victims?"

"Tom Addington."

"Right. And he was a ranch hand for . . ."

"Lakeland Ranch. Big outfit. And no, they don't supply Anglin with cattle."

"So there's no connection there," I mused. "What about the other two?"

"Mike Reese, the bank teller, was killed in his sleep," said Bear. "He too, had been shot in the back."

"So he slept on his stomach. I mean, if he was shot in the back. He wasn't awake nor was he disturbed."

Bear shrugged. "Who knows? As a teller at the Clearview Bank and Trust, he handled transactions for Anglin Cattle, but so did the other tellers."

"Which leaves us the accountant."

"Terry Hill," said Arrow.

"He handled the books. Tell me about his murder," I said.

Arrow spoke, "He went to the office late one night. Someone came in and shot him in the back of the head."

"The guards making their rounds didn't hear anything?"

"They heard the shots, came running, and saw a man in black, wearing a mask, flying down the street on a steed. They found Hill up in the office, dead."

I nodded in thought. "If he was at his desk, what was he working on? Was the ledger there?"

"The security men called Featherston. He was in charge. It was decided that it was an attempted robbery," said Arrow.

It had been a cover up. "Didn't the guards hear the gunman breaking in?" I asked.

"There was no break-in," said Bear. "Apparently Hill left the door unlocked. He felt safe with the security men there, making their rounds."

"Convenient. The gunman knows there's security. He knows Terry Hill is working late. He knows the door is unlocked."

Bear nodded. "And Featherston controlled the investigation."

I folded my hands. "Do you think the sheriff is involved? Because in this case he seemed to be very uninvolved."

Bear laughed. "The sheriff used to be a jeweler. When he started to lose his eyesight and his hands began to tremble with age, it was over. His brother was the sheriff, but he died of a heart attack. No one wanted the job, so Daily put in for it."

"That's odd," I said.

"Not really," said Arrow. "Daily couldn't set stones

anymore, but actually knew a thing or two about law enforcement. His father had been a marshal in Kentucky. His other brother is a sheriff down in Texas. By most standards, Clearview was pretty civilized. All Sheriff Daily had to do was handle paperwork."

"Except . . ." said Bear.

"Except what?"

"Except about two years ago, the sheriff started losing mental toughness."

"Old folks disease," added Arrow.

"He started forgetting things. One of his deputies who worked part time security with Anglin suggested that Daily deputize Featherston. After that, Featherston and his men became the major law enforcement group in Clearview."

"Very convenient," I said.

"Very," Bear emphasized.

The next day, I made a surprise visit to Benita. Her eyes lit up when she saw me walk into the office. I felt my own heart do a flip-flop. She looked so pretty, so happy.

"Randy!" She waved me over to her desk. Two men who had desks nearby, looked at me sharply.

"I'm sorry to disturb you at work, but I thought I could take you to lunch."

"I would love that. There's a great place over in the Mexican Quarter that makes the best tortillas."

"When do you get off?" She looked at the grandfather clock in the corner. "Give me twenty minutes."

"I'll be outside." I nodded to the other two men. They stared holes through me. Friendly people.

Pee Wee's shoe shine stand was next to Anglin's Cattle, so while waiting for Benita, I decided to give my boots a treat. "Howdy," I said, stepping up on the box.

"Howdy yourself," Pee Wee replied.

I put my boots up on the iron shoe stands. "You're Pee Wee, right?"

"Every soul in town knows me." He took out a rag and immediately went to work. "I hear you're a teacher."

"Yes I am."

"Why are you over at the paper then?"

"They needed my help."

His entire focus was on my boots as he dusted them off with the rag before applying the polish. "I hear you teach reading."

"I do."

"I don't read," he said this with pride as he took out the boot polish.

"Why not?" I asked.

"Don't see no reason."

Apparently he saw no reason to learn English either.

"What good is reading? I done all right."

I didn't answer.

"I mean, readin', writin'—it's all a waste of time." He spread the boot polish evenly, then took out a brush. Pee Wee was fast and very efficient. He must have polished a million boots.

"I don't know Pee Wee. Being able to read can open up a whole new world for you. The great philosopher Socrates said that a man is not complete if he can't read." Socrates, Aristotle, one of those guys said it, I'm sure.

Pee Wee buffed my boots in silent meditation. Then he spoke. "Soc . . ."

"Socrates."

He nodded. "Yeah, I know him. He's a trail cook with the Munger Ranch down Texas way. Skin is black as midnight. Makes a mean biscuit."

My boots were like mirrors when he finished. I flipped him a quarter. "Thanks Pee Wee. Nice job."

He eyed the two bits. His rate was four cents a polish. He bit down on the coin, giving it a molar inspection. Then he grinned broadly, revealing yellow teeth and cherry red gums. "You come back when your boots drink up too much trail dust."

The cantina was small, but lively. A band played fast, peppy Mexican tunes while hot plates of beans and tamales were served with rice. Señor Rodriguez, the owner, took us to a table near the back.

"It's nice meeting you, Mr. Foster." He gave Benita a sly smile. "Usually Señorita Brooks is with a handsome, distinguished man. Mucho older, of course."

Benita laughed and waved him off. "Don't listen to him Randy. This is one of Mr. Anglin's favorite watering holes."

As we sat, I wondered if it was Featherston's favorite spot, too. We ordered tortillas, beans, and tea. Benita sat in her chair, gazing at me with intensity and longing. As I said before, I'm terrified of women. But with Benita, it was different. We could sit in silence and be comfortable. I could take her intense gaze like an easy ride. I decided to take the plunge.

"Speaking of Mr. Anglin, I was wondering if

he'd like to have an article in the *Journal* written about him."

"I don't know. He's had stories about his life done before."

"What about the way his company works? Since Anglin is the biggest outfit in town, I thought people would be interested in how it operates."

Benita furrowed her brow in thought. "Maybe. Anglin is a big name in this town. For that matter, it's the biggest name in several states."

I pointed at her. "Right. You could show me what goes on in accounting and filing."

"I don't think it's the kind of work that's very exciting."

"It's about money. People love stories about money."

She shrugged. "I suppose."

We got back to her office early. Benita introduced me to the two men who continued to stare holes in me. "This is Mr. Chapman and Mr. Brown. They also work for Mr. Leslie."

She had mentioned Leslie before. She must have seen my face, as I tried to remember the name.

"Mr. Leslie's the lawyer for Anglin Cattle. He's the man you should talk to."

"I'll talk to him. Now what about the vault? Can you get into it?"

She looked at me suspiciously. "You're not planning on robbing us are you?"

"Not with Pandora. She's the slowest horse in Kansas. And Texas, Oklahoma, and Colorado."

Benita motioned me over to the safe. "Just don't look while I turn the combination."

I scanned the office, listening for the click of the tumblers in the lock.

"You can look now." With an effort, she pulled the massive safe door open. "We not only keep money here, but company papers, contracts, and other legal filings."

"What about company figures? Profit statements for example."

She nodded. "We keep those in a ledger."

My plan was to memorize the latest figures and dates entered. Then I would compare it with Lt. Martin. "Do you keep the ledger in the safe?"

"Oh no, that's in Mr. Leslie's office."

"The lawyer?"

"Yes. Mr. Chapman and I add our figures and turn them in to Mr. Brown. He totals the numbers and gives them over to Mr. Leslie."

I saw the file cabinet at the back of the safe. "What's in the file cabinet?"

"That's where we keep all of the former employee files." She led me out of the safe. "Now that's enough about dry numbers. Let me take you out back to the corral. The gentleman there will give you a hair raising account in herding Brahma bulls."

"I'll check on that next week, Benita. You've given me plenty to chew on for this week's edition."

She caught hold of my hand. "Randy, if you're not too busy with the article, I thought maybe we could go to the theatre tonight."

Theatre. It was as good as the opera. Maybe better, because it was usually in English. "Of course. What's the show?"

"Shakespeare's *Macbeth*."

Very English.

"The troupe that's performing it has come all the way from Philadelphia."

I touched her on the nose. "I'll be by to pick you up."

She gave me a wink back. My heart melted.

Later, at the *Journal*, I asked Arrow about Mr. Leslie, the lawyer.

"Mr. Leslie handles everybody's business in southwestern Kansas," said Arrow. "We'll get Bear to go see him. It's a break that the ledger's at his place instead of the vault."

I was just happy to be off the hook. "What can Bear do?"

"She'll think up a reason to go see him. If she can get into that office, she'll figure out a way to see that ledger."

As I left the *Journal*, I saw an old friend. It was Cracker Barrel and he walked with a pronounced limp. Apparently my kick to his groin had made an impression. Of course Lamppost had made an equal impression on my sore, swollen shoulder. Cracker Barrel scowled at me and kept limping. At least he was no longer tailing me.

The ice cream parlor was on Main Street. I decided to treat myself to a confection. As I turned the corner, I was met with a towering man wearing a badge. It was Featherston. He had three other green shirts with him. We both stopped and eyed each other. One of us was going to have to give way to the other. A woman saw this confrontation and hurried her child past us. Should I play the timid school teacher or be myself?

"You're in my way," I said evenly. I liked being a man of few words. This was a sign of toughness.

Featherston was a man of fewer words. "Watch yourself." To my surprise, he waved to his deputies and they all walked around me. One of them was Lamppost. I didn't like the smile on his face.

Chapter Twelve

When I came back from the ice cream parlor, I found Noah sitting at the desk, laboriously writing down his *ABC*s.

Arrow stood over him, pointing at the tablet I'd given Noah. "What's that letter, Noah?" he asked.

"It's an *N*, Mr. Farly. Like the N you see in the name Noah."

Farly scratched his head. "Then what's that next letter you wrote down?"

"That's an *M*, Mr. Farly."

Arrow looked up at me. "Noah keeps putting the *N* before the *M*, but he wrote all twenty-six down."

Noah beamed as he held up the tablet. I walked over and took it. The letters were just as I taught him. Block style.

"Very good. Farly's right. *M* comes before *N*." This did not drag down my pupil's enthusiasm.

"I worked on them all night. And I found the signs you told me to look for, Mr. Randy."

Arrow gave me a quizzical look. I put a hand on Noah's shoulder.

"What word starts with an *A*, Noah?"

"Apple."

"What about *H*?"

Noah looked stumped. For a long moment, he pondered. He shook his head in frustration. "I thought you were going to go in order of the letters. I was ready for *B*." He tapped the floor with his toe. "Board," he said proudly.

"*H*," I repeated firmly.

"That's a hard one," said Arrow.

I don't think Arrow realized that he'd used a word that started with an *H*.

Noah caught it and said, "*H*, ha-ha-hat!" He tapped a finger on his hat that lay on the desk.

Arrow leaned over and whispered to me. "What word would you give him for *X*?"

"Tell me about *X*, Noah."

Noah was comfortable with his two man audience. He leaned back in his chair and folded one leg over the other. "Well suh, *X* is the mark that most men use when they can't spell their name."

"I thought you'd give him something hard like xylophone," said Arrow.

"That starts with a *Z*, Mr. Farly."

I shook my head. "No, xylophone starts with an *X*, but you are right about the *Z* sound."

A dismal look crossed his face. "There's just too many words out there, Mr. Randy."

"Yes, but you use many of them and someday you'll be able to write and spell any word you want."

Arrow put his hat on. "I'm getting a headache

from all of this education that you're cramming into Noah's head. I'm going to go have a beer."

"See ya around, Mr. Farly. Enjoy your beer. Beer. That starts with a *B*."

Farly hid a smile as he left.

I'd been doing a lot of thinking about Noah Smith. He would be a perfect recruit for The Service. There were two men of his color who worked in The Service. They were Gleaners. A Gleaner was like . . . a fly on the wall. Hmm. A fly on the wall. Yeah, I had thought of the perfect comparison. A Gleaner's job was to find out information. As porters, janitors, and waiters, black men were an invisible race. People spoke in their presence about all sorts of business and personal affairs. If a Gleaner thought he had any useful information, he would pass it along to The Service.

Noah Smith was not a Gleaner. His incredible fast draw and aim would be wasted listening to idle chatter. Unfortunately, his opportunities were limited. Forget the prejudice he faced. God had given him skin that made it hard to blend in with a gang. Undercover work was lost to him. After my Clearview assignment, I would talk to Harlon. Perhaps he could find a place for Noah.

Forgoing the McGuffey Reader, I pulled out a beginner's reading book with the simple title, *Reading #1*. It was the first book in a series of ten that taught simple words. Gradually the words got longer and the stories were more sophisticated.

"Let's try something easy. I'll teach you the first three pages of this book. Then you can figure out the next three pages." I turned to the first page. On it was the picture of a dog walking down a trail. I pointed to the word under it. "Okay, what's that word?"

Noah looked at the picture and word with silent intensity. "Dog?"

"No, you're guessing." He looked at the book again with furrowed brow. I detected a slight tremor in his hand.

"Don't worry Noah. This is not a test."

"Wolf! It says wolf!"

"You're still guessing. Concentrate. What's that first letter?"

"*T.*"

"Make the letter sounds like I taught you."

"*Tuh. Tuh.*"

"Good. And the next letter?"

"*O. Ahh.*"

"And the last letter?"

He pressed his lips together with great effort, then hummed. "Mmmmm. *M.*"

"Okay, good. Now put *T-O-M* together." Like air escaping from a balloon, Noah strung the sounds together. "Tuh-ahh-mm."

"What does that say?" With a second effort, he repeated the letters, melding them together more efficiently. "Tahhmm." Then it hit him. "Tom! His name is Tom!"

"Exactly."

His eyes rolled in excitement. "I really thought that word was "Dog". I never thought he would have a name."

The next page showed milk in a bowl. The word below it was "milk." This time, Noah broke down the letters. With the help of the picture he figured it out quickly. I had forgotten my own arduous task of learning to read. As my eyes glided over sentences in a newspaper, I took it for granted. Seeing Noah's excitement brought back gratification I used to feel as a teacher.

"Let's take the next one." I turned the page and it showed Tom the dog, slurping up the milk. Under the picture was the word, "Drink." Using the picture as a cue, Noah conquered the word effortlessly.

The story of Tom eventually turned to sentences about a dog on a ranch and how he learns to herd sheep. As Noah turned the pages and looked at the pictures, I was sure he'd be asking for more stories with larger words and more complicated plots. We were both so involved in Noah's "reading", I didn't notice the shadow spreading across the floor.

"T-Tom r-runs. Tom runs." Noah read.

I finally saw the shadow and turned. It was Benita. She stood there, staring at Noah, her mouth agape. She didn't take her eyes off him as she inched into the room.

"Benita."

She was speechless.

"This is Noah Smith, my new pupil."

By now, Noah had realized her presence and was standing respectfully. An unpleasant frown was on her face. Did Benita harbor ill feelings for someone of another race? The smile on my face was frozen.

She stopped in the middle of the room, never taking her eyes off Noah as she spoke. "I came in to remind you that the play tonight starts at seven-thirty, not eight o'clock like the opera."

I nodded, afraid to speak. What was going through Benita's mind?

Her eyes left Noah and took in the jar of honey and baked bread he'd brought in payment for the day's lesson. "Well . . ." she said, attempting a smile.

Noah, too, had an emerging smile.

I'm not an interpreter of smiles so the tension was still thick in the room. At least to me, it was.

Benita swallowed. "I'm sorry to stare . . . Noah . . . but I'd never seen any person of your color, read. It's quite shocking."

Noah waved his arm at the bread and honey.

"Would you like to try my bread? I baked it this morning."

She strode over to the table. "It really smells divine."

Noah sliced a piece and placed it on the tin plate I'd been using.

Benita dipped the bread in honey and daintily chewed off a small piece. She nodded as she ate. "It's very good, Noah. Are you a cook?"

"No ma'am."

"Who taught you how to bake bread?"

"My grandpa."

She dipped the bread once more. As she took the bite, a bit of honey dribbled down her chin. Noah offered his blue checkered napkin. She took it and quickly wiped her chin.

"Pardon me," she said and handed him back the napkin. "I've seen you over at the Mercantile sweeping up."

"Yes ma'am."

She had a lopsided smile on her face. "It was an odd sight, watching you read like that."

Noah looked embarrassed, but pleased as he humbly looked at the floor. "I'm just beginning. I hope to be able to write, too."

"I'm sure you will, Noah."

He eyed the floor, not looking at Benita. She chewed the last of the bread with a delicate grace. I loved the way she chewed.

"I-I hope to be good at it someday." He took the canteen and poured tea into a cup. "You need something to wash that down."

As she took the cup, I realized neither of them had acknowledged me. I was like . . . a fly on a wall.

Benita suddenly looked over at the fly. "You're a good teacher, Randy. I knew you would be."

"Students like Noah make me look good."

The three of us formed a comfortable triangle in the room. Then, Benita broke the triangle and headed for the door. "I've interrupted your lesson long enough. Thank you for the bread, Noah. It was very nice to meet you."

"I feel the same way ma'am."

Benita looked at me brightly. "Remember, the show starts at seven-thirty."

"I'll pick you up at seven o'clock."

With that, she was gone. I could have kissed her. "That was Benita. I didn't really introduce her. Benita." Talking about Benita, saying her name out loud brought a shyness over me. Why was that? "I'm . . . I'm taking her to the theatre tonight."

Noah did not say a word. He stood there, enjoying the teacher's discomfort.

"She uh . . . I mean we . . . we are seeing each other. It's just . . ."

Noah sat down and held up the book. "I didn't bake enough bread for a long lesson, Mr. Randy."

"Of course." I sat back down. My demeanor turned businesslike as I pointed to the next page. "Try that one, Noah."

He looked at the picture of sheep in a pasture. Then he laughed.

"What is it?"

He kept laughing.

"You really like that Miss Benita, don't you, suh."

It was a statement, not a question. I blushed, but felt a pleasant warmth course through my veins.

"She's a good woman. I felt it as soon as she came into the room."

Not that I thought otherwise, but it was nice to know that Noah's sixth sense confirmed what I already knew.

Chapter Thirteen

The Grand was again filling up with well dressed theatre goers. Out in front was a poster advertising *Macbeth*, produced by the Penn Theatre Company from Philadelphia. Benita surprised me by pinning her hair up. She looked beautiful.

When I picked her up, I had to remark, "Your hair is very . . . classical. I like it."

Her smile blinded me. "I'm glad it pleases you, Randy."

I took her hand and held it during the entire ride to the theatre.

As we entered our familiar box, I looked at the throng of people coming into the auditorium. Arrow was in the front row, ready to write a review for the *Journal*. I did not see Bear or Lt. Martin, although there were several soldiers from Ft. Carmel in attendance. All wore their dark blue dress uniforms.

I caught the eye of a young woman who was looking up at me. She gave me a long, slow, sexy wink.

Embarrassed, I sat up straight. Had Benita noticed?

"Are you all right?" Benita asked.

"Me? Yes. Yes I am."

She put a cool hand on my brow. "Your face is red. Do you have a fever?"

"No, I'm fine. I'm just anticipating a great show."

A few moments later, I sneaked a glance at the young lady who winked at me. Her head was buried in her program. She was quite beautiful. Her hair was auburn and the blueness of her eyes was startling. Her bodice was cut low, allowing a very fine view of her generous bosom. It was almost scandalous.

After memorizing this beauty, I was about to turn away when she was joined by a gentleman in an ill-fitting tuxedo. It was Featherston. He looked up at me and doffed his top hat.

"I'll be," I said to myself.

"What?" Benita asked.

"It looks like Mr. Featherston has a girlfriend."

Benita followed my gaze and looked down. Her face fell.

Was she jealous? Did she have feelings for Featherston?

Then she rolled her eyes.

"That's just Sophie. She's one of Madam Tinsley's girls."

I was amazed. A working girl usually had dyed hair and wore a pound of make up. This young lady with Featherston was beautiful and looked innocent as a newborn calf.

"Where's Madam Tinsley's?"

She elbowed me sharply. "Never you mind."

"I was just wondering if all of her girls looked like Sophie."

Benita looked down at Featherston's date. "No. Sophie cleaned up good for this one. Most of Madam Tinsley's girls look like what you'd expect. Dyed hair and a pound of makeup."

"At least Featherston is looking for female companionship in other quarters."

She shook her head. "No. Lewis and all of his deputies do their part to keep Madam Tinsley in business. He's looking at me for wife material." She hugged herself in a shudder. "Let's not talk about this."

I put a comforting hand behind her thin neck. "Don't trouble yourself, Benita. I'm here."

She looked up at me just as the lights began to dim. The look was a mixture of curiosity and . . . lust? I felt my heart do another unfamiliar flip-flop.

The evening of Shakespeare was invigorating. *Macbeth* was full of violence. It was very exciting. I had read the play before and even thought of having my students in Pleasant Valley read it. Seeing it on the stage was a whole different experience. The actors were very accomplished swordsmen. Benita gripped my arm at the clanging of steel on steel. It was very realistic.

In the theatre, I looked down at Featherston. His eyes were glued to the action on stage. I wondered how I would fare in a sword fight with him. I wouldn't mind ramming a shaft of steel through his stomach. In my mind, I could see the look of dread on his face as the blood drained from it. I could see his rough hands holding onto the thin blade. It was an enjoyable thought of pulling the sword out, hearing his anguished cry, and seeing the blood and guts coming out. What made it even more enjoyable was the thought of Featherston wearing lily-white tights like the actors were wearing. Okay. Perhaps my imagination needs a little curbing, but drama and opera always stimulated my senses. Give me a good sword fight over a showdown anytime.

After the play, we walked to The Sagebrush. It was a fancy restaurant that promised big T-bone steaks and generous portions of potatoes, beans, and various kinds of cakes for dessert.

Sitting near the front was Mr. Anglin and a bald man with a bushy mustache.

"Who's that?" I asked.

"That's Mr. Leslie," said Benita. "Come on, I'll introduce you."

Mr. Anglin rose from his chair as we approached. "Benita, what a nice surprise. Hello Randy."

I nodded. "Sir."

"Would you like to sit with us?" asked Anglin.

"Oh no, sir, I just wanted to introduce Randy to Mr. Leslie."

Leslie didn't get up. He looked at both of us like we had come in and tossed a saddle on his steak.

"This is Mr. Anglin's lawyer."

I offered my hand. After a brief moment, he wiped his mouth with a napkin and gave my hand a quick shake.

"Pleased to meet you," he said shortly.

Mr. Anglin ignored the man's rudeness as he smiled and pointed at me. "Randy is Benita's beau from Colorado. He is a school teacher, but he is presently working over at the *Journal*."

Mr. Leslie gave me one more glance, then went back to his steak. Benita took the hint.

"I hope we didn't interrupt a business meeting."

Anglin lightly touched her shoulder. "Don't worry your head about it my dear. Leslie and I have had our business meeting and decided to relax with a pleasant dinner."

Mr. Leslie didn't look relaxed, and dinner at ten o'clock at night suggested a long, after hours meeting.

The waiter appeared and showed us to our table.

"He wasn't very friendly," I said as we sat.

"Oh, Mr. Leslie's an old grump. He's very good at what he does though. Rumor has it, he's convinced Mr. Anglin to buy some oil leases in Oklahoma."

"He looks like a shrewd customer."

"Mr. Leslie knows all the angles when it comes to business. When I start my dress shop, he's the first person I'm going to go see."

When our chocolate cake arrived, I noticed Mr. Anglin and Mr. Leslie enjoying cigars. Mr. Anglin said something and to my surprise, the lawyer laughed.

"Hey, the man has a smile."

Benita waved a hand in front of my face. "Hey, how about my smile? You haven't taken your eyes off of Mr. Leslie since we sat down."

"Sorry. Mr. Anglin seems to attract interesting people. People like you." Sometimes a smooth line flowed out of my mouth.

Mr. Anglin got up from his table and walked over to us. "I envy you young people. You can eat all of that food and still sleep at night without the gas."

Benita gave her wonderful, throaty laugh. Mr. Anglin hid a smile.

"Actually I came over here to invite you both to my Cattleman's Ball."

Benita's face went from mirth to surprise. "Why Mr. Anglin, thank you very much, sir."

"Thank you very much, sir," I echoed Benita.

Before I could stand, he put a hand on my shoulder. "Mr. Foster, you are to escort my favorite employee. I've arranged for a red fringed surrey to pick you both up in front of the courthouse two weeks from Wednesday at five o'clock." He gave a half bow and went back to his table, leaving a speechless Benita.

I was perplexed. "What's a Cattleman's Ball?"

She found her voice. "It's the biggest party in Kansas. Mr. Anglin's been giving it for five years, but this is the first time he's invited me."

"Should I brush up on my square dancing?"

"Do you know how to waltz?"

Thanks to my Service training, I did. "I am clumsy at it, but I can waltz."

Excitement gleamed in her eyes. "There will be dancing, fireworks, barbeque, and an orchestra from Denver. I will need a new dress."

I thought of Featherston's ill-fitting tuxedo. "What should I wear?"

"Wear what you wore to the opera, Randy. You are quite handsome in any outfit."

I blushed.

As we left The Sagebrush and headed for Benita's house, I figured it was time to bring up the subject that had been weighing on me since that shave in Clement's Barber Shop.

"Benita . . . I have to ask you something."

She took my arm and laid her head on my shoulder.

This was not going to be easy. As the buggy bumped along, I tried to form the best words I could string together.

"I'm not asking this because I'm jealous. I'm asking because I'm concerned for your welfare." She was looking up at the moon in total contentment. Would my question shatter her? "Mike Reese."

I felt her stiffen. She looked up at me. "What about Mike Reese?"

"Well . . . you were seeing him, right?"

Benita pulled away from me. "What about him?" she repeated, her voice patient, with a tingle of coolness. "Have you been delving into my past?"

I held up my free hand in protest. "No, no, of course not. It's just that . . ." Okay, now I had to go into quick thinking mode. A story. I needed a good story . . . a believable story that would make her not hate me. I started over. "It's just that your cousin Jacob told me to watch out for you. And . . . and on my first day in Clearview, a man was murdered. And, well . . . Farly at the paper told me about Terry Hill, the accountant at Anglin, and Mike Reese . . . and how they'd been killed the same way. By shotgun."

She was still for a very long time. Her face was dark, as if a cloud had passed over the moon.

I felt I had not said enough. Plus, my story was incomplete. "And so . . . I was just sort of asking around about Terry and Mike. I'm not sure where I heard it, but someone said you knew Mike well." That was good. I didn't have to mention any specifics like white carriages and going to the hoedown. Now to clinch it.

"So you see Benita, I was just worried about you. I mean, you knew Mike Reese and I've got to assume you knew Terry Hill since he worked at Anglin's. You are a common factor and it grieves me to think that you might be in danger."

She bowed her head. A tear dribbled down her cheek like rain on a window. "It seems like I've gone to too many funerals lately, but I don't think any of that involves me. Terry Hill was Mr. Anglin's right-hand man. He worked with Mr. Brown and Mr. Chapman."

"So you took his place."

She shook her head. "No. Terry Hill was a vice president and senior partner."

I had no idea that Hill was this important. I wondered if Bear and Arrow knew this.

Benita continued. "I came from the general pool. When Mr. Hill was killed, Brown and Chapman both took over his duties. I was moved in to help with the work load. They hold seniority over me, but they aren't my boss. I answer to Mr. Anglin directly."

"So you are vice president, not the other two."

She gave me a small smile. "Not yet."

"Benita, do you have any idea of why Terry Hill was murdered?"

"No. I always figured it was a robbery, but when the killer saw that safe, he fled. People think that as accountants, we handle a lot of money. We do, but most of our work is in ledgers."

I scratched my chin. As far as Terry Hill was concerned, Benita didn't know anymore than I did.

"Do you think someone was after information in the ledger?"

"I don't know. There weren't any ledgers missing.

In fact, nothing was missing. We did have to replace a ledger and contract that had his blood on them, but it was all standard paperwork and figures."

I was satisfied about Terry Hill. I wasn't about Mike Reese. "Tell me about Mike," I said gently.

Benita took a deep breath. It caught in her throat and her voice was shaky. Maybe it was the bumps in the road.

"Whoever told you about Mike and me was either lying or misinformed. He wasn't wooing me if that's what you think."

"No, Benita, that's not what I thought." It was exactly what I thought, but I needed to let her tell it in her own words.

With a sad sigh, she continued. "I make the deposits for Anglin at the bank. I got to know Mike and all of the tellers. Mr. Biggs, Taylor, Gil"—she pursed her lips in thought—"there was another one, but he got married and left. Frank. Frank someone."

"Go on," I prompted.

"Anyway, I knew them all. Mr. Biggs has such a sense of humor, always joking. And Mike always had a smile on his face. Very friendly. Sweet. He, like you"— she touched my cheek—"didn't seem to mind my starting a dress shop. Of course he had the heart of a banker. He once asked me to the annual hoedown."

Now we were getting somewhere.

"I wasn't seeing anyone, so I thought why not? Then he picked me up in this white carriage. The black horses wore white plumes on their heads. I was so surprised. It had to have cost him a fortune. He presented me with a dozen red roses."

Her eyes misted over and my right hand clinched the buggy reins tighter.

"I felt like Cinderella. I just hoped I wouldn't turn into a pumpkin before midnight."

"I believe the carriage turns into a pumpkin."

She didn't seem to hear me. "It was such a sweet gesture, but it was a little too much. I had no idea that he had a crush on me. I mean, I liked him, but . . . I just didn't feel anything but gratitude for his effort."

My hand loosened on the reins.

Benita continued, "I let him down gently. Riding back after the hoedown, I told him how wonderful he was and how wonderful the evening had been. I would cherish it, but I couldn't return what feelings he had for me."

"How did he take it?"

"He looked disappointed. Not crushed or devastated. I was thankful for that. He looked at me and said, 'I thought you might feel that way, but I had to find out.' So he took me home. I kissed him on the forehead and that was it."

We rode in silence for a long time.

"The next week he was found dead in his house." A new tear trickled down her cheek. "At his funeral, that white carriage was there with the black horses. A dozen red roses lay on the front seat."

"But who . . . ?"

She looked forward, down that dark road. "Nelson, the blacksmith said he found an envelope with a lot of money in it. Inside was a note, instructing him to take the carriage and leave it at the grave site for the duration of the service.

Who would have been motivated to do that? Mr.

Anglin had the money to do it. Maybe he thought Benita loved Mike Reese and it was his idea of a sentimental, romantic tribute. But why anonymous? Then a darker thought hit me. Maybe it was Featherston. Maybe he was jealous of Mike Reese. Maybe he killed him, or had him killed. Maybe he rented the carriage for the funeral as a cruel act to break Benita's heart.

I could not do anything about that. I pulled her head back to my shoulder and we rode along in silence.

Chapter Fourteen

By the time we got to her cottage on Cedar Dust, Benita had lost her gloom. She invited me inside for tea. Pandora, who was in back, munched grass and gave me a scowl I did not like.

Benita's parlor was small and I delicately sat on a settee with my hat on my knee. Benita bustled about her kitchen, finding a kettle and putting it on the stove after pouring a bucket of water in it.

She entered the parlor, radiant. I loved her sparkling eyes, the gentle slope of her neck and the slight hook in her nose. I stood as she entered, letting my hat hit the floor. She took my hands.

"Randy, will you forgive me?"

"For what?"

Her face turned serious. Her lips were slightly parted as if she was trying to speak, but couldn't.

"What is it, Benita?"

"I-I know you're here to ward off Lewis. I know we . . ." She looked at the thin, brown rug on the floor as she spoke. "I think you are the most handsome man. At first, it was your looks that I liked." She continued to look down as she spoke. "But I really love talking to you. You know, opera, theatre, history . . ."

"That's because I'm a teacher."

"It's more. You like me. I know. And you don't care that I want to start my own business. Most men would think that's scandalous. And you seem so interested in people and everything around you."

I felt a pang of guilt. My interest in everything was purely professional.

"I . . . Randy . . . I think I love you."

My heart shuddered. Emotions took over. "I love you," I replied. That was it. My own declaration and it was ice clear. After this assignment, I would resign my commission. I would get a proper school teaching job and settle down with Benita.

"Darling," she cooed. Our faces drew close. We kissed. Her mouth was hot and delicious. I heard bells. Big brass church bells that gonged Happiness and Never Ending Love. No, it was the whistling from the tea kettle. Benita broke the kiss.

"The tea," she whispered.

"Forget the tea," I whispered back.

As she hurried back into the kitchen, I turned and looked out the window. My heart stopped. A face was staring back at me. It was Pandora and she didn't look happy.

"We're in love!" I told her. Then I closed the curtains on the window, ignoring the hurt whinny on the other side.

* * *

The next day, Arrow found me at the desk, reading a letter to the editor sent in by Mr. Leslie. It was about how oil was the future of America.

"You look different," said Arrow.

"What do you mean?"

He tilted his head and gave a half smile. "Happy. You look too happy."

My thoughts zoomed from the letter to an image of Benita sitting on her porch, smiling. "Of course I'm happy. This letter is pretty good."

Arrow glanced at it over my shoulder. "Ah, another opinion from Mr. Leslie. Every month he sends us a four page letter about politics, or how to farm better, why we need to settle the Comanche Nation . . . stuff like that. He's a writer of the highest degree."

"Does he always quote Thoreau?"

"Almost exclusively."

"He's very intelligent."

"Some say he's almost as smart as Mr. Anglin."

Arrow looked in the back room. "Where's Mr. Bartly?"

"At the saloon, I suppose."

"No, I was just there. No one had seen him."

"He hasn't been in this morning," I said.

Then a look of awareness hit his face. He nodded to himself. "He's at his room."

"What's he doing there?"

Arrow gave a dignified "harrumph." "He's sobering up."

"And why is this news?" I asked.

"He's really sobering up so he can go to Anglin's Cattleman's Ball. Every year he sobers and cleans himself up. He'll go over to Madam Tinsley's and get himself an escort."

My thoughts went straight to Sophie. Featherston had to pay her a lot of money to keep him company. I was sure of it.

"I got invited too. Well, Benita was invited. I'm to be her escort."

Arrow shook my hand. "Good move man. People come from as far as Chicago to attend Anglin's soiree. You'll get to mingle with Anglin's buddies. Maybe get some information for us."

While I felt guilt about deceiving Benita, I felt more guilt for Arrow. Should I tell him that I was going to ask Benita to marry me? That I was quitting The Service? To quell my misgivings, I refocused.

"Has Bear had a chance to speak to Mr. Leslie?"

"Actually she had some luck. In fact, she wants us to meet again tonight. Same time, same place."

At three o'clock, it was time for Noah's lessons. We agreed that he would bake a cherry pie and I would meet him at his shack. It was my third trip there and I was becoming a familiar figure in Shanty Town. On my second trip, I handed out candy canes to the kids. I got some appreciative nods from the older folks. This time, I brought chocolates from the Mercantile. The kids came running up and shouting when they saw Pandora coming.

"Heeeehere! Heeeehere!" they cried, their hands in the air. Without stopping, I tossed the sweets to the kids who scrambled for the reward. An ancient black woman gave me a toothless smile. I doffed my hat.

I found Noah chopping wood as I rode in.

"Hello to home."

He wiped his brow and gave a short wave. "Hello Mr. Randy."

I'd saved a small box of chocolates for him. "I've got something for you."

He said hello to Pandora and she nodded her head up and down. She gave him that broad, horse grin.

"You like chocolate, Noah?"

"I make the best chocolate pie in all of Kansas, suh."

"Well here's a little treat for you."

His eyes lit up when he opened the box. "Chocolate bars. These are real fine, Mr. Randy."

Suddenly Pandora had her head between us, nosing at the chocolate.

"No Pandora. These are for Noah."

He patted her face. "I think I can spare a bar for Pandora."

"You'll spoil her," I whispered.

"Don't matter. This horse is spoiled already." Pandora nickered in agreement. It was two against one.

"Go ahead," I said in disgust.

Noah held the bar to her mouth and she took it.

"Happy?" I asked her.

She chewed on the chocolate, ignoring me, ignoring the world.

"Let's get to that reading, Mr. Randy. I'm on chapter ten when Tom the dog happens on a nest of rattlesnakes." He headed for the cabin.

It had been my intention to ask Noah to teach me how to draw my gun faster. I wasn't slow, not like Pandora. But my father always stressed that if you can improve yourself in any way, it would make life easier.

An instructor of mine in The Service told me to lower my holster—it was riding too high. Another trick was to work oil in the holster, then wax it. And keep it waxed. This helped considerably, but it wasn't enough.

I would probably never use a fast draw in my work . . . not like in a showdown or something. But on occasion I needed to get my gun out of the holster in record time. It might save my life someday if I was faster.

"Hold on there, Noah."

He turned. "Yes Mr. Randy?"

"First of all, I'm looking forward to having that pie. In fact, I look forward to anything you cook."

He smiled proudly. "Thank you, suh."

"But the truth is . . . I've gained about five pounds since I've been teaching you." I patted my stomach, which was indeed getting broader. "I thought we could do another kind of trade."

"What do you have in mind?" he asked.

"The truth is, Noah, I've never seen anyone pull a gun as fast as you."

"Am I really that good?" He was serious. He had no idea of how fast he was.

"Yes, yes you are. And I know I'll never be as fast as you, but I would bet you that you could teach me to be faster."

He looked at the ground, mulling this over. Then he spoke. "So you're saying, instead of giving you food for lessons, I teach you how to use a gun?"

I shook my head. "I already know how to use a gun. In fact, I'm as good a shot as you . . . just not as fast."

"Well Mr. Randy, knowing how to use a gun is the

whole thing. Learning how to draw fast is a whole new thing. But if you really want to learn, I'll try to help you."

I nodded. "Okay, let's go."

"You mean now?"

"Why not? We can get to Tom and the rattlesnakes later."

He shrugged. "It's all right with me. Wait right there." He walked into the cabin for a moment and returned with a green apple. He held it up. "I'm saving a few of these for our next apple pie. Catch it."

He tossed the apple toward me and I caught it. Was he going to teach me how to draw fast or teach me the finer points of baseball?

"Now throw it back."

I did so.

"Now Mr. Randy, let's play catch for a while." He saw the doubt creeping into my face. "Don't worry, I'll teach you."

So we played catch. As we did, he talked. "Just keep that long, steady throw. We aren't going anywhere."

We definitely weren't.

"Nice and slow," he repeated.

Before long, we were tossing the apple back and forth in a steady rhythm. Noah chanted his *ABC*s as the game continued. After a while, he recited the story of Tom just as it was written in the book.

As I was about to toss it to him for about the hundredth time, he held up his hands. "Hold on, Mr. Randy."

I had noticed something. He caught the ball awkwardly. Maybe he wasn't lying about his clumsy ways. His throws were lazy spirals, but then, so were mine.

"Now I want you to throw the apple at me as hard as you can."

I was pessimistic. "What if you don't catch it and it hits you?"

"Well suh. Then it's going to hurt. And it's going to be a mess. But try it. Throw that apple at me as hard as you can."

"Okay Noah, but it won't have a lot of control. Don't blame me if I pop you in the eye or something."

He crouched down like a catcher and held his hands in front of him, forming a target.

Did he know baseball?

"Come on now. Throw it in here."

I had seen those big league pitchers with their fancy windups. I knew just how to do it. I rocked forward and back, building my momentum, swinging my arms round and round in wide circles. After a few of these, I reared back and flung the ball. I mean, the apple.

It was a wild pitch. Noah dove to his left and stabbed at it. He caught the apple with the tip of his fingers. Pandora neighed in delight.

"That's good. You've got a strong arm."

I felt like I'd pulled every tendon I had in that strong arm. I waved off the pain. "I played a little ball when I was younger."

He walked up to me, tossing the apple from hand to hand. "Now suh, see that tree?" He pointed to the tree where he had shot the four tins.

I nodded.

He handed me the apple. "I want you to throw this apple at that tree. But first, don't do your wind up. Stand still and hold your breath just like before you pull the trigger.

"Okay."

"Now this will take some of your best thinking," said Noah. "You need to put pictures in your head. There's a word for that . . ." His eyes stared at the ground as he tried to think of the word.

"Imagination?" I asked.

"Yes. That's the word. Imagin . . ."

I stood there, looking at the tree. Noah's voice grew quiet, but strong. It was an old voice coming at me from down through the ages. It hardly sounded like a young man.

"Now you take that apple and before you throw it, see the apple hit the spot you want to hit. See the apple leaving a green trail in the air, humming toward that tree. See that apple bullet shooting in a straight, true line."

I tensed, preparing to throw. He put a soft hand on my shoulder.

"No, just relax. Just picture that apple. It's a green blur. It's going so fast, it's punched a hole in that old tree and is still going strong, miles away."

I relaxed. His voice seemed far off. "When you see that apple do that, put it in your mind, and with all of your heart and all of your mind, and all of your strength, throw it. Throw it with all of your weight behind it. Leave nothing left."

I centered. I focused. I was completely relaxed. I saw the apple piercing the tree a blink after it left my hand. It was twenty feet away, but I could see the bark. I could see the green skin of the apple colliding into it. I cocked my arm and reared back. The world grew dark, except for that one spot on the tree. Suddenly, I was flinging the apple with all the force I could muster. My legs, my arm, even my stomach muscles were behind the throw.

The apple left my fingers and flew those twenty feet at a speed I never knew I had. Just as I envisioned, I felt the apple leave my hand and it was already shattering against the hard tree trunk. There was a *thwop*! A splash of white and green exploded on the tree and splattered onto the ground below it. Chunks of the apple were all over the spot that I had thrown at. Green apple skin, clung to the bark. Noah's eyes were wide.

"Man, you are fast."

My body was trembling. I almost fell to my knees from the effort. "What happened?" I asked.

"Nothing miraculous," he said with a grin. "Just a man throwing an apple against a tree. It was a sight to behold."

I wiped sweat from my brow. The effort had taken a lot out of me. "Right," I said. "You taught me how to throw an apple fast. What does that have to do with drawing a gun? It's not even the same motion."

Noah's eyes glazed over. His mind was somewhere else as he recited.

"*Abcdefghijklmnopqrstuvwxyz*." His *ABC*s came out like a Gattling gun.

"You're scaring me, Noah."

The glaze look left his eyes. "Sorry," he said. Without the glazed look, he repeated his *ABC*s in rapid order.

I still didn't get his point.

"What did you tell me about my *ABC*s, Mr. Randy?"

I didn't know what answer he wanted. "Learn them?" I said.

"Right. Practice them until I knew them. You said practice them until I could do them in my sleep."

"Yes, I did."

"Remember how I got my *N*s and *M*s mixed up?"

I nodded.

"Remember how slow I was at first?"

I nodded once more.

"It's the same thing with the fast draw. Think of pulling your gun like you thought of throwing the apple. See your target. See the gun coming out of your holster like summer lightning." He let that sink in, then continued. "Then you practice it. A lot. Then you practice it some more. At first, it will be hard. You will sweat and tremble from trying, but the more you do it, the easier it gets."

I was dumbfounded. How many times had I told my students those very words? Well, maybe not the part about the sweating and trembling, but I was seeing his point. The answer to the quick draw had been staring me in the face for years. All I had to do was practice what I preached. I clapped a hand on Noah's hard shoulder.

"I will Noah. I will do exactly that."

Chapter Fifteen

That night, Callie, now known to me as Bear, closed the café, and Arrow and I made our way up the dark stairs. By the time we got to the room, she was waiting for us. She had a piece of paper in her hand.

"I saw the ledger. The numbers matched exactly what Jerry . . . Lt. Martin had in his."

I wondered if Bear had fallen for Lt. Gerald Martin, or was it just a job to her? I had fallen for Benita. It could happen to Bear.

"How did you see the ledger?" asked Arrow.

Bear couldn't hide the smile on her face. "Mr. Leslie has his breakfast at the café every morning. I put Witches Wake in his eggs."

I shook my head. "Witches Wake? What is it?" I asked.

"Bear is a chemical genius," Arrow said admiringly.

"What is Witches Wake?" I repeated.

"My own concoction," Bear said proudly. "In fact, I might get a patent for it some day."

"What is it?" I repeated, again.

"It's a combination of prune extract, a touch of quinine, cloves, and sheep syrup to hide the taste. I stirred it in his scrambled eggs. Witches Wake mixes in his stomach with the eggs and sausage. As it starts to digest, Mr. Leslie would have a great urge to visit the outhouse."

I laughed.

Bear continued, "It takes three hours to work. I made an appointment with him to discuss a will, just before lunch. During the meeting, his face got red, and he held his stomach. Then he excused himself."

"Genius," mused Arrow.

"I had plenty of time to pick the lock on his file cabinet and look at the ledger."

"What else did you find?"

Bear spoke with quiet authority as she told her story. "I found the ledger first. Then I tried his desk drawer. The lower drawer was locked with an Iron Betty."

Iron Betty was a nickname The Service gave to a combination lock. How it got the name, I have no idea. They were the ultimate locks.

"He must have wanted to hide something bad," said Arrow.

Bear smiled. "I couldn't take it with me, but I read all I could."

"What was it?" I asked.

"A file on Alan Coletrane, alias Lewis Featherston."

Arrow and I were stunned. We both gave low, impressed whistles.

"Apparently Leslie had come into some official records. His handwriting was meticulous. There were also letters from Illinois, Kentucky and Ohio."

That was Coletrane's territory.

"The letters were from various law agencies, including a court paper from Wheaton, Illinois. That was where Featherston broke out of prison."

"That was the last record we had of Alan Coletrane," said Arrow.

"Until now," I added.

"But it doesn't prove Featherston is Coletrane," said Arrow.

"Actually, it might," said Bear. "Mr. Leslie also had copies of old wanted posters. He drew beards and mustaches on several of them. He is quite a good artist."

"Yeah, but The Service had that done. And it too, looked like Coletrane."

Bear shook her head. A hint of a smile creased her face. "He also had letters from Pilsbury, Missouri and Ft. Worth. They were less official, claiming never having heard of a Lewis Featherston."

It hit me. "The references he gave Mr. Anglin."

Bear nodded.

Now I was getting excited. We could finish this case, I could resign and ask Benita to marry me. Arrow asked the question I should have asked.

"So what's in it for Mr. Leslie? Is he protecting Featherston? Is he building a case to prosecute him? Is he looking for blackmail money?"

"Whether he's on our side or not, to get a conviction, he will be a valuable source," said Bear. "We need to know his motive."

"So what do we have?" I asked.

Bear spoke, "Tomorrow, I'll post a report to The Service. We sit on this until we hear from them. As a federal official, I have the authority to take possession of Mr. Leslie's evidence. I have a feeling Harlon Shanks will want to check up on Mr. Leslie's background first."

I swallowed my disappointment. This could take two or three more weeks. The three of us were quiet, lost in our own thoughts.

Arrow shrugged. "Guess we can be patient and see how this irons out." He stood up, scraping the chair on the floor.

Then we heard it. Someone padding down the dark hallway outside the door. Bear put a finger to her lips as she turned out the lamp. Arrow rushed quietly over to the window and peeked out. A lone figure was loping across the street into the shadows. He was carrying his boots. The man ran with an awkward gait, as if he were bowlegged.

"Who is that?" asked Arrow.

Neither of us recognized him. And how much he had heard at the door, we had no idea.

Chapter Sixteen

That very next weekend, the town of Clearview celebrated it's annual spring carnival. The carnival was always held a week before Mr. Anglin's Cattleman's Ball as a prelude to the summer party season. Folks from Midvale and soldiers from the fort attended as well as farmers and ranchers in the surrounding area.

The carnival was held at the rodeo fairgrounds just east of town. Pandora was not happy when I knotted her reins around the metal lamppost in front of Benita's house. She was delighted, however, when Benita came out and laid a slice of blueberry pie at her feet.

"Enjoy this while we're at the carnival girl," said Benita.

I shook my head and clucked, "She's already spoiled rotten."

Benita ignored me as she stroked Pandora's mane. "I'm bringing her back a blue ribbon to tie in her mane."

"A blue ribbon?"

"Of course silly. I am going to win the blue ribbon for my blueberry pie."

"But you'll have a piece missing," I said as I watched Pandora scarf the pie down. There was a blue ring around her mouth.

"I think I can find another one lying around my kitchen. You can help Pandora finish this one."

As we headed for the fairgrounds on the buckboard, I wiped the corner of my mouth, relishing the taste of sweet blueberries. Benita held an entire pie in her lap, covered by a cloth.

"If you don't win a ribbon for this, the judges have no taste. This was as good as Noah's."

"Last year my apple pie took honorable mention. It really should have won a white ribbon for third place, but Mr. Kithen's wife was the judge and her best friend is Irma Jones."

"And she took third place?"

"Of course. It's all politics. But this year, the judges are different. Plus, I'm going to fool 'em."

"How can you fool them?"

"The winner is always a berry pie. Last year it was Emma Lindsay's blackberry. The year before it was Irma Jones' Staussonberry."

"Stausson-what?"

"Irma's own recipe with all sorts of berries. And I've been asking around. Only one other lady is baking a blueberry, but she does better with apple and cherry."

"Well you'd get a blue ribbon from me, that's for sure." I patted my stomach to emphasize my enthusiasm.

We arrived just as the sun was going down. Pee Wee opened the gate. "You can put your buggy over by that water trough."

There was an assortment of vehicles from carriages to wagons, all lined up in an orderly manner. Nelson, the blacksmith and Hank, his bald friend took people's horses and led them into a large barn.

"You folks enjoy the carnival," said Nelson. "Benita, if you see my wife, tell her that Hank and I will meet her at the quilting booth."

Benita gingerly alit from the buckboard. I handed her the pie. She held it up for Nelson and Hank to see. "Does it look like a winner?"

They both nodded.

Booths were lined up on both sides of a narrow road about fifty feet long. Some sold eats such as popcorn, peanuts, taffy, and corn on the cob. Buttermilk Dairy had a long booth where Trev Olfman's son and his family sold ice cream in cardboard cartons. Other booths sold merchandise from paper fans to rocking chairs. There were booths manned by professional carnival barkers who offered up games of chance. There was a roulette wheel, a shooting gallery, and a dart throw. Lanterns were strung up over the road. Benita called it "The Midway".

She pointed to a series of tents at the end. "That's where they're judging the pies. In the next tent is jams and preserves and the big tent is where the farm and ranch exhibits are. They even give ribbons for the biggest hog or bull."

"I thought they did all of that at the rodeo?"

"The rodeo is the biggest. Mr. Anglin always wins the Brahma competition. He donates the prize money back to the town."

"Is he here tonight?" She shook her head.

"He never comes to the carnival. He's spending all of his time getting ready for his Cattleman's Ball."

Benita went to enter her pie while I strode along the midway. Scattered among the carnival goers were green shirts. They patrolled the grounds and tent areas. Featherston was there, but he wasn't in uniform. He was at the shooting gallery, attempting to win a kewpie doll for Tula Morningstar, an Indian girl who worked at the local brothel. I stopped to watch and heard a voice behind me.

"Hello Mr. Foster."

I turned to see Clarence Biggs watching over my shoulder. "Are you going to try your hand at shooting those moving targets?"

A roustabout turned a crank, which moved the assorted ducks, bears, and fox targets on a pulley. I knew that these games were rigged. I would not indulge.

"No Mr. Biggs. I'm not that good a shot." Not good enough to beat the house. "Besides, I only have a small amount of nickels to waste on such a risky venture."

"Dadgumit!" cried Featherston. Apparently he had already wasted some nickels at the shooting gallery. He plunked another nickel down. "Let's go," he demanded.

The barker snatched the nickel up and dropped it into his apron pouch, heavy with coins. "That's right, that's right!" cried the barker. "The more you play, the better your chances of winning."

I watched Lewis aim the pellet gun. He drew a
bead on a bear and shot. *Clang* went the metal target
as it popped back.

"That's one!" yelled the barker. He looked over the
people who were crowded around his booth. "Just
two more and you win a kewpie doll!"

Tula had her hand on the small of Featherston's
back. It seemed like an intimate gesture, considering
the characters of this play. "Come on Lewis, you can
do it."

Featherston was an iceberg. He bent over the
counter, resting his elbows with the stock of the gun
at his shoulder.

"Aim a little to the left," Biggs, the banker/
sharpshooter advised.

There was a pop and a tin fox fell back with a
clang. Some of the onlookers cheered.

The barker looked at his audience as he spoke to
Featherston. "Just one more my good man. One more
and your lady gets a kewpie doll."

What was unseen by everyone and known only to
me, the barker, and the roustabout, was a pedal under
the counter. I knew this, because The Service actually
held a class on carnival scams. The barker tapped a
nickel on the counter to distract the shooter, while he
pushed the pedal with his foot. This raised the counter
up an inch. If the customer felt the movement, it was
so slight and quick, he dismissed it as nerves or the
shudder of his arm. This resulted in a slightly higher
shot, just over the head of the target. At times, the shot
grazed the top, but not with enough force to knock the
target over.

If the customer was standing, the roustabout

pushed a pedal with his foot and the pulley lowered. Again, the shot would be high.

"Round and round the targets go. One clean shot and down it goes!" cried the barker.

Lewis was sweating as he leaned on the counter. Tula was looking at the full faced plastic kewpie dolls that hung over the shooting area. "Come on baby, you can do it," she encouraged.

Featherston swatted at her hand which now lingered on his shoulder. He didn't speak. She put her hand behind her back. Another fox was in his site. The barker was tapping the nickel on the counter. Just as Featherston gently squeezed the trigger, I saw the leg of the barker move. He was pushing the pedal. The pellet just missed the fox's head. The crowd groaned.

"Dadgumit!" screamed Featherston. He threw down another nickel. "Once more! Let's go!"

I didn't think of Lewis Featherston as stupid. Maybe it was blind pride making him continue. Surely being a "lawman", he realized he was being scammed. Maybe.

I decided to leave him and Tula to their futility and check out the rest of the midway. I nodded to Bear and Lt. Martin who walked arm in arm past the popcorn booth. I didn't want to be too familiar with her. We played our parts . . . the private tutor and Callie the waitress. Arrow was also there, taking pictures for the *Journal*. I saw that as he took a picture of people along the row of booths, he was getting a good shot of a green shirt.

"Getting some good ones, Mr. Wilson?"

"Of course, Mr. Foster." He looked around to make sure no one was paying attention, and quietly said,

"I've shot four of the deputies. I'll send the pictures to Dodge. Maybe The Service can match them up to some wanted posters."

"Keep up the good work." I patted him on the shoulder and noticed A.J., the ten year old barber watching Featherston. He was smiling. He knew. He knew that the game was rigged. And he was having a good time watching Lewis lose his money. He got my attention by pointing at the big bully. He mouthed, "Bad Tipper."

I walked over to him. "Where's you father, A.J.?"

"He's helping my mother sell her quilts. They're five booths down to the right."

"I'll go say hello," I said, leaving A.J. to laugh at Featherston's fruitless quest.

Clement was handing a quilt to a young couple. The man was giving him some dollar bills. His wife was talking to an older woman. A calico quilt lay on the counter between them. I was right about where A.J. got his red hair. His mother's hair was flaming under the lights. She had green eyes and a pert nose. She could have been a McMahon.

Clement waved at me. "How are you, school teacher?"

My eyes were glued to the amazing quilts that hung in the booth or were stacked on a table. They were made with various patterns in all colors.

"I'm fine, Clement."

"Do you need a quilt?"

"Not for now, but I know who to go to if I ever do need one."

He shook my hand. "Margie here, is the seam-stress."

The redhead glanced my way. She smiled and nodded as the other woman kept speaking to her.

I touched the brim of my hat in greeting. "She's very good, Clement."

"Margie spends all year-round, quilting. She usually sells most of them in just one evening here at the carnival. We get a booth at the rodeo and sell what we don't sell here." He held up his hand at a very decorative piece. It showed yellow sunflowers on an eggshell background. "She named that one 'Kansas Morn'. She sews the title in the corner of the quilt." He pulled the corner of the quilt back so I could see. In script style, sewn in black thread were the words, "Kansas Morn."

I pointed to a quilt that hung behind him. It was mostly black with a big, white moon and the silhouette of a ship steaming across a calm, green sea.

"What's that one called?"

Clement had to look at the corner and read the title. "Oh yeah, this one here is called 'Midnight Crossing'. Pretty, isn't it?"

"Very. How much does it cost?"

Without blinking, Clement said, "Five dollars. They all cost five dollars."

I had no idea of how much a quilt cost. Five dollars was a lot of money, but these quilts were works of art. On top of that, they served the practical purpose of keeping you warm. Five dollars was beginning to sound like a bargain. That was a hundred nickels. A hundred nickels might buy you a kewpie doll. The barker had to let someone win occasionally to encourage others. On the other hand, a hundred nickels could buy something to treasure . . . something you could share with a young wife. Yes, my thoughts were on Benita. Then, I noticed that Margie was speaking to me.

"I'm sorry, what were you saying?"

She spoke in a lilting, Irish brogue. "I said it's a pleasure to make your acquaintance, Mr. Foster."

"Yes, yes, of course. Forgive me, but I was so struck by your wonderful quilts."

She let out a lusty laugh, then eyed me as a serious customer. "Aye. They were put together with love."

Exactly my thoughts. One particular blanket caught my attention. It was blue like the sky. White, puffy clouds seemed to drift across it. Some were lighter, as if the sun was trying to break through. Others had a purple hue near the bottom to suggest they were pregnant with rain. It was a happy quilt. It lifted my spirit to see it.

"What did you name that one?"

"Ah, that's one of my favorites. It touches my heart." She put a pale, white hand over her chest. I do believe she was about to cry. "It's called 'Clouds'. A simple name for a simple little quilt, eh?" Margie lovingly traced a finger over the title. There was a catch in her throat when she spoke. "Unassuming little fellow. 'Clouds' has plenty of simplicity. That's its genius." Margie bowed her head.

Clement put his hand on her shoulder. "Margie grows attached to her creations. I believe she loves some of them more than A.J."

She gave him a playful slap. "Enough of your nonsense, boyo. I love the lad with all my heart." She took the blanket and put it on the counter in front of me. "You can have it for free." Before I could protest, she held up her hand. "I don't want money for it. In return, I want you to teach my Andrew history."

That was one request that took me like a raccoon getting into the buttermilk. "History?"

She nodded. "A.J. knows his letters. And he can count money like those fancy adding machines you see in banks. I taught him," she said proudly.

Clement nodded in agreement.

She continued, "But he doesn't know the history of the old country. All he knows is this town. He's never been beyond the limits."

"A.J.'s been to Midvale," said Clement.

"I meant in general," she countered. Her startling green eyes were bright. "He hasn't seen much of the world, Mr. Foster. You could take him to places with your books, your knowledge." She put her hand on "Clouds." "'Tis a small price I ask, eh, sir?"

In that moment, I wanted so much to teach A.J. I wanted so much to stay in Clearview with Benita and have a passel of students to teach. It sounded a lot better than being thrown down a mine or dragged by a stagecoach. Okay, I'd never been dragged by a stagecoach, but in my line of work, it was bound to happen. The problem was, I couldn't commit to another student until the case was over. I went into a story that was mostly true.

"Margie, I would very much like to teach your A.J. I currently have a full slate of students"—that slate being one, Noah Smith—"however, I should have an opening by summer"—or as soon as the Featherston case was finished—"and it will give me time to order a very good book on the history of the Emerald Isle." I would have to find such a book if it ever existed. I

put a hand on "Clouds." "Why don't you hold this for
me until I can fulfill my obligation to A.J.?" Truth-
fully, I hoped she would let me keep it.

She pushed the blanket toward me. "I'll be having
none of that. You keep the blanket and when you're
ready, I'll send A.J. to you."

I just couldn't accept the quilt unless I was sure I'd
be staying in Clearview. I took out some money.
"Here's five dollars. It might be a while before I get
to A.J. It might not be until the fall." For a moment,
I thought she was going to refuse the money. She
looked over at Clement.

"Take the money, Margie. Mr. Foster is a man of
his word."

How he knew that, I have no idea.

She thought about it. "Okay Mr. Foster. But as
soon as you start teaching A.J., this five dollars goes
on his account."

"Thank you kindly, Margie. Now, could you do me
a favor?"

"Anything, Mr. Foster."

I pushed the quilt back toward her. "Keep this for
me. I'll be by the barbershop tomorrow to pick it up.
I'm, uh . . . with the young lady who . . ."

Again, she held up her hand. "I understand sir.
Speak no more of it. Clement will keep it for you at
the shop."

I gave them a farewell and headed down the
midway. Another barker ambled among the carnival
goers, yelling into a megaphone. "Come one, come
all! The wrestling matches have begun behind the
livestock tent!"

Wrestling or a pie contest? I had a choice to make.

Of course the choice was obvious. A good wrestling match with the sound of bones breaking and cries of agony was appealing . . . but Benita's blueberry pie . . . woof. I was in love.

A mixture of coconut, apple, and chocolate wafted from the pie tent. I entered and found a place on a long bench. Sheriff Daily was there with two small girls. Perhaps they were his granddaughters. There were several familiar faces occupying the benches. Up in front was a long table. Benita stood there with seven other women. All had their pies before them. Benita gave me a wink as I sat. The judges were Sheriff Daily's wife, Captain Finley from Fort Carmel, and Brodie Simon, a chef at The Sagebrush. All three were huddled near the back of the tent in deep conversation. Captain Finley broke away and clapped his hands together.

"Ladies and gentlemen, we are sorry for the delay. We have been waiting for another judge, Mr. Bartly."

There were murmurs and soft twitters of laughter among the spectators. Words like "sot" and "drunk" seeped from the conversations. Unfortunately it was true. Editor Bartly was probably sitting in an alley somewhere, sharing his whiskey with an imaginary friend. Or maybe he was still sequestered at his place, trying to stay sober for Anglin's Cattleman's Ball.

Captain Finley continued, "The judges have decided to distribute the point total three ways. We will now commence with the contest."

Everyone applauded. Each judge took one fork each, off a tray. They started with contestant number one, Thelma Billings and her maple walnut concoction. Each judge took a small bite of the pie, swallowed it, drank from a flask of water, then took a new fork for the next pie.

Millie Winters, a sweet little old lady who sent cooking recipes to the *Journal*, sat by me. She whispered in my ear, "Thelma Billings will win this year. She used my recipe."

"Why didn't you enter, Mrs. Winters?" I whispered back.

She shook her head and held up two, trembling hands. "Lost my touch years ago. I have a whole room full of blue ribbons."

Sheriff Daily's wife was at contestant number two. She took a bite and rolled the contents around in her mouth, savoring the flavor. Her face went through a mixture of puzzlement, delight and finally, satisfaction. As she swallowed, the other two judges joined her. She waited for them to take a bite before proceeding to contestant number three.

Benita was contestant number five. It seemed to take hours before they got to her. I felt my back tense up. The entire tent was silent. All eyes were on the judges and their reactions. People were trying to read their faces to get a hint of the results.

When they finally reached her, Benita gave each judge a smile as they dug into the golden brown crust sprinkled with cinnamon. She did not look nervous. I was feeling nervous. I had been in high stakes poker games that felt like pillow fights compared to this. The whole place brimmed with tension. One man, the husband of contestant number six, coughed and walked out of the tent. The poor fellow could not stand the heat of the competition.

Captain Finley took longer to make up his mind before leaving Benita and going on to contestant six. Did he have a smile on his face? No, it was a grimace. Maybe he was sick. This was very nerve wracking. I almost got up and went outside with the husband of contestant number six. When the judges took their last bites, Captain Finley addressed the audience.

"We will break for a few moments and confer. The judges hope to make a decision within a few minutes."

It was as if the tent itself, sagged from its metal stakes in relief. A collective sigh erupted from the benches. The contestants joined family and friends. Benita walked up to me, her eyes aglow.

"What do you think, Randy?"

"I think they liked blueberry pie."

She squeezed my hand. "I think they did, too."

Her confidence was admirable. My lack of spine was embarrassing. Would she be shattered if she lost? Would I? I kissed her on the forehead.

"So have you decided on where you'll put your blue ribbon?"

"On my kitchen wall would be nice. Maybe I could start a scrapbook."

Before I could reply, Captain Finley clapped his hands. "The judges have reached a decision."

The nervous laughter and chatter stopped. The spectators took their seats as Captain Finley motioned to Benita and the seven others. "Will the contestants please come forward and stand behind your pies?"

"Good luck," I told her.

She gave my hand a second squeeze and headed for

the table. I saw half a face peeking from the entrance of the tent. It was contestant number six's husband. I sat back down and crossed my fingers.

As an agent, I've had ample opportunity to testify at trials. One challenge was to watch the jury return with a verdict. Generally the verdict was guilty, thanks to the mounds of evidence The Service compiled. Yet, it was never easy to read the faces of the panelists. Every once in a while, if the case concerned gambling or other nefarious activities, the accused party's lawyer would poke a hole in the law. He exploited that hole and despite the evidence, a jury was swayed to favor the defendant. I watched all three judges. They didn't have poker faces. They were generally smiling.

Brodie Simon, the chef, stepped forward with the white ribbon for third place. He cleared his throat, enjoying the moment. His voice was full of self-importance. "After strong consideration, the judges have made their decision. For third place, we have chosen a blueberry pie."

My heart stopped. Chef Simon headed for Benita, but he walked to the end of the table. "Miriam Townsend!" he announced. He laid the white ribbon in front of the Townsend pie to the applause of the crowd. The elation I felt melted away. What were the chances of *two* blueberry pies winning?

Sheriff Daily's wife handed Brodie Simon a red ribbon. "And in second place, we tasted a very good chocolate pie, made by Alice Franklin."

Contestant number six squealed with delight. Her husband rushed into the tent and did some steps of a dance I was not familiar with. "You did it Alice! I knew you would, honey!" he screamed.

Everyone laughed. Captain Finley handed Chef Simon the prized blue ribbon. I stole a glance at Benita. She was looking at the ribbon, almost leaning toward it. Chef Simon held the blue ribbon up for all to see.

"And now ladies and gentlemen, the highest award, the blue ribbon goes to"—only then, did I feel my breath still in my lungs—"Benita Brooks' blueberry pie!"

Benita's shoulders sagged in relief. Perhaps she'd been a lot more tense than I thought. She beamed as the chef placed the blue ribbon in front of her pie. People got up off the benches and surged forward to congratulate the winners. I waved at Benita and caught her eye. She held up the ribbon.

I cupped my hands over my mouth. "I'll be outside!"

She nodded.

I made my way against the flow of people and found myself outside the tent. Arrow was headed inside with his camera, slate, and flash powder.

"Hey you missed Benita winning her blue ribbon."

"It's okay. I've got good pictures of several of those deputies."

"Guess I'll check out the wrestling matches."

"You'll be in time to see the final bout."

"Who is it?" I asked.

"Our own Mr. Featherston and Nelson, the blacksmith."

I hightailed it over to the livestock tent. I wanted to see Lewis Featherston in action. As I arrived, both contestants had their shirts off. Nelson looked very muscular, but it was hard to tell with all the hair. The man was a grizzly. Featherston had a belly that drooped over the belt loops, but his arms and shoulders looked rock hard. He had a few inches on Nelson in height, but he just didn't look that powerful.

The fights were conducted in a holding pen made with oak planks. Sawdust covered the floor. A carnival official was talking to both men, but he didn't look like a referee. The place was crowded with drunk, rowdy men. Bets were being thrown around like horseshoes made of feathers. The only female there was Tula. She clutched a kewpie doll to her breasts. So old Lewis finally won one. He'd probably spent two dollars to win a ten cent item.

The man between the wrestlers left them and addressed the crowd. "The winner of this match will be the carnival champion. There are no rules, winner takes all!"

The man held up a fist full of cash, then a bank bag that looked like it was also full of cash. A cheer went up. I noticed one fellow with his arm in a sling, and another man with two black eyes and a swollen lip. They had been Nelson's and Featherston's victims.

"Let's go!" yelled the man as he climbed over the fence of the holding pen. Another man rang a cowbell. The crowd went into a frenzy of shouts and curses.

Lewis and Nelson wearily circled, sizing each other up. The crowd was going wild, having worked up into a lather during the previous bouts. I felt a spray of beer on the back of my neck. I turned to see a green shirt. He was the one in the barbershop that day. What was his name? Fryer, that was it. Had he spit beer on me?

He was laughing and joking with another deputy. "Come on Lewis! Make him yell 'Uncle', let's go!" cried Fryer.

"Pull his hair out, Nelson!" cried a teenage boy in the back.

"Kick him between the legs!" shouted Tula.

There were several green shirts cheering Featherston. Shadow and Cracker Barrel were there. I didn't see Lamppost.

Quick as a bobcat, Nelson lunged at Lewis, grabbing nothing but air. I was impressed at how deftly Lewis sidestepped him. Then, while Nelson was off balance, Featherston kicked the blacksmith forward. The crown of his head collided with the hard oak of the pen.

Nelson slowly sat up and shook his head. As he was doing this, Lewis kicked him in the face. I saw a tooth fly out and land in some hay nearby. A roar came from the crowd. Featherston wasn't going to let the man get up.

"Kill him!" screamed Shadow. Nelson had fallen back. Blood was flowing from his mouth and nose. Glassy-eyed, his arms trembled with effort as he tried to push himself up. Lewis stood over him, tightening his fist into a ball. He looked at Tula. She nodded vigorously. Just as Nelson made it to his knees, Featherston punched downward. It was a deadly blow as his fist caught Nelson between the eyes. He fell back like an anvil, knocked out.

Those who won bets, jumped and cheered. The man running the show leaped into the pen and held up Featherston's arm. "The winner!"

There were more cheers. Hank stood over Nelson and dumped a pail of water on him. Nelson sputtered and coughed. Hank pulled him into a sitting position.

The man gave Featherston the bag of money. He

held it high over his face. "Drinks on me!" he cried
in triumph.

The entire fight had taken about fifteen seconds.
Nelson's face was swelling up. His eyes were
unfocused as Hank held up a couple of fingers in
front of his face. I knew one thing. I didn't want to
meet Lewis Featherston in an alley.

I met Benita at the tent where the pie eating contest would be held. "I can't wait to have a slice of that
blueberry," I said.

"You can't. All eight pies are the first ones to be
eaten in the contest. Here." She reached over and
pinned the blue ribbon on my chest. Any other time I
would have felt like a fool, but I was so proud of
Benita, I wore it without embarrassment. Men in love
do foolish things.

Arrow set up his camera on a platform overlooking the stage and a long table with eight contestants.
Benita's blueberry pie and the seven others were
placed in front of the "eaters"—Hank, Trev Olfman,
A.J., Bill Kithen, Brodie Simon, the chef who had
judged the pie contest, two soldiers from Fort Carmel,
and Mimi Helfer, a woman of large proportions and a
moon shaped face. She was dressed as a dairy maid.
Benita told me that she worked for Trev Olfman.
Trev's two daughters, also dressed as dairy maids,
stood near a cart that was stacked with pies. They were
ready to lay a pie down in front of a contestant as soon
as he or she finished their first pie.

We found a seat behind Peter Washington and his

wife, Cynda. Peter owned a boot store in town and always bought plenty of advertising at the paper.

"Hi Mr. Washington," he turned.

"Mr. Foster. You've met my wife, Cynda?"

"I haven't had the pleasure." I shook her hand.

"How do you do, Mr. Foster."

She smiled at Benita. "Congratulations Benita." She eyed the blue ribbon on my chest. "Thelma Billings told me."

Before Benita could respond, the emcee banged a pie pan with a spoon. "The pie eating contest will commence! Are all of the contestants ready?"

The eight eaters nodded. A.J. gave an "okay" sign to Clement who sat in the front row.

"The rules are as follows: The object is to eat the most pies in a five minute period. On the count of ten, you will begin eating."

The emcee pulled out a pocket watch and counted to himself. Then he found his mark and began to count down. "Ten, nine, eight, seven . . ."

The crowd joined him. "Six, five, four, three, two, one!" The eight eaters buried their heads in the sweets. Their jaws chomped down on the crusts, letting the pie filling slide down their throats.

People were cheering and waving their hands. A.J. lifted his blueberry face. A dairy maid had a cream pie ready. In one action, A.J. came up for air, then dove into the creamy topping. One of the soldiers and Mimi were next. The others followed suit.

"Come on Joseph!" came a call from the back. It was soldiers from the fort, cheering their fellow cavalrymen along. Hank pulled up the rear with a big burp.

He gamely dipped into the next pie. Various shouts of encouragement came from the onlookers.

"Chew! Chew!"

"Come on, Mimi, you can do it!"

"Let's go Brodie!"

Everyone had someone cheering for them. Benita had picked Hank to encourage. "Come on Hank! Faster, faster!"

I was soon coaching A.J. "Swallow the filling first A.J.! Then eat the crust!" Right. Sixty-four seconds into the contest and I was an expert.

Mimi began to pull ahead. On his fourth pie, A.J. was slowing down. I hoped he wasn't getting sick. The soldier named Joseph threw his napkin down on his fourth pie. It seemed that the fourth was the hardest. This action brought jeers from the soldiers.

"Don't give up!"

"Don't stop, Trev!"

"Faster, Mimi, faster!"

As he chewed furiously, Trev was checking out Bill Kithen on his left and Hank on his right. Mimi started to cough. Brodie Simon was motioning for his fifth pie, but the judge shook his head.

"Finish the crust," he said.

Brodie looked at the two chunks of crust like they were cow patties.

"Go, Hank, go!" screamed Benita. Hank had started to slow, but he'd also developed a rhythm. He was chewing and swallowing methodically and gaining on the others.

"Use your hands!" I shouted at A.J.

As if he heard me, A.J. scooped up some chocolate and slammed it into his face.

Before we knew it, the emcee called "Time!"

In the same motion, the contestants immediately stopped eating and sat back in their seats. Burps and other various sounds emitted from the eight eaters. There were six empty plates and half a pie in front of A.J. Mimi had six empty plates and one quarter of a pie left. The winner was Trev Olfman who had eight empty pie plates stacked in front of him.

"The winner!" declared the emcee. Everyone applauded. Trev held his stomach and stood, rocking back on his feet slightly.

"What's the prize?" he asked.

The emcee held up an apple pie. "Mr. Olfman, for your outstanding accomplishment, you win this apple pie, baked by the ladies Fire Auxiliary."

Mimi and A.J. groaned in unison. Joseph the soldier ran out, holding his mouth. The audience laughed at the sour look on Trev's face.

Later, Benita and I walked the midway. I plunked down a nickel for three darts. If I could bust a balloon, I could win Benita a kewpie doll. Since I had secretly bought her the blanket entitled "Clouds", I didn't feel bad when I failed to break a single balloon. The game was probably fixed anyway.

As we headed for the buggy, there was a disturbance in the lot. I saw three green shirts struggling with a man in the moonlight.

"Hold him! Don't let him get away!" It was Lamppost and two others. They had the man pinned against a buckboard.

"What's going on?" I called out. I didn't like what was happening. "Stay here Benita."

She backed away, sensing the danger of the situation.

When Lamppost saw me, he was immediately on guard. "Now this ain't your fight, teacher." His hand was on the butt of his holstered gun. That's when I saw the man they had was Noah.

"What did he do?"

Noah's eyes were wide with fear. He shook his head at me in warning.

"I said get out of here," repeated Lamppost. He stepped toward me. I didn't back down. We were almost nose to nose. Someone else had come up beside us. It was Lewis Featherston. He was chewing tobacco and holding the tin in his hand.

"What was he doing?" he asked. Lamppost took his eyes off me.

"We found this young buck skulking around the horses."

Featherston looked at Noah. "Thinking of stealing a horse, boy?"

Noah's voice squeaked as he spoke. He was terrified. "N-no suh. I was tending Mr. Simon's buggy. He's paying me ten cents."

"He was next to the buggy all right," said Lamppost. "And he was reading this." He took out a leaflet advertising the carnival. He handed it to Featherson. Lewis read it. I was surprised he didn't move his lips as he read. Then he looked at Noah.

"You know how to read?"

"I was-I was just picking out some words."

Featherston frowned. He spit a long stream of brown into the dirt. Then he wadded up the leaflet.

Was this it? Was I about to get to wrestle Lewis Featherston? I couldn't let him hurt Noah. I tightened my fist behind my back. Just like throwing the apple, I concentrated on Featherston's throat. The others might get me, but the big man was going down. Then, the unexpected happened.

"Let him go," said Featherston.

Lamppost hesitated. "But we—"

"Let him go." Lewis's voice was low and threatening.

Lamppost and the other green shirts took a step back. Then Lamppost said, "Let him go boys."

Featherston jerked his head in one direction. "Take off," he said to Noah.

Noah looked at me and gave a short nod of thanks. Then he shot out of there and never looked back.

Featherston looked at me levelly. "Boy like that shouldn't be reading."

I wasn't sure if he was talking to me or just making a general statement.

"Just ain't right," he said quietly.

With that, Featherston and his men walked away, leaving me and Benita alone in the lot. Somehow, that seemed more menacing than wanting to fight me.

Chapter Seventeen

Mr. Anglin hired three fancy surreys to take his employees to The Cattleman's Ball. Each surrey held up to six people. Benita and I rode with Mr. Chapman and Mr. Brown, her two morose co-workers. Also riding with us was Rowdy Holman and his wife, Clara.

Rowdy was a trail boss who lived up to his name by talking loud and telling ribald jokes, to the embarrassment of Clara. Benita tried to hide her laughter while Mr. Chapman and Mr. Brown stared stoically at the passing landscape.

"Here's a good one!" said Rowdy. "A wildcatter was shot in the stomach by a whore. When the doctor said he would have to dig the bullet out, the wildcatter said, 'You can dig anywhere Doc, I feel like a gusher today!' Get it?" He slapped his knee and guffawed.

It wasn't funny, but I had to smile at Rowdy's enthusiasm. Clara just lowered her head and shook it.

Mr. Brown finally spoke. "Your stories are pointless, Holman. Make sense man."

Rowdy threw a thumb at Chapman and Brown. "Accountants," he said, as if that explained it.

For some reason, that made Benita laugh. It was infectious, and soon, Rowdy, Clara, and I joined in. Brown and Chapman watched the setting sun with sourness that only a mortician would love.

As the sun got lower, we came to the Anglin property. A white, boarded fence stretched for what looked like miles. The gate was a single bar that was raised by one of Featherston's green shirts who stood guard.

As our surrey approached, I recognized the guard. It was my old friend, Shadow. He raised the bar and doffed his hat. When he saw me sitting next to Benita, he looked like he'd swallowed skunk meat soaked in elephant sperm. For a moment, I thought he was going to draw his gun right there and shoot me in the chest.

"How much farther?" I asked.

"Anglin's spread covers half of southwest Kansas," said Rowdy. "His mansion's up past the next ridge."

Mansion? I had seen mansions in Denver and St. Louis. Who had a mansion in the middle of nowhere?

A patch of trees and shrubs topped the ridge. The road led down into a valley. The land was suddenly green and lush. A brook ran into a lake and next to the lake was the largest mansion I'd ever seen.

"I'll be a blue nosed mule," I said, forgetting proper English.

Benita's hand gripped mine. "Isn't it grand? It has twenty-three rooms. All have running water and there's a gaslight chandelier in the main ballroom."

"The main ballroom?"

"He has a large room in the back for private parties and banquets."

I clucked my tongue in amazement. "I thought you said it was your first Cattleman's Ball."

Benita looked excitedly at the mansion as she spoke. "I delivered some contracts once and Mr. Anglin gave me a personal tour."

The place was already lit up. Carriages and surreys filed up a brick, circular road in front of the house. A fountain, with the marble statue of a horse spouting water out of its mouth was in the middle of the curved road.

"Mr. Anglin lives here all by himself?" I asked.

Benita shook her head. "He comes here on weekends. Mr. Anglin has a suite at The Majestic in town."

"Hell, he owns that hotel," said Rowdy.

"Rowdy, watch your mouth," said Clara with serious resignation.

The surrey stopped, we got out, and were ushered into a vast room with mirrors on the walls. There was a long table filled with food, from fresh lake fish to barbeque. The dance floor was the size of a large corral. Dancing couples filled up the room. An orchestra played a slow, serene number. It was definitely classical. I thought I recognized the composer.

"Vivaldi?" I asked.

Benita took me by the hand and led me onto the dance floor. My newly shined boots clopped clumsily to the slow number, but I held Benita close, avoided her toes, and managed not to bump into other couples.

"You're not a bad dancer, Randy."

"Thanks, but we both know I'm an imposter out here."

She laughed. "Hey, any man who can hold his girl close and dance without counting is a good dancer."

I began to relax and enjoy the movement. Benita was smooth and graceful. She seemed to slow down to my level.

"Where did you learn to dance?" I asked her.

"Mrs. Phipps School of Dance," she said proudly.

"I must admit, Mrs. Phipps is a heck of a teacher."

As Benita glided and I awkwardly slid across the floor, I kept an eye out for Lewis Featherston. His men in green shirts were all over the place. I recognized Cracker Barrel and Lamppost moving around the room, watching for someone to steal the furniture I supposed.

Suddenly, the orchestra went into a rousing number where couples broke apart and formed a line. It was a reel that I'd learned at The Service. It involved a lot of hand clapping, foot stomping, and yee-hawing.

From that, the orchestra went back to a waltz. This went on for about five minutes before Rowdy took the floor with a megaphone and called out a lively square dance, peppered with lines bordering on obscenity.

"Turn your partner round and round, bend 'er over and take her to town!" On the words "bend 'er over", the real gentlemen bowed and the ladies curtseyed. How Rowdy got away with the ribald lyrics, I'll never know. Maybe it was the champagne, but a lot of the couples were laughing lustily along with Rowdy's rendition.

After a few more numbers, we walked outside. Benita wanted to show me the garden. Garden. It was an acre of blooms from all over the Midwest. A glass house on the side of the mansion contained some exotic flowers from Japan. Behind the glass house was a pond where goldfish swam peacefully. Stones surrounded it.

"Can you believe all of this Randy?"

"It's a lot of nature contained in a small space."

Benita touched the petal of a pink and white flower with red speckles. "Smell it," she said.

I did. "Nice."

Her eyes drank in the splash of colors. I vowed that I would make enough money to buy her a glass house. "Would you like a place like this Benita?"

She shook her head emphatically. "No. This is the type of spread you want to visit, but you don't necessarily want to live there." She leaned against me, watching the movement of the goldfish in the pond. "I like the simple things, Randy. If I had a thousand dollars, I'd live in a little gingerbread house with a picket fence."

I hugged her.

A voice came from behind some shrubs. "I heard that." Mr. Anglin came out from behind the bushes and walked over to us. "You need to aim higher, Benita. You should have a house with a maid and a grand piano to play your opera music." His smile was warm, fatherly.

"You have a very impressive place here, Mr. Anglin," I said.

He put a cigar in his mouth and for a moment, his eyes were watery. He looked up at the large mansion. "I built this for Edna and John."

"Your family?" I ventured.

He nodded soberly. "I know it's ridiculous. I lost them a long time ago."

Benita took his arm. "You shouldn't be sad Mr. Anglin."

At that, he brightened. "You're right. This is an evening to celebrate. And remember, we're having fireworks on the terrace at ten."

"Fireworks! I can hardly wait!" she exclaimed.

Anglin patted her on the shoulder. "My dear, could I have some time with your man here? Just for a few minutes?"

Benita looked pleasantly surprised. "Of course Mr. Anglin."

She kissed me on the cheek. "I'll fill a plate of bar-beque for you." Benita headed back inside.

Mr. Anglin pulled out a cigar. "Would you like a smoke, sir?"

I took the cigar. "Thank you Mr. Anglin."

He produced a match and lit it. I held the cigar over the flame and puffed. The man put on a "business" face.

"That girl is a treasure," he said.

"I agree."

"Mr. Foster . . . Randy. Unless I've misread you two, I would predict that it's a match."

"You would be right sir."

"It seems only fair that I tell you about my plans."

I puffed on the cigar thoughtfully, letting him speak.

"Benita is smart, loyal, and handles herself well with the businessmen who come through the office."

"I can't argue with that."

"What are your plans, Randy?"

"I'm staying at the *Journal* for now. I hope to get a teaching position in the fall."

"Ah, the new school. Clearview Technical will be accepting applications when they open in the fall."

"Yes sir."

"But you might be more interested in a position at Kansas Teacher's College in Topeka."

This was a turn in the conversation I hadn't expected. "Sir?"

"Benita doesn't know it yet, but I'm going to promote her. She is the perfect choice to head up the accounting department in my new branch office."

This was definitely good news.

"In a large town like Topeka, a woman in charge is more palatable to the citizenry."

"Of course," I said as I puffed a perfect ring in the air. "But what about Mr. Chapman or Mr. Brown? Don't they have seniority over Benita?"

Anglin waved his cigar in the air. "Those two are settled here like clams. Neither one would want to move." He blew out a long stream of smoke and leaned into me. "Besides, they don't like working with Benita." He winked.

"Yeah, I sort of figured that."

He pulled himself up to his full height. "Randy, I am on the board of directors at Kansas Teachers. You can have your choice of classes."

I was overwhelmed. "I don't know what to say. Thank you sir."

He shook his head. "No, thank you. You're the right man for her. And maybe I'm still looking for someone to fill that family role." His eyes were watering again.

I didn't know if it was smoke or real tears. Then his voice broke with emotion. "Don't tell her about Topeka. Not yet. I'd like it to be a surprise. I just want you to take care of her."

I felt like hugging the old gent. "I won't tell her sir. And yes, I will take care of her." I thought about the case. "And sir, I haven't asked her to marry me yet. But I will. For now, that's just between us." I winked back at him.

He gave me a heartfelt handshake.

To Pandora's chagrin, I saw Benita every night the next week. Pandora liked it when I went to teach Noah at his cabin. She braved rocks, thistles, and all of the road hazards on that narrow trail to his place. But as soon as I turned on to Cedar Dust, she would slow down until she resembled a moving statue. On Saturday, I took Benita to the Little Cimarron River for a picnic. Pandora kept trying to pull the blanket out from under us. She nipped at Benita's head and I had to scold my errant horse.

"Stop it Pandora! Behave!"

Benita put a hand on my shoulder. "Don't yell at her Randy." She stood up and walked over to Pandora. "I hear you do tricks Pandora. Why don't you show me?"

I wasn't sure, but I think Pandora rolled her eyes. She wasn't going to give Benita the satisfaction. Then, she suddenly did her fainting trick. Her eyes rolled back in her head and she plopped dead into the dust.

"Oh my!" screamed Benita. She bent down and frantically patted Pandora's forehead. "Pandora! Pandora, speak to me!"

"She can't talk, Benita."

"Please Pandora! Get up!"

It was then I realized Benita was playing along.

"Randy, what can we do? Pandora has fainted!"

On that cue, Pandora rolled over and slowly got up.

Benita clapped briskly. "Oh good! Very good! You had me fooled!" With encouragement, Pandora pranced in a circle, high stepping it like a prima donna. Benita continued to applaud. "She's better than an opera!"

"A horse opera," I said under my breath.

Pandora reared up on her hind legs and whinnied. Then she turned a full circle on two legs.

"That's impossible," I said in quiet awe.

Benita was shouting, jumping up and down. "Beautiful! You're beautiful!"

Then, Pandora did something strange. Well, not really strange since it was Pandora. She leaned over and gently licked Benita's face.

"I like you too girl," Benita said, patting her lightly on her face. She gave me a sly look as she spoke to Pandora. "Would you be my horse?" Without waiting for an answer, Benita hiked up her blue dress and put her tiny foot in the stirrup. Before I could assist her, she was up in the saddle with both legs draped down Pandora's left side.

"Riding her sidesaddle is dangerous," I warned. She might try to buck you off." Of course I gave Pandora a stern look. I wasn't talking to Benita more so than warning Pandora to behave.

"Pshaw! Pandora is my best friend."

I was waiting for Pandora to roll her eyes at all of this sweetness and light Benita was sending her way.

"Let's go girl," Benita said.

To my amazement, Pandora gently took Benita along the bank of the river for about half a mile. I watched until my horse was a tiny black and red dot with a spot of blue atop her. When they returned, Benita was talking to her.

"You are one fine, little filly."

Pandora was literally prancing with delight.

Later we walked back up the hill from the river. Pandora followed docilely. The mischief in her had left with all of the tricks. I put my arm around Benita as we walked and looked back at Pandora. She was smiling.

Chapter Eighteen

At three o'clock on that following Monday, I was at the *Journal*, practicing my fast draw before Noah was to show up. I stood in the middle of the room, which in my mind, was a bar. Also in my mind was a surly cowboy at the end of the bar. He was insulting me.

"What's the matter scarface?" he was asking. "I'm telling you now, you've got the slowest horse in the west, and you're a lousy teacher." Real fighting words. This bad varmint in my mind took a long swallow of whiskey and slammed the glass down on the bar. Everyone in the bar jumped. The cowboy wiped his mouth and smirked. "'Fraid? Going to go run home to your mama?" He let out a rough laugh. So did the other characters in this mind play that I was writing, producing and directing. They were all laughing—the cigar chomping piano player in the brown derby, the dance hall girl in the tawdry, blue sequined dress, and rheumy eyed hound dog, lying under a table with the smell of beer on his breath. Okay, maybe my imagination was jumping the fence.

I focused on the invisible bad guy across the newspaper office. I envisioned the gun coming out of my holster and the man already falling at the moment of the gun blast.

"Show your hand, hombre," I say in a low, threatening voice. I am relaxed. I am looking at the spot where his bad, black heart beats wildly. He starts to draw. I slip the gun out of my holster and fire. The loudmouth clutches his punctured chest . . . and falls. In reality, my gun is not smoking. Not here in the office. Maybe in the imaginary bar. Although I pulled the trigger, it is not smoking, because it's empty. Concentrating with all my might, I thought it best to practice without bullets as long as I was pulling it inside. Of late, I'd been taking it out into the country and applying the principles that Noah taught me. My accuracy had suffered as I shot at boxes and tin cans. Was I getting faster? Did it matter?

The clock in the office showed five minutes after three. Noah was late. He was never late. I was not alarmed. Everyone was entitled to be late once in a while. I went back to practicing my fast draw.

Shutting out the world, shutting out imaginary bad men and dance hall girls, I focused on a point in the room. Envisioning the gun coming out of the holster, the bullet already hitting the target . . .

I lost track of time. I was awash in fast draws. It was three-thirty. Farly came in just as I pulled my gun.

"Hey, you're getting pretty quick with that .45."

I turned and holstered my gun. "Just a matter of a little practice."

"Where's Noah?"

Then it hit me. Noah. "I have no idea." A bad feeling came over me.

Arrow saw it on my face. "Where do you think he is?"

I scraped the bullets off my desk and loaded my gun. "I've got to go see about him."

"You want me to go with you?"

I was flopping on my hat as I hurried to the door. "Stay here. If Noah shows up, tell him I went to his shack. Tell him I'll be back."

Pandora sensed my anxiety. Not that she sped out like a fire horse, but I didn't have to encourage her. She lit out of town at a slow, but steady gallop.

When I got to Shanty Town, something was wrong. The children weren't there to catch treats. Not that I had treats to throw to them. I saw their faces inside the tents, watching me. Something else. They looked scared. And the adults were inside their tents and cardboard houses. No one was coming out to greet me. I headed for Easy Springs.

A lot of the brush and limbs were crushed and broken on the narrow trail toward Noah's shack. It looked like a number of horses had trampled through. This was not good.

As we neared the cabin, Pandora began to creep. She neighed quietly.

"What is it girl? What do you see?"

We entered the clearing. I was half expecting to find it burned to the ground, but the cabin was there. I stopped. "Hold on Pandora, hold on." I got off Pandora and drew my gun. "Noah?" I called out. "Noah Smith!" Silence. I crept closer. There were no windows to check out. I would have to go to the door. I listened as I crept.

The door was ajar, inviting me to enter. Enter into what? I stood off to the side, and listened for movement inside. Nothing stirred. What was behind that door? I stayed to the side and figured the angle. One swift side kick would do it. I took a beat. Here goes.

With my big, brown boot, I smacked the door. The hinges screamed and the old door crashed into the inside wall. Nothing. I eased my head around and squinted into the dark shack.

"Noah?" It was quiet. The place looked undisturbed. What was going on? I turned to leave and was met with the barrel of a rifle.

"Who be you?" the old woman asked. I put my hands up.

"I was looking for Noah." She did not wear glasses and gave me a hard squint. A look of recognition hit her face.

"You Noah's friend."

Then I recognized her. She was from Shanty Town. "What happened here? Where is Noah?"

"Gone. Chased off."

"What?"

She lowered the rifle and walked into the cabin. I followed.

"Have a seat. I'll make you some tea."

I didn't want tea. I wanted to find out about Noah. Instead I said, "Yes, thank you. Tea would be nice."

She bustled about, pouring water into a teapot and lighting the wood inside the stove. I tapped my boot impatiently on the dirt floor.

"You said he was chased away?"

The old woman eased into a rickety chair. "My hip

don't sit like it used to. I'm Ola. I knowed Noah and his grandpa. We be friends."

"What happened, Ola?"

"I was in Shanty Town. Noah come running down the road. He was all bloody . . . his face was swollen. He been beat up real bad and was scared. He asked me to hide him, so I took some branches behind my cardboard box. I always keep branches to make a fire. I told him to lie down and I covered him up."

"You said he was all bloody and beaten up. Who did it?" I was beginning to talk fast, because I was anxious and worried.

She held up a calming hand. "I didn't have time to inspect him. A thunder of horses was coming down on us. Old man Hankins and the widow Wilks helped me put the branches on Noah."

"And so you covered him up . . ." I prompted. The woman didn't seem to be in a hurry to tell her story.

"Just in time before those mean town men showed up. They rode up like they owned the world. The leader asked me about Noah." She stopped and readjusted herself on the chair. "We told 'em we ain't seen him. One of them baddies grabbed little Sudie Jefferson. He told us that if we were lying, they'd hurt her. I seen the branches move. I knowed Noah was going to give himself up to protect that little girl. I pointed up this way and said, "He's out at his place". That leader man dropped Sudie and they hightailed it into the woods to come over here."

"Were any of those men wearing green shirts? Did any of them wear badges?"

"Not that I recollect. They were dressed in normal clothes, but they did put a scare into us."

"Is that what the people were afraid of? That the men would come back to Shanty Town?"

She nodded. "At first I was feared that they'd come back and burn the place down, but they didn't. Something made them go back to town."

"Could you describe the leader?"

"My eyes ain't so good. He was a big man. His voice sounded like two rocks being rubbed together."

It could have been Featherston. Lamppost also had a voice that could sound just as Ola described.

"Did the man have a crooked nose?" Lamppost had a broken nose. I wished I'd been the one to give it to him.

Ola looked thoughtful. She suddenly produced a corncob pipe from her tattered apron and chewed on the stem. "I do recollect how his nose was all bunched up on him."

Lamppost. It was easy to figure. Featherston's men had beaten Noah up. For what reason, I had no idea. Most likely it was his pigmentation that pricked their wrath. But being "lawmen", they couldn't beat him in their uniforms. Bad publicity for Anglin. And something made them return to town. That sounded like men on a schedule . . . men who had to return to duty.

"So then what happened?"

As Ola chewed on the pipe, her eyes grew wide. A high pitched scream erupted behind her. I jumped.

"Tea's ready," she said. The old woman struggled up and hobbled over to the whistling tea kettle on the stove. "You like sugar?"

"Yes ma'am. Just a touch."

"I don't think there's any sugar in the cupboard presently."

"That's fine. I know for a fact that Noah's been baking a lot of pies lately."

She nodded knowingly. "For his schooling."

"Yes ma'am."

She poured the tea and brought the cup over to me. As she poured herself a cup, she spoke, "Noah was on his way to town."

To see me, I thought.

"He said a man stopped him and said he was needed over at the Mercantile. He was led into an alley and several men jumped him."

I wondered why Noah didn't sense the badness in the men, but like he told me, it didn't always work.

"Go on," I said.

"They beat that boy to a pulp. How he made it back here, I'll never know."

"Did Noah say why they beat him?"

She sipped her tea and lifted her hip off the chair, then readjusted. "Noah don't believe in soft chairs. I'm going to have to sew a cushion or lay some hay around here." She readjusted once more, then continued. "He said they were hollerin' and cursin' him . . . said he wasn't going to learn how to read . . . said it weren't fittin' for his kind."

My heart sank. It was my fault. There were still people in the world who held to old ways, old beliefs.

"They busted his head open with a pipe, and kicked him in the ribs and stomach . . . and his nether regions."

I was feeling sick to my stomach. Every punch, every blow had been my fault. If I'd had half a mind, I would have refused him when he asked for lessons. At the very least, I should have conducted the lessons at night in some attic or basement. Who was I kidding? I had enough on my docket with the Featherston case. I was so lost in my misery, I didn't catch what she said.

"I'm sorry, could you repeat that?"

"I said he was close to being knocked out, but he played possum. He heard the men laughing. One said, 'Looks like we killed him boys.' Then they left him bleeding in the alley."

It had to be Featherston's men. Lewis was using Noah to get to me.

She continued. "As soon as the men left, he crawled out of the alley and ran. They must have come back and found him gone."

"So where did he go?"

Ola took another long sip of her tea. She shifted the pipe from one side of her mouth to the other and commenced to chew harder. "He willed this house to me."

I don't think she was talking from a legal position, but I got her point.

"He told me to tell you thanks for all you done for him."

For all I had done "to" him really.

"He said he was going away to heal up. Then he was going to Abilene to see if he could get on a trail ride as a cook."

That was that. I swallowed the rest of my tea and stood. "Thank you, Ola. And I thank you for Noah. I hope he gets on."

She got up. I heard a creak as she did. I didn't know if it was the rickety chair or her old bones.

"He's gone, suh. And he won't be coming back for a long time. But"—she said this last part with a smile—"he said he would write." She held up her head proudly and said, "Yes suh. That boy can write."

Chapter Nineteen

The next day, I took my usual table at the café for breakfast. I had to forget about Noah and concentrate on the case. He was gone and that was a shame. The best way I could help him was to do my job, then use all of The Service's resources to find him. Callie walked up to my table.

"What's good today Callie?"

Bear, playing the waitress, handed me a menu and pointed. "Our sausage can't be beat. Coffee with cream?"

"Yes ma'am. And I'll have the sausage with two eggs."

She headed back toward the kitchen. I looked at the paper menu where Bear had pointed. There was a message in her handwriting. It read: *Tonight 11:00 Horseshoe.*

Horseshoe was a public park not far from Anglin's massive holding area where all major cattle drives ended. Pandora and I approached The Commons, a grassy field that was outlined with oak trees.

Arrow had picked a spot under a tree. Sounds of mooing cattle wafted gently from the holding pens.

"Where's Bear?"

"She'll be along. I'm surprised you didn't bring Benita."

I took the mild rebuke. It was a major sin to get emotionally involved in a case. Arrow had sensed that I was now emotionally involved. It would be okay. When I told him my plan, he would understand. There was no sin to be emotionally involved if you planned on leaving The Service.

"Is that what this meeting is about? Me and Benita?"

Arrow was chewing on a weed. He patted the ground next to him. "Calm down. Have a seat." I tied Pandora to a low branch, next to Arrow's horse. I sat next to him. I thought about bringing up Noah being run out of town by Featherston's men, but decided that now was not the time. We had plenty of meat on our plates as it was.

"I hope we don't see some stranger running away, carrying his boots this time."

Arrow laughed softly. "I guess that's why we're meeting here."

We sat and listened to the cattle in the holding area. We never heard Bear, who suddenly appeared from behind the tree.

"You're both here. Good."

"What took you so long?" asked Arrow.

"I was reconnoitering the area. I don't want anyone else in on this conversation."

"Any developments, Bear?"

She was facing us. "I heard from headquarters. They want me to prepare my notes so they can have a detailed report. I'm taking the train to Dodge tomorrow morning."

"Why don't you get a summons for Mr. Leslie's office?"

She shook her head. "Harlon doesn't want to warn him. The plan is to bring in some more men to help us. Once we go after Leslie, it might alert Featherston."

Arrow and I both nodded in agreement.

"What do we do until then?" I asked.

Bear pulled out a piece of paper. "This name was in Leslie's files." She handed it to Arrow. "You've been here a lot longer than I have. Recognize it?"

Arrow read the name. "Carmen." He shook his head.

"I didn't recognize it either," she said.

She looked at me and I shrugged. "The only Carmen I ever heard of was an opera."

"It's a woman's name," said Arrow.

"It could be a man," I said.

"There's more," said Bear. "Next to Carmen's name, was another one. Sophie."

"I know her," said Arrow. "She's one of Tinsley's girls."

Bear and I looked at each other.

Arrow didn't miss it. He looked defensive. "Hey, I know a lot of women over there. I'm not going to dicker with any of them."

We both gave him unconvinced stares.

"It just so happens that Madame Tinsley cooks the best dang steak in Kansas."

"You go there for the steak?"

Arrow's face was stone determination. "The meat is tender and seasoned with a Mediterranean herb. And the bartender there has a liquor selection fit for the President."

"So you've frequented that den of painted ladies and you never heard the name, Carmen?"

Arrow stared at the ground. "Girls come and go there. Right now there's about twenty of them. I know most of their names."

"While I'm in Dodge, maybe you should go over there, have a steak, and ask around."

Arrow patted his stomach. "That's a job I'm trained for."

"What about me?" I asked.

Bear was quiet for a long time. Then she spoke, "Someone heard our last conversation. Whoever it was, is trouble. I don't know how you can do it, but work on that. Find out who was listening at the door, Rattler." She stood up. "One more thing, gentlemen. Keep playing the reporter and the school teacher. But from now on, start toting weapons."

The next morning, I unpacked my gun and wore it in my hidden shoulder holster. The Service issued a switchblade to each agent. I took mine and put it in my boot. It felt good to be armed.

I went to the café for breakfast. Martha, an older woman and wife of the owner, was taking orders.

"What's good today Martha?"

"If you see it on the menu, it's good."

"Where's Callie?" I asked innocently.

Martha seemed put out. "She's got a sick aunt in Mission City. She took the milk train early this morning. Woke up me and the mister long before dawn."

That was Bear's genius. Her alibi had a touch of authenticity by waking up Martha for an early morning emergency.

I ordered bacon and eggs and watched Martha wipe tables and take orders. I wondered how I could get every man in town to take off his boots and run for me. The first one I saw running bowlegged would be the man.

I hiked over to the *Journal* and found Teddy Bartly pouring his first drink of the day. He toasted me when I walked through the door.

"Ah, here comes my editor. Hair of the dog?"

I waved him off. "A little too early for me, Mr. Bartly. Where's . . . Farly?" Farly. I almost said Arrow.

"Farly's off to report a rabid dog spotted outside of town. One of the school kids saw it."

On a hunch, I sat down next to Bartly and decided to see if he knew a Carmen. He squinted up at the ceiling in deep thought. "No. Never knew a Carmen."

"I had a dog once," I said, prompting him. "I named him Carmen after my favorite opera."

Bartly was still sober as he drank scotch out of a shot glass. "Never heard of that one. In my early days, I reviewed an opera for the *Wichita Ledger*. Fell asleep before the fat lady sang."

"What fat lady?"

"There's always a fat lady," he said with a slight slur. He poured himself another.

I kept venturing the name. "A lot of kids made fun of me for naming a dog for an opera. They'd never heard the name Carmen before." I adopted a relaxed pose as I leaned back in my chair. I let forth a mirthful snort and shook my head. "Carmen. What a silly name. It could be a male or female. Are you sure you never heard anyone called by that name?"

The old editor in chief downed his drink. His eyes

were turning glassy. One more drink and he would be useless.

"Hey, that was some shindig over at Anglin's the other night," he said. "I love watching fireworks in the night sky."

Okay, I'd tried. Mr. Bartly was on to another subject. He pushed a piece of paper towards me. "Here's a write up of the Cattleman's Ball. You might want to check my spelling."

"Yes sir."

He put his hat on and stood up. He wavered for a moment and caught the back of my chair to steady himself. "I'll be over at the saloon if you need me." His slur was more pronounced, but he walked to the door without bumping into the furniture. He stopped and looked down the street. Bartly looked like he was trying to gather his thoughts.

"Carmen," he said. "Never knew a Carmen." He gave a short laugh. "Funny. That's the second time I've heard that name in two days."

For a moment, I thought I'd messed up. Of course, Arrow would have asked him. But he said "two days". We had not heard the name Carmen until last night.

"Where did you hear that name before?" I asked casually, my blood racing.

Bartly took out his pocket watch and squinted at it. "Saloon is open."

"Mr. Bartly, where did you hear that name before?" I repeated.

He motioned to himself. "Here. Here in the office. One of Anglin's deputies came in . . . asked me if I knew a Carmen."

Anglin's deputy. No. Featherston's deputy. Featherston was looking for Carmen too.

* * *

I headed for the schoolhouse on the edge of town. There were students, parents, and various other people watching the woods. Arrow was interviewing a young boy.

"Yes sir. The dog was walking funny. I saw him behind the schoolhouse and told Miss Parker."

I looked over and saw the elderly school teacher and several students with their noses pressed to the window. Sheriff Daily was there with his shotgun. A man stood next to him, pointing toward the trees.

"He's in there somewhere, Sheriff. I saw him scrounging around and growling in the brush."

Suddenly, a blood chilling howl came out of the woods. The sheriff turned toward the crowd. "Everyone stay clear of the woods until I can investigate!"

Like ghosts out of the mist, four of Featherston's green shirt deputies rode up. One of them dismounted. "We're here, Sheriff. We'll take care of it for you."

Sheriff Daily's shoulders sagged. I couldn't tell if it was disappointment or relief.

Arrow held up his camera at the deputies. "Can I get a picture of the dog when you kill it?"

The deputy smiled. "You can gut him, cook him, and eat him if you want." He motioned to the other three. "George, you, and Sam go around his left flank."

An ex-military man. He waved at the other deputy. "Charlie, take his other flank and we'll flush him out."

The rabid dog had a growl that was low and full of threat. I couldn't see him, but that sound was enough. The kid who had seen him first, spoke to no one in particular. "That devil dog had white foam leaking out of his mouth."

Arrow heard this and jotted it down. The deputies started moving toward the growling sound and made noises like men herding cattle.

"Yeehaa!"

"Yaw! Yaw!"

Without warning, a huge brown blur leaped out of the bushes at Charlie, the lone deputy. He raised his rifle, but was going to be too late. With a quickness of a cobra, the deputy who was in charge, pulled up his rifle at the hip and shot the dog in midair. It dropped at Charlie's feet.

For a moment, there was stunned silence. Charlie looked like he was going to faint. Then, everyone was cheering and applauding. With gloved hands, the deputies dragged the dog out into the open. Arrow shouted at them, moving his camera into place. "Let's get a picture for the newspaper!"

All four deputies posed over the dead dog, their rifles on their hips. With expert quickness, Arrow set up the camera and held up the tray of flash powder. People were respectful and quiet as the moment was preserved for history.

"Ready?" shouted Arrow. In a puff of smoke, he took the picture and the deputies relaxed. They slapped each other on the shoulders as the people applauded some more.

Sheriff Daily looked confused. "What's going on?" he asked no one in particular.

One of the deputies took the sheriff by the arm. "I'll see you to your office, sir." He led him off.

I pulled Arrow to the side. "Mr. Bartly told me that one of Featherston's men came by the office asking about Carmen."

Arrow took the news with a poker face. "Come

with me back to the office Mr. Foster. I will show you how to develop a photograph."

As we entered the *Journal* office, Arrow headed for the back room. "That rabid dog showing up was lucky. I've got a picture of four of those deputies. I'll send it to Topeka with the mail courier in the morning to see if any of them are wanted anywhere."

"Good idea. Maybe one of them will be recognized. But what about Carmen?"

Arrow was pouring a solution into a shallow pan. "While I'm developing this, why don't you go over to Madam Tinsley's?"

"Why me?"

"You're new in town. You can ask questions about all of the girls without raising any suspicions."

I sighed. "Why didn't you say something last night?"

"Because I just thought of it this morning."

Madam Tinsley's was a two story affair situated between a pool hall and a saloon. There was no sign out front and it's location was obvious. There was an outside back stairway for the married customers. I had recognized that it was a house of ill repute and had avoided it. Piano music came from the saloon, while shouts and curses came from the pool hall.

I nervously walked up the front steps to the door. It looked dark inside. The place seemed quiet, but then it was eleven in the morning. As I walked in, a bell tinkled above the door. The room had a thick, furry rug. There were various love seats placed around a winding staircase. A grand piano was over in the corner by a bay window. The drapes and walls were grey and brown. I was expecting brighter colors and more decoration. A woman about fifty years old glided into the room.

"May I help you?"

"Miss Tinsley?"

"No, I'm her daughter, Estelle."

"I'm, uh . . . I'm a little nervous."

She could have been a preacher's wife. She gave me a warm smile and laid a soft hand on my shoulder. "There's no need to be. Can I get you some tea?" Before I could answer, she led me over to a love seat. "Sit down and tell me your name."

"Foster. Randy."

"What would you like Mr. Randy?"

"I, uh . . . I was wondering about the uh . . . the . . . your . . ."

"The ladies?"

"Yes ma'am."

"Did you have someone in mind? Of course, most of the girls are asleep."

I held up my hand. "No. Don't wake up anybody."

She clasped her hands together and gave me a bright smile. "Not to worry. We always have a couple of girls in reserve."

Again, I held up my hand. "You misunderstand. I'm not looking for companionship."

She looked perplexed.

"You see Madam . . . uh, Miss . . . uh, Estelle. I'm actually looking for my sister. She was engaged to be married, but the man left her. So she . . . she turned to your line of work."

"I see," she said sympathetically.

"I've been looking for her for two years. Her name is Carmen. Do you have a Carmen here?"

She shook her head. "No, but that doesn't mean

she's not here. Most of the girls work under an alias."
She moved her face close to mine and whispered,
"Their pasts tend to follow them around. A new name
doesn't hurt."

"Yes. I figured that. I just thought you might know
their real names."

"Let me see her picture."

Picture. Of course. "I don't have one."

The perplexity on her face, grew. "That's odd. It
seems you would have a picture."

It was time for my quick brain (according to
Harlon Shanks) to think up a plausible story.

"I had a picture. I lost it in Hallsville. I'd been
asking around for Carmen and these men followed
me into an alley."

She put her hand to her mouth. "Oh, my goodness."

"They took my money, my wallet . . . Carmen's picture, which was in my wallet."

"You poor dear."

A woman in her mid-thirties walked into the parlor.
She wore a silky gown and her face was caked with
makeup. She brought a tray of tea cakes over to a settee
and put them down. Estelle was shaking her head.

"You poor, poor man."

"Yes, well . . . I'll keep looking for Carmen. If any
girl should come here with that name, let me know.
I have a room at The Berkshire."

"Carmen, yes. I'll remember."

I stood. "Thank you, Miss Estelle."

"Of course, Mr. Randy."

The girl in the silk gown walked over to me. "Do
I have a customer, Miss Estelle?"

I smelled a very pleasant fragrance. She was short.

She reached up and twirled a lock of my hair into a curl. "Hello handsome."

"Leave him alone," said Estelle. "He's not here for that."

There was something familiar about this temptress.

She had the same idea. "I've seen you before, Mister. I never forget a handsome face."

"I said leave him alone, Sophie."

Sophie. It was Sophie? That was the other name that Bear had said. And I suddenly realized who this Sophie was. She was the young girl who had been Featherston's date at the theatre. The makeup that she was wearing now, was heavy. And seeing her up close, I could see the lines in her face. She was not a young girl. I put a thumb and forefinger to the brim of my hat and gave it a light tug.

"A pleasure ma'am," I said to Sophie. Was Sophie really Carmen? Not likely. When I mentioned the name to Estelle, Sophie didn't let out an "eek!" Not even a quiet one. Maybe Sophie knew Carmen, yet she had not reacted when I mentioned the name.

As I stepped out into the street, another idea hit me. I could go see Mr. Leslie. Of course I'd have to improve my story. And what did Carmen mean to him?

Heading up Main Street, I saw Pee Wee come out of the café with a sack.

"Lunch for Mr. Featherston," he said as he passed.

I shook my head and walked on. Something. I turned. Pee Wee was walking faster. He wasn't quite running, but he was walking fast . . . and sort of bowlegged.

Chapter Twenty

My story for Mr. Leslie would have to be simple. I had questions for him. What was his relationship with Carmen? Somehow I had to work the name into the conversation. Before I could be brilliant, I came to his office. It was closed. I peered through the glass. The place was dark.

I went across the street to a saloon and had a beer. After waiting an hour, and Mr. Leslie didn't show up I headed back to the *Journal* to see if Arrow was there. He wasn't in, so I edited the story on the rabid dog.

Around four o'clock, I walked back over to Mr. Leslie's office. It was still closed. There was no note on the door, so I went looking for Arrow.

Arrow's place was on the top floor of a rooming house on Water Street. He had carrier pigeons on the roof, a necessity for any serious newsman. It was even more valuable to an agent in The Service.

I didn't have to knock on Arrow's door. The room was open and I walked in. It was a small affair that had a short bed with two broken springs poking out of the mattress. There was no evidence that an agent of The Service lived here. Dime novels, the *Police Gazette*, and other literature of a questionable nature lay about. The one object with a truly personal touch was a framed picture of Arrow and a young woman. He was all dressed up and held a top hat stiffly in one hand. He looked about ten years younger, perhaps in his late teens. The young woman was beautiful, wearing a high collared dress and a most serious expression. It said so much, yet so little. Was Arrow married? It was funny how you could work with someone and talk intimate details about the job, but not know a thing about that person's life. That was part of the duties. I left the room and headed up to the roof.

Arrow was with his pigeons, tending to a broken wire on a cage.

"Nice room," I told him.

He turned and smiled. "It gets me by. You, Bear, and the landlord are the only people who have been up there. At least, those are the ones I know of." He turned away and twisted the wire around a nail. Without turning back, he spoke. "It's my sister."

"I beg your pardon?"

"The picture in the frame." He turned and wiped his brow. "You were wondering if she was my wife."

I dropped all pretense and the story that "I never saw a picture, let's have a look," instead choosing just to whistle. "She is a looker."

"It was taken at the President's Inaugural Ball."

I was caught off guard. The President?

"The President of the United States at the time," he clarified. "President Grant when he was re-elected in

'72. Our family knew the Grants. Slightly, of course," he added.

Slightly my eye. Arrow had probably been some rich kid in Washington or New York even. I doubt if he would tell me. I got back to the matter at hand.

"I went by Mr. Leslie's office. He wasn't there. The place looked all closed up."

"Maybe he's out at Mr. Anglin's ranch," said Arrow.

"Maybe, but for a busy lawyer, you'd think he'd put a note on his door."

Arrow used a scoop to put some seeds in the cages. Four fat pigeons hopped to the feeder. "Here you are girls. Mess time."

He was thinking pigeons, I was still thinking of Mr. Leslie. "Maybe he went over to Midvale to see a client."

"Not likely," said Arrow. "Like you said, he would have put up a note on his door."

"Yeah." I walked over to the ledge and looked down on the street. The sun was setting and a gas lighter was putting a flame to the street lamps. A row of electric lights had been installed at Main and Second Street. They would flicker on after dark. "What if he's not here tomorrow?"

Arrow poured water into the cage trough.

"We could have a problem, Arrow." I told him about Pee Wee. "He's Featherston's errand boy. Featherston knows." I sat on a barrel that overlooked the ledge.

"Okay, so Pee Wee tells Featherston about us. But what does he tell? What did he hear?"

I propped a boot up on the ledge. "We need to be very careful my friend."

Arrow sat on the ledge next to me. "Are you seeing Benita tonight?"

"She's having me over for dinner."

"Watch your back. No telling who's out there in the shadows watching."

I was at Benita's around seven o'clock. She greeted me with a cold, brief kiss to the cheek. "Dinner's ready," she said with an unfamiliar curtness.

What was her problem? "Am I late?"

She didn't answer. Benita was not her usual happy self. Her eyes were dark.

I followed her into the kitchen. On the table were peas, cooked carrots, potatoes, and a big slab of roast beef.

"It looks good." I leaned over the food and sniffed.

"Sit!" she commanded.

I sat. "Is anything wrong Benita?"

She slammed a glass of tea in front of me.

Yep. Something was wrong. "Did I say something wrong?"

Before she could answer, Pandora stuck her head in the kitchen window. Benita whirled around and yelled, "Get out, Pandora!"

Pandora's eyes widened. She ducked out and dashed behind a tree in the back. Well . . . she loped.

Then Benita turned on me. "Eat your food Randy!"

I meekly spooned peas onto my plate. "What's wrong?" I asked softly.

She sat down hard and plopped a large spoonful of potatoes onto her plate. Bits of potato flew across the table. I felt some of it spray on my cheek.

"You know what's wrong," she spat.

My mind flipped through possible reasons that would make Benita mad at me. I picked my teeth at breakfast, but that was at the café where she would not have seen me. I didn't ask her to lunch. That was it. No, I did ask her to lunch, but she told me Mr. Anglin had a company lunch with his employees on Wednesdays.

"I have no idea," I confessed.

Benita had a look on her face that gave me a headache. "Clara Holman told me."

"Told you what?"

"She was buying ribbon at Stickman's this morning. She said she saw you coming out of Madam Tinsley's."

Then to add insult to injury, she really laid the heavy timber on me.

"At eleven in the morning! Eleven in the morning, Randy!"

It was a pretty big sin to dabble with painted women, but at eleven in the morning, it was plain hedonistic. I frantically searched for an excuse.

"Yes I was," I said, stalling for time.

Benita's face turned red. Her eyes narrowed. I tensed, expecting to get a face full of mashed potatoes.

"Go on," she said darkly.

"I was at Madam Tinsley's because I was looking for . . . Farly."

"Farly?"

"Yes. Mr. Bartly needed him to develop pictures of that rabid dog down by the schoolhouse."

"She said you were in there for quite some time."

"They had to check each room. And it was finally

determined that Farly wasn't there. I, of course, stayed down in the parlor with Estelle."

"Estelle?"

"Old Estelle . . . Miss Tinsley's daughter. Very old. At least fifty years or more."

I could see Benita start to teeter. The anger left her face. At least she believed me.

"I really was looking for Farly. I found him over at the ice cream parlor."

A smile slowly played across her face. "Oh Randy." She got up and hugged me around the neck. "Will you ever forgive me?"

"Of course, sweetheart."

"I'm just a jealous biddy. I should have known you wouldn't deceive me."

My guilt increased. She thought I was a school teacher. I was a fraud. To assuage that guilt, I made a bold proclamation.

"I'll tell you what. Why don't we take a trip over Denver way."

Her face lit up and she hugged me tighter. "When?! When, my darling?"

My resolve to quit The Service was strengthened. The Colorado Hotel would be a perfect honeymoon place. As soon as this case was over, I'd pop the question.

"We'll go before the new school year opens . . . before I take a new teaching position." Before Mr. Anglin sets us up in Topeka. Benita would work in his Topeka office and I would accept a position at Kansas Teachers College. We would be so happy.

"Oh Randy, I'm so happy. I hear they have an opera playing in Denver almost every night."

"We will dine on opera."

Benita felt so good, she immediately rushed outside with some sugar. She was making amends to the newly cowed Pandora.

I got back into town late that night. Pandora clip-clopped to the front of The Berkshire and drank water from the horse trough. I dismounted and patted her on the flank.

"Rest girl. I'll bring you some oats in the morning."

She gave a tired nod and winked an eye at me. I walked up the steps and into the hotel.

As I got to my room, goose bumps raised up all over my body. The metal plate on my door where the keyhole was, was scratched. Someone had tried to break in. Or they succeeded, and were waiting for me. I took out my gun and quietly put the key in the lock. I turned the key, but the door was unlocked. I slowly opened the door. The light from the hallway spilled into the room. Two dainty feet under a purple dress became visible. She was sitting on the edge of the bed.

"Who is it?" I asked.

"Carmen."

Carmen? She found me. I cautiously opened the door, letting the light fill the room, and kept one eye on Carmen.

"Hurry. Get in here." She got up and lit the lamp in my room. I noticed she had drawn the shades. Then I got a look at Carmen. It was Sophie.

"So you are Carmen."

She wasn't wearing makeup. Her natural beauty shone through and her wrinkles were softer. She was older than me by five years. Right now, she looked scared.

"Who are you?" she asked. "And don't tell me you're a teacher."

"I'm Randy Foster."

"No, I mean what are you? You're a U.S. Marshal, aren't you."

I looked at her evenly, not answering. I decided to plunge ahead with the questions. "Why is your name in Mr. Leslie's office? What do you have to do with Featherston?"

She looked toward the door.

"Are you expecting someone Carmen?"

"I might have been followed. And Pee Wee is known to listen through key holes."

"Yeah, I'm familiar with Pee Wee's habit." I decided to give her some information. "He heard me talking to a confederate about Featherston."

She nodded.

I continued, "He told Featherston and it's stirred up a pot."

"You might say that."

"How do you fit in, Carmen?"

She licked her lips and sat back on the bed. "His name is not Featherston. He's a man named Allan Coletrane."

I felt a tingling at the back of my neck. We had him.

Carmen continued, "Back east, seven years ago, he raped and killed my sister. He also raped me and beat me within an inch of my life. He was wanted under the name of Cole Allan at the time. After he had his way with me and slit my sister's throat, he disappeared."

I was suspicious of her story. "I saw you at the theatre with him. Are you saying he doesn't know you?"

"After what he did to my face? My own mother wouldn't recognize me."

"But you're beautiful."

She pointed to her nose. "This used to be long and straight."

For the first time, I noticed the slight bump near the bridge of her nose.

She put a finger to her left eye. "This eye droops slightly lower."

It wasn't obvious. Maybe all the makeup she wore hid these "imperfections", but despite my observation skills, I'm still a man. Sophie might have compared what she was before to what she was now, but all I saw was a good looking woman.

"And I changed my hair color," she added.

"It took me four years of living in every whorehouse between Kentucky and Kansas to find him. That's where I first met him."

"You were a . . . working girl?"

She shook her head. "Elsie, my sister. She was seeing him a lot. I was actually a member of The Temperance League. I was trying to get her out of that Louisville slum house. I'd send up a little money now and then, and promised her a better life out west." She started to unbutton her blouse. I was not expecting this.

"Uh, ma'am . . . Sophie . . . Carmen . . . I don't think . . ."

She opened her blouse, revealing a long, ugly scar on the lower part of her neck.

"Featherston?"

She nodded.

I was convinced.

Then, Carmen's eyes flitted toward the door. I slowly bent down and looked through the key hole. Nothing. I looked at her and shook my head. She shrugged and continued talking.

"So I was trying to get Elsie out of that life. Coletrane didn't like my interference. To punish me, he broke into our house. He tied me up and made me watch what he did to Elsie. Then he took me."

I thought about the file I had seen on Coletrane. His cruelty was well documented. My heart went out to this broken girl before me.

"I'm sorry Carmen."

She continued as if she hadn't heard me. "He disappeared after that. I vowed to chase him down. I knew he liked the whorehouses." Her face was stone as she told the story, but a wet tear dripped down her cheek. "I guess my faith wasn't strong enough. I became what I hated."

I didn't say anything, letting her collect her thoughts.

"About a year ago, I traced him here." She looked up and gave me a sad smile. "By then, he was using my family name, Featherston."

I didn't know what to say.

"He had raped so many women, had so many whores . . . I was confident he wouldn't recognize me."

"Apparently he didn't."

"My sister didn't mean anything to him. I looked a lot like her, but he never remembered." She gave a bitter laugh. "He changed my face enough so that it fooled him. I'm one of his regular girls. Every time

I'm with him, I fantasize about cutting his throat while he sleeps."

"Why don't you?"

"I spent seven years thinking about how I would cut him up . . . slowly . . . sticking hat pins in various parts of him . . . shooting him in the knee caps . . . anything that would cause him pain . . . anything that would kill him slowly . . . slowly, so I could watch and talk to him in a calm voice, telling him about Elsie and me and how he destroyed us."

I repeated my question.

"So why didn't you?"

Her eyes rolled to the side and the smile on her face was now haunted. "The first time I saw Lewis here, he was walking down the street with his badge and that green shirt with "Anglin Security" sewn on it. Something came over me."

"You didn't want to kill him."

Her face drew open in surprise. "How did you know?"

We stood in the room, still and silent. Even as a tough character who's seen his share of rough scrapes, deep down, I still had my humanity. Call it compassion, call it soft, but I still didn't enjoy seeing someone suffer, including varmints like Featherston. "I just know," I told her.

She gave me a sad smile. "I don't understand. I've had him in a vulnerable position many times."

"Maybe it was your religious background. Maybe your faith is stronger than you think. You conscience overrode your vengeful hatred."

Her head lolled to the side in thought. "Something deep, welled up inside me. 'Vengeance is Mine, saith the Lord.' That's in Romans. And yet, I keep waiting for the moment. I keep waiting when I'll be able to shut God out and do the deed. After all, I've soiled my soul. I'm as lost as Coletrane is . . .''

Before I could speak, she held up a hand. "I know, I know. God forgives. Jesus told the woman to go and sin no more. Maybe I can't forgive myself. I just know that whether I kill Coletrane or not, I'll face eternity alone."

My heart went out to this doomed woman. There was nothing I could say to comfort her.

She continued, "I couldn't kill him. I thought I could at least turn him in to the authorities. After a few weeks in Clearview, I realized I couldn't trust the sheriff with my knowledge of Featherston. I thought of going to Mr. Anglin myself. He's a decent sort, but why would he believe a Tinsley girl?"

I had no answer. She was right.

"After asking around, I realized Mr. Leslie was my man. He knew law and according to the locals, he was honest."

"So you told Mr. Leslie."

"He advised me to be patient. Featherston isn't a well liked man. He's rough, uncouth, dangerously likes power. But he's been clean as a whistle since he arrived in Clearview."

"Maybe, maybe not. I have a feeling we don't know everything he's done in Clearview."

"Mr. Leslie is a lawyer to the bone. He wanted to build a case that would put Featherston away forever. He had me write down everything I'd told him about Lewis. Over the past few months, he's been doing some subtle investigating. He wanted to get evidence that agreed with my story."

"Do you know where Mr. Leslie is?"

The fear returned to her face. "No. I'm afraid for him."

"Where does he live?"

"He has a small house just out of town. I went over there, but he wasn't home."

"Why do you think you're being followed?"

Just before she could answer, a loud blast shook the room. My heart stopped. The window shade shredded and glass flew through the air. Carmen was pushed by some invisible force into my arms.

"Uhh," she moaned.

I heard a horse galloping off. My hands were slippery with blood. A fist sized hole was in her lower back. Her eyes were dull.

"Go get him," she murmured weakly. Then she slumped into a dead weight in my arms.

Chapter Twenty-one

My room was suddenly filled with the hotel clerk, several excited guests, and an Anglin security man who had been on patrol.

"What happened?" asked the security man.

It was on the tip of my tongue to say, "Ask your boss." Instead, I told him what I knew. "We were talking. Car . . . I mean, Sophie was standing next to the window."

"It was the same man who cut down Tom Addington!" cried the clerk. He'd seen the assassin on his horse through the glass door of the hotel.

The deputy looked down at Carmen's body. He gave me an accusing stare. "You were talking. What was she really doing in your room?"

The room was still. I looked back at the faces. Curious faces. Faces anxious to know every sordid detail of the story between the school teacher and the prostitute.

"We weren't doing anything. We were just talking."

The deputy nodded, but the look on his face told me

that he wasn't buying my story. "I've never known a Tinsley girl to be much of a talker."

"Know many of them?" I shot back.

The people laughed.

He scowled as he eyed her open blouse. "Nope, not much talkers. Most of them are doers."

I wanted to smash his face. "She was here because she heard that I was a teacher. She wanted to learn to . . ." Read? That wasn't a good answer. Maybe there were people in the room who already knew that she could read. ". . . do mathematics. She was hoping to better herself and eventually ask Madam Tinsley for a job in accounting."

The deputy, clerk, and guests looked at me like I'd just told them that I was George Washington.

"Really," I added.

The deputy's eyes narrowed. "Why didn't she come see you during the day?"

"She's working . . . days this week. Tonight was her only chance."

A little old man I'd seen smoking cigars in the lobby, started to nod, believing my story. Before the deputy could drill me some more, I pointed at the window.

"What about the man who shot her? Shouldn't you be going after *him*?"

Everyone looked at the deputy, wondering the same thing. At that moment, Featherston strode in. Some guests stepped aside, letting him through. He looked down at Carmen.

"That's too bad. Sophie was a good one." He looked at the deputy and jerked his head to the side. "Go out there and check the hoofprints out in the street." Then he looked at me. "Did you see which way he went?"

"No, but it sounded like he was headed north."

Featherston called back at the deputy. "Check for hoofprints headed north." Featherston waved at the people in the room. "Okay folks, back to your rooms. Unless you are a witness, there is nothing to see here."

They all reluctantly headed back to the lobby to chatter about this new, exciting chapter of Clearview crime.

Featherston gave me a hard look. "I want you to see Sheriff Daily tomorrow and file a report."

"Of course." I looked at him evenly. "I guess you were wrong about Nick Starrett."

Featherston looked like he was trying to place the name. "Who?"

"The man you told me was responsible for the shotgun killings. You said Nick Starrett was the man. You killed him. That's what you said."

He looked like a rabbit in a snare. "Yes . . . yes, you're right. Uh, I guess we were wrong." He definitely was not good at thinking on his toes. Hoping to quickly change the subject, he looked down once more at Carmen.

"I'll send some men over to get her. We'll bury her in Pauper's Field."

"How do you know she doesn't have any relatives?"

Featherston froze. Did he remember Carmen? Did he remember Elsie?

"No. Girls like that don't have any relatives." With that, he left.

I sat down in the chair, looking at the poor, sad girl who never had a chance. I also realized that the final insult for Carmen Featherston was, she'd taken a bullet that had been meant for me.

* * *

The next day, the whole town was buzzing about Sophie's murder. Unfortunately, I was a major player in the sordid drama. Walking over to the *Journal*, I could feel the pointing fingers and whispered gossip behind my back.

Arrow shook his head as soon as I entered. He had figured it out without me telling him. "So you found Carmen."

"More like she found me. She did confirm that Featherston was Coletrane. She and Mr. Leslie were building a case against him."

"I guess I'd better do the story. People are already talking, they might as well read the facts." He picked up his notebook. "What exactly are the facts, Rattler?"

"For publication purposes, I'll tell you what I told the deputy last night. Then I'll tell you what Carmen told me."

After relating the story I told the deputy about Sophie coming to my room to ask for math lessons, it sounded lame in the light of day. Also I thought that with the story raging through Clearview like a wildfire, Benita would soon be getting a juicy version of it.

I waited for Benita to come out of the Anglin office for lunch. She came out around five minutes to noon. She walked a little stiffly and had a stern look on her face. I steeled myself for the jealous wrath I was about to face.

"Benita!" I called out.

She turned. I froze there on the boardwalk. Then her face melted into a smile.

"Randy!" She rushed into my arms and hugged

me tight. She buried her head in my shoulder. "Oh darling, I was coming to see you."

"You were?"

She broke the embrace. "I heard what happened. Are you okay?"

"I'm fine." Sensing I was on a roll, I added, "A little shaken, but I'm better. It was quite a scare."

"Poor Sophie."

"Yes," I agreed. "The poor girl. All she wanted to do was learn arithmetic." Benita was putting her total trust in me. It hurt my heart to continue to lie to her.

"Who would kill an innocent, young girl like that?" Benita bit her lip as she amended her question. "I mean, a professional girl, truly, but she was trying to improve herself."

Apparently she'd gotten my story through Featherston. The fact that Sophie wanted to become an accountant had impressed the businesswoman in Benita.

"I don't know my dear," I said. "Maybe it was a client of hers. There are all sorts of unscrupulous characters who frequent houses of ill repute."

"Lewis said it was the same gunman who killed that ranch hand a few weeks ago."

I remembered my conversation with Lewis the night before. I'd caught him red-handed in a lie. It would do no good to mention it to Benita.

"Yeah, that's what the clerk said." I was ready to get off the subject. "I was hoping you'd have some tortillas with me at The Cantina."

She squeezed my hand. "Let me buy you lunch. You've had a rough night."

We strolled down the street, arm in arm. This beautiful, trusting woman didn't deserve a cad like me. I began to count the days when this case would be over and I could ask Benita to be my wife.

After lunch, I escorted Benita back to her office, then headed over to the *Journal*. I was anxious to tell Arrow everything that Carmen had told me, but Arrow wasn't there. Mr. Bartly sat at his desk snoozing off a hangover.

I left and walked over to the building where Arrow had a room. I met him halfway up the staircase. He looked worried.

"I was coming to see you," he said.

"What is it?"

"Not here. Come up to the roof."

The pigeons were cooing softly in their cages as a cool breeze blew over the roof. Arrow had a piece of paper in his hand. He held it up.

"Bear never made it to Dodge."

"What?"

"Headquarters said she never showed up." He read the little slip of paper. "Bear no show. Proceed with caution."

I cursed. Arrow tore up the strip of paper and let the breeze scatter it. "What do we do now?"

"Bear never got on that train. Mr. Leslie is missing. It was Pee Wee who heard us at the door that night."

It was Arrow's turn to curse. He did.

"Apparently Pee Wee heard enough. They got Bear. Last night they tried to get me," I said.

Arrow went over to one of the cages. He reached under it and pulled out a gun. "Guess it's really time I started carrying this."

We talked for an hour making our plans. Featherston was coming out, getting desperate. He knew that someone was on to him. I would start to shadow him. Sooner or later, he would make a mistake. Arrow sent a pigeon with a message to Dodge City, requesting more manpower. I headed back to my room to get my handcuffs.

When I got back to my room, I found a note stuck on my mirror. It shattered our plans to pieces.

Chapter Twenty-two

The note was short. It simply read: *We've got your friend*. I ripped the note off the mirror and ran out of the room. I tore down the street, almost knocking over an old lady with a parasol.

"Pardon!" I screamed after her. A pigeon flew from the roof of Arrow's building. He was probably carrying the request for more agents. I took two steps at a time as I ran into the building. My boots created a loud clamor as I sped up the narrow stairway.

Arrow was on the roof, feeding the pigeons. I waved the note at him. "They've got Bear!"

He looked at the note and frowned. "Why do I get the feeling that another note is on the way?"

I nodded. "They want us to panic, Arrow."

"It's working."

"I wonder where they have her?"

"The next note will tell us."

I had no idea of what to do. I took a breath and thought hard. "Why don't I ride out to Fort Carmel? Lt. Martin can give us some men. You wait here until you hear from Featherston. We'll get a note asking us to come to a specific place. That's where Bear will be. If she's . . ."

He knew I was going to say "still alive", but we both just stopped and looked at each other.

"It will be a trick," he warned.

"That's why we need extra men."

Pandora and I headed out of town. I was sure I was being watched. That was fine. Keeping an eye on me would spread out Featherston's forces.

"No one's going to do anything to us," I told Pandora. "They want to get me, Bear, and Arrow all together before they kill us. But first they'll want to know what we know."

Pandora looked a little anxious. I'm not sure that my words were reassuring.

Fort Carmel was five miles northwest of town. I took the Federal Road which led straight to the fort. After we were well out of town, I sensed a presence. Pandora did too as she looked back over her shoulder.

"What do you see girl?"

She went into that easy gallop. Then I heard a gunshot behind me.

"Go girl! Go!"

Pandora sped up to her maximum speed which was half as fast as the average horse. What did I expect?

Four men in green shirts were about two hundred yards behind me. Apparently Featherston didn't care if he killed us together or separately. I kicked Pandora, urging her to go faster. More gunfire. They were getting closer.

"You realize this is very serious!" I shouted at her. This did not spur her on, but she looked scared, so I knew she was really trying.

My only chance was to pull off into a wooded area and try to lose them. "Through those pines, girl!"

Pandora might not have been fast, but she was smart. I didn't have to lead her. She jumped over the shallow ditch that bordered the road and headed into the woods. On instinct, she zigged and zagged between the trees and climbed up a steep hill.

I looked back and saw no green shirts. "Keep going Pandora! You're doing good!" She veered sharply around a rock and down a gulley. We splashed into a brook. She stayed in the water for several hundred yards, leaving no track for the deputies to find. I kissed her on the back of her bobbing head. "You are truly a horse of The Service."

A shadow appeared on our right. It was two of the green shirts. They had flanked us.

Pandora nickered and shot out of the stream. I pulled my gun and aimed for the kill. Of course shooting from a moving horse on uneven ground isn't a guarantee. I aimed for the chest, but got the man in the shoulder. He dropped his gun and held his wound, letting out a tortured howl. The other man shot. I heard the zing and ducked.

"Go! Go! Go!" I screamed. With astounding agility, Pandora wove in and out of closely set trees, trying to evade the men. I had seen this manner of horse maneuvering in barrel races at the rodeos. Pandora was in a class by herself.

Again, we lost the deputies as Pandora kept weaving up a ghost trail. I had to duck branches and felt the scrape of thorns on my legs. Pandora slowed and made some graceful turns around several more pine trees. I pulled up on the reins and listened. Nothing. I patted Pandora greatly.

"Who says you need a lot of speed?"

As an answer, the bark on the pine tree next to me exploded with a gun blast. I felt a splinter bury into my cheek. Without having to say a word, Pandora flew up a slight slope.

Two more shots hit branches just over my head. I couldn't see them, but the green shirts were getting closer. The slope shot upward, and Pandora shot upward with it. It seemed to rise forever. I leaned forward, my face in her black mane.

As Pandora hit the rise, she stopped on a dime. Before us was a vista of flat land. We were at the pinnacle of the cliff. Seventy feet below was the green and white water of the Little Cimarron River rapids.

"We're cornered Pandora! We've got to jump!" Pandora shook her head. Her eyes were wide with fear. The words of Cavez came back to haunt me. "Told me Pandora was worthless when it came to diving off high places," he had said.

I leaned down and whispered to Pandora. "We are going to die. You have to jump." She stood there, thinking about it. Two more gun blasts made us flinch. They were close now. I could hear them yelling.

"We've got him, boys!" came the shout. They were close. Too close. I leaned back down to Pandora, who was doing a wonderful impression of a statue. She was frozen in fear.

"You hear that Pandora? They've got us." I was determined to inspire her to courageous acts. My voice turned bold, commanding. "You can do it Pandora! Show 'em your stuff! Now!"

She bolted forward. Grunts of effort flew out of her nostrils. The vista got large fast as we hit the ledge. Then she stopped.

I flew over her head and into the air. "Pandora!"

Her face showed a mixture of regret and curiosity. Before I disappeared over the ledge, I think she smiled.

The river and the world rushed up to catch me. I prayed that the river would be deep enough to swallow my body. It was a cold that I'd never experienced before. Like a huge, icy fist, the water gripped and held me under. My sinking body touched hard rock, but the descent had slowed. I was numb, terrified, and shocked, but I had the presence of mind to roll into a ball. The current rolled me, then spit me to the surface. I had time to gulp air before the liquid cold pulled me back under.

I rode the rapids, tumbling about seven more times before the river slowed and the current began to weaken. Soon I was able to tread water. My body temperature adjusted and I swam to the bank.

Since the river had two sharp bends, the deputies were nowhere in sight. I hoped they were up on that cliff, assuming I'd broken my back and drowned. Clearview was closer than the fort, so I decided to walk back to town. Staying off the road, I kept my eye out for green shirts. Apparently, they had figured I was done in.

Taking the long way through the woods, I saw a rider, wearing a long, black coat, toting a shotgun. Tom Addington's killer. Carmen's killer. I dove behind a bush. The man was searching for something. He was searching for me.

I could see the shoes of his horse as he drew nearer. The shoes were caked in mud. Yep, he'd been down by the river. He was looking for me. I put my hand on my gun and held my breath.

The rider was very close. The flank of his horse brushed the bush I was behind as it passed. I tensed, waiting for his slowly swiveling head to turn and see me. He didn't.

I waited a long moment, trying to gage his course. He might double back and see me. There was a good reason to think he would turn due north once he cleared the woods. How did I know this? Because he wasn't wearing a mask and I saw his face. It was Lt. Martin.

It was after dark when I got back to town. I took the back alleys over to the *Journal*. The lights were still on, and I could see Arrow and Mr. Bartly sharing a drink. Bartly was in his usual drunken stupor and in the middle of a rant. Arrow was listening patiently and pouring drinks.

It was around nine and the streets were quiet. I left the safety of the dark alley and snuck across the street. Bartly's back was to me. I waved at the window and caught Arrow's eye. His face went white. I ducked into the alley next to the *Journal*.

Not long after that, I heard the door open and Bartly was singing a ribald song about senoritas with red underwear. Arrow was speaking, "You head on over to the saloon and I'll lock up."

"You're a good, good, good man, Farly!" slurred Bartly. He tripped down the street, singing the song in a key I wasn't familiar with.

Arrow stood by the door, whispering my name. "Randy? R . . ."

I dashed from the alley and sped past him into the office. "Douse the light!" I said as I disappeared behind a desk.

Arrow blew the lamp out and looked down at me. "I've been trying to get rid of Mr. Bartly for an hour. He was on a tear about the new Indian Bureau set up in Wichita."

I stood up.

He pulled a piece of paper from his desk drawer. "This was on my desk. I found it about two hours ago."

It was a note. It read: *Your friend is dead. Your other friend is at the farm in Spring Branch.*

"They think I'm dead, Arrow. We want them to keep thinking that."

"You gave me a good scare when I saw you in the window. I really thought you were a goner."

"What's the farm? Where is Spring Branch?"

"There's only one farm out at Spring Branch. It belongs to Mr. Leslie's sister. It's about eight miles northwest of here, near Midvale."

Arrow began to pace. "Okay, they think you're dead. I could get you a horse that is actually fast and . . ." He looked at me. "What happened to your horse?"

"She tried to kill me on a cliff."

He looked at me like I was wearing a wigwam on my head. "Tried to kill you? Never mind. Tell me later. We need to get you a fast horse and you high-tail it up to Fort Carmel to get help."

"Fort Carmel is no longer an option."

"What do you mean?"

I told him about Lt. Martin. "Right now we can't

trust anyone at that fort. Martin might be the only rotten apple, but we can't risk it."

Arrow thought hard. His face scrunched up in concentration. "I know someone who can help. He's good with a gun and he's tough."

"Who?"

"Rowdy Holman."

"The trail master? How do you know he's not one of Featherston's men?"

"He's a good guy. Since I've been here, he and I have shared a beer or two. He and Clara had me out at their ranch a couple of times." Despite his dirty jokes and loud manner, Rowdy seemed like a good natured sort, but Arrow assured me that he was tough. Being a trail master required leadership and responsibility. "And he hates Featherston," said Arrow.

"Why?"

"Remember the guy that Featherston beat up?"

"Yeah. Benita actually saw it happen."

"He was Rowdy's brother-in-law. Clara's brother."

"I see."

"Rowdy knew that his brother-in-law was tapping the till. He thought that Anglin was a good boss and didn't like his wife's blood stealing from him. Rowdy was going to turn Clara's brother in, but Featherston caught the guy first. Rowdy didn't realize that Featherston was going to beat the man to a pulp. Which he did."

I grinned. "Rowdy believes in responsibility and justice. I like that."

"And Rowdy's still in town. Next week, he'll be leaving."

"Get him."

Chapter Twenty-three

We found Rowdy just where Clara said he was—in the north pasture, tending to a lame horse. He didn't seem surprised to see us as we approached.

"Hello boys. If you're here to beg on the Chisholm ride so you can write a story about herding, forget it. You don't need to know about all those women I have along the trail." He winked at us as he applied a white, pasty poultice to the horse's fetlock.

"Something else," said Farly.

We told him about our being in The Service and how we needed his help. He looked at me, then Arrow, whom he thought of as Farly, the reporter, then back to me, whom he thought was a school teacher. Then he burst out laughing.

"That's a good one Farly. Are you writing one of those dime novels?"

I didn't crack a smile as I said, "It's Featherston. We're here to bring him in."

In an instant, Rowdy's good-natured face turned

hard. He looked like a tough trail boss, ready to put his fist up to a lazy hand.

"What do you want me to do?" he asked quietly.

"Are you a good shot?" I asked.

Before Rowdy could reply, Arrow did his bragging for him. "The last two years at the Anglin Rodeo, Rowdy won the sharpshooting contest in both rifle and pistol events. And he also won a blue ribbon in the quick draw."

My thoughts went to Noah. How would Rowdy match up against him?

Rowdy took us to his barn. He had a storage bin under it. He also had several Colt .45s and an assortment of rifles and shotguns. "My father was a gunsmith," he told us.

I had no doubts about that.

Arrow said that Featherston had eleven deputies. With Lt. Martin, that made thirteen known bad guys. After some mental figuring, it was decided that Featherston could be at Spring Branch with at least two others. There would be three or four guarding the perimeter of the farm, which left the rest in town.

"I like our odds," said Arrow. It was brave talk from a man who would be the one in their gun sites. But the deputies didn't figure on Rowdy in the deal, or a dead man named Randy Foster backing him up.

The plan was for Arrow to go straight to the farm, armed with a shotgun, two pistols, and a Bowie knife. If he made it past the checkpoint, he would confront those in the farmhouse. Chances were, he'd be stopped at the front door. He would then surrender his weapons, after "finding out" he was outmanned. He was to ask how many were in the house as he laid down his arms. If he got an honest answer and it was likely that he would, he would put that number of weapons to the right of the front door. If he didn't have enough weapons, he'd stab his knife in the dirt.

Meanwhile, Rowdy and I would be ferreting out the checkpoint guards and taking care of them. Dangerous but simple? Right.

Rowdy knew the lay of the land. He suggested that he go first where he could find the guards and quietly take care of them. Since Arrow nor I saw a flaw in that, he went with our blessing.

We gave Rowdy an hour's lead. Arrow went to the livery and got a horse for me. We met outside of town so no one would see Arrow with a dead man. He shook my hand.

"Don't let this horse's speed throw you. He's not that fast, but compared to Pandora, he's a bullet."

"Good luck Arrow. We'll get Bear back." He gave me a wink and mounted his steed. I had never seen an agent that well armed.

I gave Arrow a half hour lead before following his map. I left the main road a mile before I got to Spring Branch. Rowdy had drawn a line of where he was going to search. I was to go on the opposite side of the road.

The rocks and crevices in a heavily wooded area provided plenty of places for a green shirt to hide. The good news was, they would hide where they could see the road. That left a lot of acreage I could ignore.

I saw the horse tied to a tree near a crag. It would belong to a sentry. Smoke came from behind a rock that overlooked the road. I was hoping to find the man asleep, but didn't expect it. There was a clump of bushes on the other side of the rock. I quietly made my approach.

He was on the ledge, looking out at the road. He also had an ice pack tied to his shoulder. He was the one I'd shot. Now was the time to finish the job. I took out a garrote that Arrow had given me. One swift move and it would all be over. I couldn't see his face, but his posture and stance were familiar. Shadow. I had been too busy running to recognize him when my bullet said hello to his shoulder. I was glad it wasn't Lamppost. That fellow was strong as a bull. Shadow would be no problem.

He tossed a cigarette over the ledge, and immediately rolled another one. This was my chance. I carefully stepped forward. He was a few feet away. Another step forward. I held the garrote steady. One more step.

I swung the garrote over his head and pulled. Using all of my strength, my arms had a tug of war against the muscle in his neck. There was a slight grunt and his hands went up where the garrote was, but he was already losing the battle. The garrote was a razor thin, but strong cord. Shadow didn't try to kick me or lash out. All he could think of was the hellish tightening around his windpipe.

He finally slumped. I felt no pulse and pulled off the bloody garrote. I looked up and was startled to see Rowdy grinning down at me from the top of the crag.

"I got me two of them," he said.

"Do you think that's all?"

"If not, we're in big trouble."

Without warning, there was a gunshot from above us. Rowdy's hat flew off and we dove behind a rock. We drew our guns.

"Where is he? Did you see him?"

I pointed to a clump of rocks. "It looks like it came from over there."

A drop of red ran out from under Rowdy's hairline.

"You got grazed."

He wiped his head and looked at his sleeve. He whistled. "Man oh, man. One pinch closer and I'm trading stories with St. Peter."

Before I could reply, there was another blast. The rock exploded between us as we ducked lower. Rowdy rolled down the slope under some bushes. I found a smaller rock that didn't provide much cover. The second shot was from some trees on the other side of the road. There were two of them. Maybe more.

The air was full of rifle reports banging in our ears. I could smell cordite as bullets rained down on the rock I was behind. I tried to make myself smaller as chunks of rocks became like bullets, and sprayed all over me.

"Rowdy! Can you see the flash?!" I was totally helpless. I couldn't see where Rowdy had rolled. For a chilling instant, I thought he was dead. In desperation, I held my gun over the rock and put as much lead as I could in the trees across the road. A bullet ripped my boot and I drew my knees closer into my body.

"Save your ammo!" I heard Rowdy shout. "I've got him!"

Relief flooded over me when I heard those words. From the brush, Rowdy carefully aimed. I couldn't

see it, but I knew he could see the flashes and smoke
from the green shirt's rifle. I heard him shoot.

"Aagguuuh!" A man screamed. I peered over the
rock and saw a body bouncing from the limb of a
high tree. His neck snapped as he hit a thick branch
and his body became semi-impaled on a short, thin
tree at the bottom.

Apparently, the other assailant was watching his
buddy die as he was descending the tree. He had
stopped firing. I used the moment to jump up and
dive behind the larger rock.

"He's running for it!" Rowdy shouted.

At that, I jumped from behind the rock and laid
down fire in the direction of the moving bushes.
Rowdy ran past me in pursuit.

"We've got to get him before he gets to his horse!"

"Be careful!" I yelled as I lit after Rowdy.

We reached a tree where the grass had been disturbed and there were bullet casings lying around.

"That way!" I pointed.

A horse was galloping away. We came to a clearing and could see the fleeing green shirt headed for
the road. Rowdy looked at me and smiled. "How
good are you?"

"I'm pretty good."

The man hit the road and sped away. He was putting a lot of distance between us.

"Aim for the small of his back," he said.

We both raised our guns. This guy was rushing to
the bend in the road where he could disappear. He
was not going to escape.

"Ready?"

"Ready," I replied.

We cocked our pistols and focused on the back of the departing deputy.

"Now," I said quietly.

We shot. For a second, nothing happened, but a spray of red appeared on his back as the man shot straight up in his saddle. His arms spread out in mortal surrender. Then he flipped off his horse and fell in a heap of dust.

Rowdy gave out a lusty laugh. "That's for ruining my hat!" he shouted at the fallen figure.

We made our way down to the road and looked at the body. It was the deputy who had shot the rabid dog.

"Guess we'd better get him off the road," I said. "We don't want to alert anyone."

"You got it," said Rowdy.

We dragged the man into some bushes on the side of the road. Rowdy held up two fingers. "That's two more bad guys we don't have to worry about."

"You got that right," I said. "Let's get out of here."

We doubled back around to where the farmhouse stood. It was in a clearing with a well and a barn. A chicken coop was between the house and the barn.

"What do you think?" Rowdy asked.

"I see a shotgun and two pistols to the right of the door."

Arrow's knife was to the left. "We've got three men inside, Rowdy. You go to the barn. I'll see if I can sneak a peek in the window."

"What are you going to do?"

"I'm going to assess the situation. If it looks good,

I'll signal you. I'll draw their attention to the front door. You go in the back and—"

A sharp click sounded behind us. I felt cold steel at the back of my ear. Rowdy froze.

"I didn't think you were dead." I turned to face the shotgun held by Lt. Martin.

"Why aren't you out soldiering?

"I'm over at Ft. Leavenworth right now, requesting a cannon," Martin replied.

I looked over at Rowdy. "Good excuse."

We stood up and raised our hands.

Lt. Martin grinned at Rowdy. "Mr. Holman. I didn't realize you were in cahoots with the law."

Rowdy returned the grin. "We need a lot of law around here to get rid of skunks like you."

Martin pointed his shotgun at me. "Okay deadman. Disarm."

I dropped my pistol to the ground.

"Let's see the knife in your boot."

My heart sank. The knife was going to be my big surprise.

Lt. Martin gave a slight wave of the shotgun at Randy.

"You too, trail master. Let's go."

Rowdy tossed his gun at Lt. Martin's feet.

"Now gentlemen, let's march to the house in an orderly manner."

With our hands raised, we headed for the farmhouse. Lt. Martin followed us close enough to blow us out of our boots, but far enough to keep us from getting any ideas.

"Hello to home!" shouted Martin.

Pee Wee opened the door and gave a little giggle. "Lookee here. We've got company!"

"Pee Wee, go back into town and tell Mr. Featherston these men killed five of his deputies."

Pee Wee's look soured. He stepped outside and headed for his horse. "Dern newcomers," he said under his breath.

Lt. Martin prodded us inside. Charlie, the deputy who was almost bit by the rabid dog, sat in a chair with a rifle in his lap. Across the room, tied to another chair was Arrow. He had a bruise on his forehead. He lisped through two missing teeth.

"Hey Randy. I tried to warn you about Lt. Martin."

Then I remembered. When Arrow laid down his arms, he put the shotgun about four feet from the two pistols. Two men inside, one outside. It was a standard signal we'd learned in The Service. I could kick myself, but I knew someone would do the kicking for me.

"Where's Mr. Leslie and his sister?" I asked.

Charlie nodded toward the window. "They're out getting water out of the well. Been there for a couple days."

Where were Bear and the other deputy? To answer my question, Lamppost came out of a room, stuffing his shirttail back into his pants. "Well, well, well, the school teacher." He threw a thumb at the door he'd just come out of. "You want to take a poke at her?"

I rushed into the room. Bear was on a bed, naked. Her arms and legs were bound by ropes. I threw a sheet over her and examined her face. Her jaw was swollen. A rivulet of blood dripped from the corner of her mouth. Her left eye looked like a big, purple mushroom. Dried blood was caked around her nose. She opened her one good eye. Her lips were cracked and dry. She was trying to smile.

"What took you so long?" she croaked.

"Can you sit up?" I untied her and with surprising strength, she sat up straight and rubbed her wrists.

Then she cursed. "They've had their way with me, but I'm ready to skin every one of them." She wiped her still-bleeding mouth.

I had to admit, I liked her spirit.

She moved close to me and whispered, "they tried to get me to tell them who you and Farly really are." She looked at the door. "They didn't get a thing from me."

I gently kissed her on the forehead and helped her up. She wrapped the sheet around her and we went back into the main room.

Lamppost was tying Rowdy to a chair while Martin and the other deputy kept him covered. Lamppost looked at me as he tied Rowdy up.

"Looks like you aren't the sportin' type."

Bear walked up to Martin. She merely stood there and stared at him. Then she spit into his face. He brought the shotgun up and clubbed her under the chin.

"Ooof!" She fell back into my arms.

Rowdy and Arrow were shouting. Martin swung his shotgun at Rowdy.

"Shut up! Shut up!" he cried.

The rage I felt was a calm storm. I had to remain focused. "Okay Lieutenant, I'd like answers before you tie me up and shoot me."

Martin wiped Bear's pink spittle from his face. "What do you want to know?"

I set up the scenario I'd been thinking in my head. "We know that you controlled the supply of stock you sold to Anglin Cattle. Obviously you were skimming funds with Featherston's help."

He nodded. "We had help. Brown and Chapman rearranged the numbers in the book before giving it to Mr. Leslie."

"And Anglin never suspected?"

"Nope."

"You killed Terry Hill, the accountant, because he stumbled on this crookedness."

Lt. Martin shrugged. "A small price."

"Then you killed Mike Reese, the bank teller, because—"

Martin finished my thought.

"He was putting two and two together when he saw my personal account. I should have kept the cash at my quarters at Carmel. My father was a banker and old habits die hard."

"So he figured you were making too much money for an army lieutenant."

"To tell you the truth, I didn't think he would notice. I was putting the money in a little bit at a time, but he couldn't ignore my large balance. It was too much for a soldier of my pay grade."

"What about Tom Addington, the ranch hand?"

"Featherston had me take care of him. Lewis misjudged the man. He thought he was a good candidate to be a deputy. The man had a mean streak, and he needed money to pay gambling debts."

Rowdy joined in. "But he found out what you and Featherston were up to . . . robbing Mr. Anglin blind."

"True," said Martin. "He made some bad excuse about Hogan giving him a raise and not needing the job, but we knew it was only a matter of time before he told Mr. Anglin." Lt. Martin had a look of calm on his face. Under the calm was pure evil. "But we took care of those problems." He looked at Lamppost. "Tie him, and my lovely Callie up."

Before Lamppost could make a move, there was a loud thump on the door. Then another. We all looked at the front door. Martin aimed his shotgun at the middle of the door and spoke in a rough, intimidating voice, "Who is it?"

I glanced out the window and caught a blur of reddish brown flash past. It was Pandora. The same two thumps were now at the back door. Everyone's head swiveled toward the back. Martin motioned for Charlie, the deputy, to check it out. With rifle poised, Charlie headed to the back door.

With a deafening blast, the front door collapsed under two hooves. Pandora had broken in. Everything happened at once. Lt. Martin swung around toward the front. Lamppost raised his gun to shoot me, but Bear threw her sheet over him and kicked him for all she was worth.

I struggled with Lt. Martin, but he wouldn't let go of the shotgun. It went off, narrowly missing Arrow and catching Charlie in his stomach. There was a burst of red and he fell on his back. A snake, white and slimy, slithered out of his stomach. It looked just like the intestines on Doc Fenton's chart. As we struggled, Pandora came forward and bit Martin's wrist.

"Auugghh!" He dropped the shotgun.

Lamppost managed to throw off the sheet and was met in the face by the chair Bear threw at him. He fell down, stunned, and Bear gave a wicked kick to his head.

Martin kicked my instep. He had the same training that I had gotten in The Service. While I was distracted, he threw a sharp elbow to my face.

It was like everything had slowed to a crawl. As I fell back, I saw Martin taking a gun from his belt. He was cocking the gun as my butt hit the floor. My back cracked against the wall and he was aiming the gun at my chest.

There was a shot. Martin dropped the gun and fell back, clutching the red river that was pouring from his throat. I looked to the right and saw Bear, standing naked, with Lamppost's smoking gun clutched in her hand.

Chapter Twenty-four

As I untied Arrow and Rowdy, Bear took Lamp-post's clothes and put them on. While he lay there in his long johns, he started to come to. Bear, now wearing his boots, delivered a vicious kick between Lamp-post's legs. He screamed. Before he could scream again, she kicked him in the face, putting him back into dreamland.

I found Pandora out in the front, under a shade tree. She gave me that smile as I approached. I laid a big, wet kiss on her nose.

"You saved my life, girl. Tonight, I'm giving you five extra cubes of sugar." Arrow came out to meet us. When he spoke, the words whistled through his broken teeth.

"Did you train your horse to break the door down?"

"I never trained her in anything."

Arrow petted her. "She's unbelievable."

Rowdy came out of the house. "Hey Randy, did you train your horse to break down that door?"

I shook my head and repeated, "I never trained her in anything."

Bear, wearing clothes that were much too large for her, came out the front door. With her beaten, swollen face along with the clothes, she looked like a man with long, blond hair. "So that's Pandora, the wonder horse," mused Bear.

I went over to her and took her hand. "Are you okay?"

Her eyes were calm and kind. "I made it through my friend." She put a hand on my shoulder. "Thanks for coming for me."

"Thanks for not telling them about us."

Rowdy walked up to Bear. He rubbed his chin and grinned. "Well Miss Callie, I know you serve a fine meal at the café, but I never knew a woman could fight like that."

"You never had to work for tips, Rowdy."

His face fell to serious concern. "Are you sure you're all right ma'am?" Before she could answer, a blast erupted from the house. A branch over my head shot across the yard.

"It's Gavin!" yelled Bear. Gavin. Lamppost. His name was Gavin. We all ducked. Pandora ran behind the tree. Another blast sent us scurrying into the bushes. Arrow's guns lay useless in front of the house. Mine and Rowdy's were up the hill where Lt. Martin had taken us captive.

Bear pulled out one of Gavin's guns from his holster that she wore. She tried to aim through the eye that looked like a purple mushroom.

"My aim's no good," she said. She tossed the gun to Arrow, who tossed the gun to Rowdy. "Rowdy's our best shot." The house was quiet. We could hear Gavin loading up his shotgun. This was my best chance.

"I'll draw him out," I volunteered. I ran from the bushes and zigzagged like Pandora had done in the woods. The shotgun barrel appeared in the window. I dove behind the well just as he shot. A clump of dust rose behind me. The good news was, old Lamppost was a lousy shot.

A stench rose up from the well. It had to be the rotting bodies of Mr. Leslie and his sister. My eyes watered as I watched Rowdy return fire. The shotgun barrel dropped from the window.

"Did you get him?" yelled Arrow. I couldn't see inside the house with my eyes tearing up and my nose revolting against the gruesome smell from the well. Rowdy was creeping out of the bushes. I saw Pandora's ears peeking from behind the tree.

"Be careful," I said. Rowdy had the pistol cocked and ready. The house was quiet. Suddenly we heard the neigh of a horse. Then, galloping hooves. All of us ran toward the side of the house, Pandora, of course, trailing behind. Gavin, in his long johns, was riding away on Arrow's horse.

Rowdy couldn't get a clean shot through the trees, but he tried. I was amazed at how close he was hitting at that distance. Leaves and tree bark moved with each shot, just missing Gavin. Rowdy looked at me expectantly.

"Well."

"Well what?"

"Get on your horse and go get him!" He tossed the pistol to me.

"It won't do, Rowdy. Pandora is a slow horse."

"Very slow," added Arrow.

"My fault," said Bear. "I should have tied Gavin up. I gave him my best kick. That should put a man out for hours."

Arrow hugged her. "You're weaker than you think. I'm surprised you can still walk."

"Well let's gather up our guns and Rowdy's horse. Chances are, Gavin's horse was hidden in the woods with Lt. Martin's. He'll go for it."

"We can ride double," said Rowdy.

We gathered all of the guns from inside the house, then went back up the hill for mine and Rowdy's.

"One thing's for sure," said Arrow. "Featherston is going to know we're coming."

Chapter Twenty-five

We didn't know how Lewis Featherston would play this. He knew he was dealing with the law instead of a reporter, a school teacher, and a waitress. Arrow didn't think he would try to arrest us for killing his deputies.

"He's going to ambush us when we get to town . . . claim we didn't identify ourselves as U.S. Marshals."

"He thinks we're U.S. Marshals? We're The Service."

"Doesn't matter. He'll kill us, and if any more marshals arrive, he'll lay everything on Lt. Martin."

"He thinks we're marshals," said Bear. "Not that that will keep us any safer. We could be killed before the reinforcements arrive."

Rowdy was taking in this talk with new wonder. He was seeing us with different eyes. "Hey Randy, you're not mad about that joke I told the night of the ball."

"Which one was that?"

"How many undercover agents in The Service does it take to solve a crime committed by a prostitute?"

I nodded, knowing the answer. Bear and Arrow

looked at him expectantly. He supplied the answer, "It depends on how many dresses The Service owns." Rowdy laughed. Arrow laughed. Bear looked puzzled. Rowdy stopped and soberly amended his comment. "Of course I didn't realize there were ladies in The Service, Callie."

"We have a few. Some of them don't like those kinds of jokes." She scowled.

Rowdy bowed his head. "Yes ma'am."

Then Bear reached over and squeezed his arm. "Of course those jokes are right up my alley."

Rowdy brightened.

Bear continued, "And Rowdy, you were always a good tipper. I appreciated that."

We debated on waiting for help. I had an idea. "One of us needs to sneak up to the roof and release a pigeon with the message that we're at Mr. Leslie's sister's farm. Then we head back there and wait."

"They'll be watching my place," said Arrow. "Any of us show up and we're dead."

"We could get someone else to go up to the roof," I said.

"Who?"

"Benita." It was time that I told her what I was up to. Time to come clean. After this was over, for the hundredth time, I resolved to propose to her and settle down.

"What if Featherston makes a run for it?" asked Bear. "Hell, he could already be on his way out of town."

"He can only go one way. That's the southwest road to Colorado. He won't come here and he won't go to Ft. Carmel."

"He could hop a train," said Arrow.

"There aren't that many trains going through," I said. "His only way out is the southwest road."

Bear took off Gavin's hat and fanned her beaten face. To see a woman in that condition made my blood boil. I didn't care if she was a trained agent in a dangerous business.

"Rowdy, if we can get another horse, you could head southwest and see about that," said Bear.

"I've got a buddy who has a ranch not far from here." He touched the horse he was riding. "I'll keep Pancho here and we'll get horses for you and Farly."

Bear nodded. "Thanks Rowdy. Randy, get Pandora and wait until dark. Ride over to Benita's and let her know what we need." I nodded. Waiting was the best thing. I'd seen enough action for one day.

There was a lamp shining in Benita's window. The buckboard was in the back. Pandora and I had taken the back way in and I sauntered up to her porch. Knocking lightly, I waited for a few moments. No Benita. She was probably asleep. There was a chance that she was across the street, visiting Old Widow Henry. Staying in the shadows, I crept to the side of the house. The widow's grey framed cottage was dark. She had already gone to bed.

Something was wrong. I took some chicken wire from a neighbor's fence and twisted it into a pick. Benita's back door was easy, and I was inside in moments. Her kitchen was dim. The lamp light seeped in from the front room. On the table was a rock. Under the rock was a note. When I read it, my heart went to my throat. It read: *Mr. U.S. Marshal. I have your woman. I also have Mr. Anglin. If you want to see them alive, come alone. We are in Mr. Anglin's greenhouse.* It was signed Lewis Featherston. There was a P.S. It read: *Told you I could write.*

Pandora wasn't fast enough to ride back to Spring Branch. Rowdy was on the southwest road, getting farther away. I was truly in this alone. All I could think of was Benita.

"Come on Pandora! We've got to hurry!"

It was one of the longest rides of my life. The road was dark and smooth, but it could hide snipers who could take a shot at me. But no. There would be no snipers. And there was no reason to go through the woods for a surprise attack. They were expecting me.

Mr. Anglin's mansion had enough lights on to show the road ahead. My eyes flitted back and forth for unseemly shadows. Despite the lights, the place was quiet. Too quiet.

I dismounted and whispered to Pandora, "I don't know how you know, but I know you know." She looked as confused as the sentence I had spoken. "Stay here, but stay near. If you see me in trouble, come help." I don't think Pandora understood, but she could sense danger. I only hoped she would repeat what she did at Spring Branch if I needed her.

I sneaked through the front courtyard. There was still no sign of Featherston or his men. I edged up to the house, and slowly turned the corner. I could see the greenhouse and gas lampposts around it. I knew they were watching. But watching from where? Then, I saw her.

Benita was tied to a chair. Her head was bowed like she'd fallen asleep. I didn't see Mr. Anglin. I stayed behind the corner of the house and looked for a small pebble. There were a few at my feet. I took one and tossed it against the glass entrance. Her head popped up. Tears streaked her face and she looked terrified.

As my heart sank, my hatred for Featherston rose. Then, a familiar voice came up from behind me. "Welcome, Teacher." It was Lewis.

I turned and saw the big man standing in the moonlight. Behind him were two deputies.

"Where's Mr. Anglin?" I asked. The nasty smile he gave me was aching to be broken into a million pieces.

"Why are you worried about him? I figure you'd be more worried about yourself. Or Little Miss Sugar Britches over there."

There had to be more deputies around. They were probably guarding Anglin.

"What I'd like to know is, how many U.S. Marshals are working in Clearview?"

"I'm not a marshal. I'm an agent with The Service. More agents are on the way to take you in Coletrane." I could see my words hit home.

His eyes went from arrogance to hatred.

"Take his guns," he hissed.

Before I knew it, there was a deputy behind me. He snatched my holstered gun. I threw down my rifle.

Featherston took a step toward me. "Well, I guess I'd better be going before your partners arrive. But first I need to do something." As Featherston kept talking, he took off his gun belt. "Back east, I beat several men senseless. There's a lawman back in Cincinnati that can't eat his peas without drooling into the butter."

The other deputies started to back away. Benita's muffled screams were trying to penetrate the thick glass of the greenhouse.

"Let's see how good you are, Mr. Agent." Featherston put on gloves with ugly iron studs sewn onto the knuckles. "You beat up three of my men in an alley. I think I owe you."

I raised my fists. "Let's go."

He laughed cruelly. "When I finish with you"—he nodded toward the greenhouse—"me and the boys are going to have some fun with your girl."

That did it. My blood went past the boiling point. I leaped at Featherston, wildly swinging my fists. I felt my nose collapse as he sent a ramrod punch to my face. The deputies were yelling for blood as my own blood spurted from my face. I couldn't breathe. Before I could recover, Lewis swung a wicked left. The studs buried into my right jaw and pulled out tiny pieces of flesh. My legs folded and I fell hard. Featherston stood over me with his hands on his hips.

"Tough guy, huh? I'm going to have to fire some deputies for letting a dandy like you to beat them up."

I was woozy. It felt like the ground was sliding back and forth under me. Nausea erupted from my gullet. Somewhere in the distance, I could hear Benita crying and calling my name. Featherston picked up his right foot and put his boot on my chest. "Good-bye Mr. Agent."

As he raised his boot, I kicked up and caught him between his legs. A mixture of surprise and pain filled his face. Then, I flung dirt into his eyes. As Lewis backed away, I pulled the knife from my boot.

"Knife!" yelled one of the deputies. Before the others could react, I was up and had the knife at Featherston's throat. In the same move, I pulled his arm behind his back.

"Stand back!" I yelled at them.

The deputies had drawn their guns, but they backed away now. Featherston was groaning.

"Now it's real simple, Lewis. You're going to release Miss Brooks and Mr. Anglin." Before I could finish my demands, the butt of a pistol cracked me behind my ear. I dropped the knife, and released Lewis. It was the man I called Cracker Barrel. He failed to knock me out, but it was enough. I staggered.

"Grab him!" yelled Featherston.

Two deputies had me by the arms. All I could do was stand impotently. I almost blacked out as the studded glove exploded against my forehead.

"I'm going to mess you up good," said Featherston.

My legs wobbled under the assault. He was punching me, cutting my face to ribbons.

"Make him look like chopped beef!" cried Cracker Barrel.

My face was numb and I felt blood pour into my eyes. Featherston was holding back, prolonging the agony. My head whipped to the right and then to the left with each punch. I felt new pain as the bone in my jaw cracked. Something gashed my lip. The deputies who were holding me had blood on their clothes and faces. My blood.

Breathing heavily, Lewis picked up my knife.

"That's a nice pig sticker," he said. He gingerly ran

his gloved fingers along the blade. "I'm going to cut all those muscles that work your arms and legs. Then I'm going to blind you . . . but not before we make you watch what we do to your princess over there."

I spat blood at him. My nose hurt, my face hurt, so spitting was all I could do.

"Go to hell!" I screamed. The fight was still in me, but my body was through. Where was Pandora? As if reading my mind, Gavin appeared from among the deputies.

"Your horse won't save you this time. She's tied up real good to the hitching post in the courtyard." Featherston was holding the knife and looking at my arm.

"Think I'll start on your right elbow." He slashed my forearm to test the sharpness of the knife. With the searing pain, blood began to soak my sleeve.

I cried out.

He nodded, satisfied. "Yeah, that'll do." He grabbed my arm and raised the knife. I was trying to wrench loose, but the deputies held me tight.

"Welcome to hell, Mr. Agent."

In one instant, shots rang out. Featherston dropped the knife and the deputies dropped their guns—all at once it seemed. Each man grabbed his wrist. For a crazy moment, I thought Pandora had untied herself and was now shooting a rifle. But only one person could shoot like that. Noah Smith.

There was another shot and Gavin looked down at his own chest where blood blossomed under his green shirt. He fell over. Featherston and the deputies scattered in panic. I fell to the ground and lay there, stunned. My mind was losing focus.

"Where are they?!" shouted Featherston. They

picked up their guns and started shooting blindly in all directions. There was return gunfire. A deputy fell next to me. I stared into his dead face. It was Cracker Barrel.

"They're over there! In the bushes! Shoot at the flash!" screamed Featherston.

The deputies found cover in the bushes behind a cart that served as a planter. There was smoke and a deafening roar as guns exploded.

Above the gunfire, I heard Bear's voice. "There! Over there! He's getting away!"

A deputy ran for his horse. He was shot in midstride. Then I saw Featherston working his way to the greenhouse behind the bushes. He was going for Benita. He was going to stop this battle by using her as a shield.

"That's not going to happen," I told myself. I reached over and took the gun from Cracker Barrel's dead hand. Amid all the smoke and noise, I lay there in a prone firing position. Featherston was almost to the greenhouse door. My hands shook and blood continued to blind me. I was aiming for his back.

Featherston opened the greenhouse door. I fired. The back of his knee shattered. Bad aim. Lewis fell at Benita's feet. He grabbed his knee and moaned. I aimed for his chest. I couldn't stop my hand from shaking. I fired and the bullet broke glass near Benita. I'd almost hit her.

Lewis was in great pain, but he realized who got him in the knee. He sat there, then raised his gun and aimed. I couldn't afford to shoot at him without risking a shot at Benita who was tied to the chair behind him. I felt like I could look all the way down the barrel of his pistol. That bullet was going to hit me squarely in the face.

Without hesitation, I rolled. As the bullet bit earth, dirt kicked up next to me. The side of the house stopped my progress, but it didn't stop Lewis. He had me in his sight. Just before he fired, Benita swung her bound feet and kicked him in his damaged knee. The bullet hit the window that was above my head. Lewis was on his butt, holding his knee and cursing.

I took a breath and calmed down. I leveled the gun at his chest and fired. His chest was clean, but a red dot appeared on his head. Bad aim. It didn't matter. Lewis Featherston fell back, dead.

The two remaining deputies threw out their guns and held up their hands.

"We surrender! Stop firing!"

Then, it got quiet. I felt a hand on my shoulder. The blood was wiped from my eyes and I saw Bear's beaten face. Arrow and Rowdy walked past us with rifles held on the two deputies.

Through swollen lips I asked, "how did you . . ." Bear looked over at Arrow. "Farly thought we should come see Mr. Anglin for help. We couldn't wait on more agents."

"What about Rowdy?"

"All he saw were wagon tracks on the southwest road. He didn't think Featherston was escaping by wheel. We left him a note and he caught up with us before we got here. Then we met this young man on the road." She pointed to a grinning Noah, who came out of the bushes.

"Hello Mr. Randy. Guess I never got to run too far away."

I looked at him in amazement.

"My grandpa told me never to run away from a

fight." He pointed the rifle he was holding at the recently deceased Gavin. "Him and two of those others beat me. I let 'em think they won. I've been living in the shadows, waiting for a good time to make my move. I ain't no cold-blooded killer like them. I wanted to catch 'em in the act."

"Why didn't we see you at Spring Branch?" I asked.

He pointed his rifle at Cracker Barrel. "I was busy following him. Can't be in two places at once." A fly on the wall, I thought. I stood there for a moment, then grabbed Noah and gave him a big hug.

"Thank you, my friend."

Bear tapped me on the shoulder. "Someone else wants to see you."

Benita, now untied, ran up to me and threw her arms around my neck. "Oh Randy! I was so afraid!" I patted her gently on the back. She seemed no worse for the wear.

"It's okay. You're safe now."

Bear handed me my knife. "Nice pig sticker."

"Thanks."

Arrow had the two deputies handcuffed and on their knees. "Now you two don't move, even if your nose itches." He walked over and shook my hand. "Good to see you, Randy." He whistled through his busted teeth.

"You too, Farly," I replied. I could feel myself stop shaking. My face was numb, but pain was making it's way to the surface. My jaw was swelling. Of the six of us, Benita, Rowdy and Noah's faces were unmarked. Benita hugged Noah. "I knew you were a good man the moment I saw you."

"At least we got out of this one alive," said Arrow.

I caressed Benita's cheek. "Are you sure you're okay?"

"I'm fine, now."

I was afraid to ask, but I had to. "Benita. What did they do with Mr. Anglin?"

She looked puzzled. "I don't know. I thought he was at his room in town."

Without warning, an explosion filled the air.

"Aaauuggh!" Arrow screamed as he dropped his gun. Rowdy wheeled toward the sound of the gun shot. Bear pulled her pistol.

"Drop your weapons!" came a voice in the dark. "You are all covered!"

Bear had left her rifle when she picked me up. All she had was her Service pistol. She dropped it. Arrow's right arm was bleeding. Only Noah and Rowdy still had their guns. Rowdy assessed the situation and surrendered his. For a moment, I saw the glint in Noah's eye. He was fast enough to take them all, but no one knew how many deputies were hidden out there. Maybe one on the roof. Maybe one over by the trees. I shook my head at Noah. He finally dropped his rifle.

A deputy came out from behind a tree. Another came out of the bushes. He was followed by Anglin, who held a pistol. "You've killed just about all of my deputies," he said. We stood in front of the greenhouse as Anglin casually waved his gun toward the mansion. "It took me a long time to accumulate all of this. Back east, I made a fortune in gold." He looked like he was trying not to laugh as he saw the questions on our faces. "Okay, it was a gold shipment from the Bank of Baltimore."

Thirty years before, the largest robbery of gold had been taken from the Baltimore-Ohio Railroad. Three bandits had used a Gatling gun to kill the eight guards. The case went unsolved.

"So that was you," I said.

Anglin looked down at the dead Featherston. "Me and his daddy. I moved to Illinois and became respectable. Lewis started working for me, getting rid of business competitors."

"Then you set up shop in Clearview," said Bear.

"It was a sweet deal. Allan . . . I mean, Lewis, was wanted back east, so I sent for him and gave him a new identity."

"You were working with Lt. Martin to steal money from the government," I said.

Anglin looked up at the moon, hiding a smile. "Among others," he said. "I finally reached a comfortable level. I was a legitimate businessman and a respected community leader."

Then it hit me. "And your accountants, Brown and Chapman kept your ledger looking clean."

He laughed. "That's why I was going to send Benita to Topeka." Benita looked surprised. "Eventually she would have known too much." The mirth left his face. "Now all of you know too much. I bought land in Mexico and built a ranch in case I ever needed to "get away". I guess it's time I got away." He pointed the gun at Benita. "Instead of promoting you to Topeka, I guess I'll fire you to hell." His eyes narrowed. His finger was white on the trigger.

"No!" I screamed.

Bear jumped in front of Benita, stumbling just as

he fired. With a look of utter shock on her face Bear slowly stood up.

Benita too, looked surprised as she clutched her stomach. Blood ran though her fingers. She fell into Bear's arms. I grabbed Benita and lowered her to the ground.

"Benita!"

She looked up at me with her eyes half closed. "Guess I won't be going to the opera," she said weakly. She smiled and touched my cheek. Then she expired. Everyone was still.

In that moment, bitterness and rage swept over me. In a blur, I took out my knife and threw it at Anglin. With a soft *thump*, the blade found it's mark in Anglin's throat. He grabbed the handle with both hands and tried to pull it out. He stood there for a few moments, then crumpled to the ground. While the deputies watched in horror, Noah dove to the ground, picked up his rifle and rolled up in a shooting stance. Before the deputies could react, he put a bullet in each of their hearts.

When a team from The Service arrived, Arrow sent them to the jail where we'd put Brown, Chapman, Pee Wee, and the two surviving deputies. After an investigation at Fort Carmel, it was determined that Lt. Martin had acted alone.

Benita's funeral was held on a Tuesday. It was nice to see so many people at the ceremony. Benita had no close friends, but many in town respected her. I could see tears on some faces, and true regret on others. Noah was there. When *Bless Be the Tie that Binds* was sung, his shoulders shook and tears rolled down his grimacing face.

No one stopped me when I walked over and put the quilt into the coffin. I liked to think that "Clouds" would keep her warm. Obviously I had not been thinking clearly. I was very unagent-like, thinking emotionally. I didn't care.

Jacob Specks and Harlon Shanks were at the graveside. I expected to be fired by Jacob. I didn't care. I deserved it. I had let him down. And I had let Benita down. Bear came to my rescue with a detailed report expounding on my effort and how I went beyond the call of duty. I disagreed with the report. There was more I could have done. I could have saved Benita. Everyone was aware of what kept Jacob from doing anything drastic. He knew what everyone knew. That Benita truly loved me. And I loved her. He had lost a cousin. I had lost the love of my life.

Editor Bartly showed up sober and dressed in a fancy suit. I had no idea that he knew Benita. When the last hymn was sung, and the final amens were spoken, I sadly walked out of the graveyard and went straight to Pandora. I mounted up.

Harlon always said he admired my skill as an agent. He liked my cool temper under fire, the accuracy of my gun, and my undercover ability.

"You lack one thing son," he had told me. "People can shoot you, beat you, cheat you, and give you a swift kick in the head . . . but it won't make you hard. And Rattler, you might not have the mental toughness that makes a complete agent."

Pandora felt my sadness as she clopped out of Clearview. I felt a hole boring through my heart. It was carving a scar that would never heal. I was a man. A man doesn't cry at lost love. Never. Instead, he turns hard. From now on, I would live up to my name.

SPECIAL THANKS to: Gary Goldstein for his expertise, support and belief. Also thanks to Bill E. Compton, Frances Doyle, Neila Petrick, and Janice Chambers for their research.